ID1029747

A DREAM OF WESSEX

CHRISTOPHER PRIEST was born in Cheshire, England in 1943. He began writing soon after leaving school and has been a full-time freelance writer since 1968. He has published thirteen novels, four short story collections and a number of other books, including critical works, biographies, novelizations, and children's nonfiction.

Priest first gained notice with short stories contributed to science fiction magazines such as *Impulse* and *New Worlds* in the 1960s and later won widespread acclaim for his novels, including *Inverted World* (1974), *The Affirmation* (1981), and *The Glamour* (1984). The success of these novels, which have gone on to be recognized as classics of the genre, led Granta to name Priest one of the top young British novelists in its 1983 list. More recently, *The Prestige* (1995) won both the James Tait Black Memorial Prize for best novel of the year and the World Fantasy Award and was adapted for a film directed by Christopher Nolan, and *The Separation* (2002) won both the Arthur C. Clarke and BSFA Awards. Priest's work has also earned major awards internationally, including the Kurd Laßwitz Award (Germany), the Eurocon Award (Yugoslavia), the Ditmar Award (Australia), and Le Grand Prix de L'Imaginaire (France). In 2001 he was awarded the Prix Utopia (France) for lifetime achievement.

In addition to writing books, Priest has written drama for radio and television, and as a journalist he has written features and reviews for *The Times*, the *Guardian*, the *Independent*, the *New Statesman*, the *Scotsman*, and many different magazines.

His most recent novel, *The Adjacent*, was published in the U.S. in April 2014. Five of his best novels are available in new editions from Valancourt Books.

By Christopher Priest

* Available in paperback and e-book
† Available in e-book

Christopher Priest

A DREAM OF WESSEX

VALANCOURT BOOKS

Dedication: To Martin Walker

A Dream of Wessex by Christopher Priest
First published in Great Britain by Faber & Faber in 1977
First U.S. edition published by Scribner in 1977 (as *A Perfect Lover*)
First Valancourt Books edition 2016

Published by Valancourt Books, Richmond, Virginia
http://www.valancourtbooks.com

ISBN 978-1-943910-23-6 (trade paperback)
ISBN 978-1-954321-49-6 (trade hardcover)
Also available as an electronic book.

Set in Dante MT
Cover by Henry Petrides

'May you live through interesting times.'
Ancient Chinese curse

I

The Tartan Army had planted a bomb at Heathrow, and Julia Stretton, who had gone the long way round past the airport to avoid the usual congestion on the approach-roads to the M3, had been delayed for two hours by police and army checkpoints. By the time she joined the motorway further down she was so late that she was able to put thoughts of Paul Mason out of her mind, and concentrate on her driving. She drove quickly for an hour, breaking the speed-limit all the way and not particularly concerned should one of the police helicopters spot her.

She left the motorway near Basingstoke, and drove steadily down the main road towards Salisbury. The plain was grey and misty, with low clouds softening the lines of the higher mounds. It had been a cool, wet summer in Britain, or so everyone told her, and now in July there had been reports of snow-flurries along the Yorkshire coast, and flooding in parts of Cornwall. It all seemed remote from her own life, and she had registered only mild surprise when on complaining of the cold a few days earlier she had been reminded of the time of year.

A few miles beyond Salisbury, on the road to Blandford Forum, Julia stopped at a roadside café for a cup of coffee, and as she sat at the plastic-topped table she had time at last for reflection.

It had been the surprise of seeing Paul Mason that had probably upset her more than anything else: that, and the way it had happened, and the place.

Wessex House in High Holborn was a dark, gloomy place at weekends, and she had been there only because she had been instructed to. One of the trustees of the Wessex Foundation, a dry, acerbic lawyer named Bonner, had called her in to see him before she returned to Dorchester from leave. The urgent summons had turned out to be about a minor, irritating matter, and when she left his office in a mood of suppressed anger, and was walking down to the car-park, she met Paul Mason.

Paul at Wessex House: it was like the breach of a sanctuary. Paul an intruder from her past life; Paul who had almost destroyed her once; Paul whom she had left behind her six years before.

Sitting in the roadside café, Julia stirred her coffee with the plastic spoon, slopping some of the pale brown liquid into the saucer. She was still angry. She had never wanted to see Paul again, and she was reacting as if he had deliberately followed and waylaid her. He had sounded as surprised to see her as she was to see him, and if he had faked it he was faking well. 'Julia! What are you doing here! You look well.' Well enough, Paul. He was still the same Paul, hard-featured but plausible, more debonair now, perhaps, than the egocentric student he had been when she fell for him during their last year at Durham. They'd lived together in London after that, while Paul built his career and she squandered three years of higher education in a succession of secretarial jobs. Then at last the break-up, and the freedom from him, and the lingering, paradoxical dependence on him she'd felt. All in the past, until yesterday.

She glanced at her wristwatch; she was still late, and all the hurrying on the road had made up no time. She had been in touch with Dr Eliot at Maiden Castle before the weekend, and she had told him she would be in Dorchester by lunchtime. But it was already past two-thirty. Julia wondered if she ought to telephone again, and warn Eliot and his staff, but she looked around the interior of the café and couldn't see a pay-phone. It didn't matter; if she was delaying them they would have to wait. Someone would ring Wessex House, and find out she was on her way.

Such indifference to the administration of the Wessex project was not like her. She had Paul to thank for that. She was still marvelling to herself at the way he had the ability to invade her life. He'd always done it, of course; while they were living together he had treated her as he would treat one of his arms, as an unquestioning, uninteresting but useful part of himself.

But now, six years after she had last seen him, she was furious with herself for letting him do it again.

It was this anger at herself that had started the row yesterday. She stared blankly at the dirty table-top, seeing Paul's face again, his eyes narrowed with cold indifference to her independence;

she could hear again his calm but provocative words, subtly insinuating her reliance on him. Playing the truth game she had called it in the old days, the destructive days of that last lacerating year with him. He had a way of playing on secrets she had once confided to him, then turning them against her to expose her weaknesses and to get his own way. Yesterday he'd done it again, and the old truths still held; the old secrets still betrayed her. He didn't get it all his own way, though: the inevitable sexual pass had been made, and she passed it straight back, as cold with her body as he was with his eyes. It was her only moment of triumph, and it was one that made her feel sordid; another strike for Paul.

The coffee, like the recollection, left a bitter taste in the mouth. She was still thirsty, but decided against having a second cup. She went to the loo, then returned to the car.

It had started to rain while she was in the café, so Julia ran the engine and turned on the heater. The weekend encounter with Paul was still foremost in her mind, and some rebellious quirk made her disinclined to drive on, the irritation transferred illogically from Paul to her job. She sat and watched the rain run bright channels down the windscreen.

She still hadn't found out what Paul had been doing at Wessex House at all, let alone on a Sunday. The only explanation could be that he had taken a job there, was working for the trustees. The thought induced a quiet panic in her; when she had started to work for the Foundation four years ago, she hadn't been able to shake off the notion that it was a refuge from Paul, and even today, deeply involved in her work as she was, she couldn't rid herself of this residual motive. But Paul had found her there, by accident or design. She could ask Dr Eliot if he knew anything about it . . . he needn't be told why she wanted to know.

It was a relief to return to Dorchester, because Paul, even if he was working for the Foundation, could not follow her. No one could follow, and like a genuine sanctuary it was impregnable and timeless.

She drove on then, still annoyed with herself for letting Paul disrupt her life again.

Three miles before she reached the town of Blandford Forum, Julia was waved down by an army checkpoint, and she drew in behind a line of three other cars. Passing through these check-points was normally a matter of routine – she carried a government pass, and her car was listed as a regular user of this road – but even so she was detained for ten minutes.

This remote area of Dorset seemed an unlikely place for acts of terrorism to happen, even though there were army-bases all over Salisbury Plain, and Blandford Camp itself was only half a mile from here. Julia stood in the rain, leaning against the side of the car under the dripping trees, realizing that guerrilla violence was now a usual, almost expected, part of everyday life in the big cities, but that the countryside continued to feel immune from the troubles. However many targets there were around here, a bomb explosion in Dorset would be an extraordinary event.

She felt cold and restless. Two soldiers came to inspect her documents and car, and they searched the passenger-compartment and boot. An officer watched them, watched her. Julia thought how young they all seemed.

Later, when she and her car had been cleared, and she was driving on towards Dorchester, she thought about David Hark-man. He was believed by some of the Wessex participants to be a soldier now, but it was just a theory, as good as any other. No one knew where he was, nor what he was doing, and in the weeks ahead it would be Julia's responsibility to find him. During her week's leave she had spent some time in London talking to Harkman's former wife, hoping to gain some extra insight into his personality; it had been a dispiriting meeting, though, with his ex-wife still suppressing resentments, seven years after their divorce.

The character profile was her only hope of finding him. A lecturer in social history, David Harkman had been at the London School of Economics before joining the Wessex project. His colleagues at the L.S.E. had spoken of him as an assertive man, stable and authoritative, but not ambitious. Julia would agree with the judgment of assertiveness; during the time the Wessex project was being set up, Harkman had often been stubborn, pressing his own ideas and opinions in the face of others. She had not much liked him, and now she found it ironical – after her disastrous meeting with Paul – that she should be the one chosen to look for him. She was escaping from one man she detested, to seek another she did not care for.

Even so, she was not discontented. She was glad to be getting back to work.

She drove through Blandford Forum and took the Dorchester road. As soon as the car had breasted the first rise after the river the rain stopped. Looking ahead as she drove, she saw the sky was brighter, but low clouds moved quickly from the south-west. It was Dorset weather: windy, wet, changeable.

She was tired from the long journey, and not in the best condition to start work. Even more unsuited, perhaps, was her state of mind; she needed to be calm and single-minded and receptive, and instead she was fretting about Paul. As she drove quickly through Dorchester, and took the road towards the south, Julia wondered again about what he wanted. She sensed an urge in him to destroy – for that, after all, was what he had done to her ever since she had known him – and she wished she knew more about what was going on. Why hadn't she asked him while she had the chance?

The gate to the car-park of Maiden Castle was closed, and she blew the horn until Mr Wentworth appeared. He came out of his wooden hut, smiling when he recognized the car.

When she had driven through the gate, and parked the car, she climbed out and waited for him as he walked towards her.

'Only a week off this time, Miss Stretton?' he said.

'It was all I needed,' she said. 'Look, Mr Wentworth, I didn't have time to go to Bincombe House. Do you think you could have these delivered to my room?'

She gave him her suitcase of clothes, and a holdall containing several books. This had been her fourth period of leave since the project began, and as she found on the other three occasions, the return to London had destroyed her concentration. She intended spending her next leave in Dorset; Bincombe House was large and comfortable, and she had a room of her own there. At Bincombe one could always see other members of the project, and so help to maintain a continuity of purpose between spells inside the projector.

'Will the car be O.K. here?' She glanced over the long line of cars, parked in three ranks, close to each other. Several of them were dirty; one of Mr Wentworth's tasks was to wash the cars from time to time, but he only did it under protest.

'You leave it there, Miss. I'll get it out of the way if someone wants to move.'

She gave him the ignition-key, and he took a paper tag from his pocket and tied it to it. Julia leaned over, and looked towards the far end of the car-park. David Harkman's yellow Rover 2000 was still there, as it had been for two years, unclaimed by its owner.

'Has anyone been asking for me?' Julia said.

'Well, Dr Trowbridge rang down earlier.'

'Yes?'

'He said to send you to see Dr Eliot as soon as you arrived.'

She turned away from him, casting her eyes towards the ground. Julia had a minor superstition, that persisted from childhood, that if she looked at anyone thinking that it was the last time she would see him – and thus hold a mental photograph – then it would come to be so. It was always there, as she went back to the Castle, this feeling of finality, the danger of never returning. As she started to climb the grassy slope of the lowest and nearest rampart of the Castle, Julia looked back in Mr Wentworth's general direction, trying to see him with her peripheral vision, so that she would have no clear memory of how he appeared on her last sight of him. This sideways look that Julia gave people as she left them was something of which she was acutely conscious. Paul used to call it her shifty look, but he was the last person she would ever have tried to explain it to.

She came to the top of the first of the earth ramparts that surrounded the ancient hill-fort. On this northerly side of Maiden Castle there were three of these, each one higher and steeper than the one before it, and there was no other way in to the Castle than to climb each one. A well-worn path took the easiest route and she followed this, her hair blowing across her face in the stiff wind. She was cold now, her thin city clothes pressed against her body, her skirt whipping in the wind. As she walked down into the lee of the second earth ridge the wind let her alone, and she swept back her hair and laughed. The Castle often engendered an elemental unconcern in those who found it, whether they were casual visitors – who were still allowed access to certain parts – or the staff of the Wessex project. The Castle was ancient and solid, and permanent; its grass-covered shoulders had shrugged off decay for five thousand years, and it would still be here in five thousand years' time. Julia felt this sense of abandonment whenever she arrived at the Castle from London, and today was no different. By the time she had reached the top of the second ridge she was running, gasping in the cold wind, and she left the path and skipped over the tufty grass.

From here she could see down into the dip between the second and third ramparts, where the entrance to the underground workings lay. No one could be seen there. Although Mr Wentworth had probably telephoned the word of her arrival to Trowbridge or Eliot, she had a few minutes to spare.

She put down her briefcase and looked about. The sky, the wind, the grass. Two or three seagulls, soaring above her in the wind-waves thrown up by the humps of the Castle; they were a long way from the sea, but gulls were common inland birds these days.

The city of Dorchester lay below her and to the left, spreading out untidily across the side of its hill. She could see the wireless-telegraphy station on the heath behind it, and traffic moving on the roads around the town. A train stood at a signal just outside the station. Beyond, the soft rolling Dorset hills around Cerne Abbas and Charminster and Tolpuddle. She stared at the view for some time, drawn to it by the images and memories she had of another time, another summer . . .

It was not far to the view across to the east, so Julia picked up her briefcase and strode out along the edge of the ridge, looking ahead. Soon she reached the place where the ramparts circled round to the south, and from here the view across the Frome Valley was uninterrupted. It was flat and windswept, the river meandering across its floor, flowing slowly towards the mud-flats of Wareham, and Poole Harbour beyond. This was Hardy country, Egdon Heath and Anglebury, Casterbridge and Budmouth . . . she hadn't read the books since school. From this position it was difficult to see why so many people liked the Dorset scenery, because it seemed grey and flat and dull. Only to her right was there a green rise of land; the downs leading to the Purbeck Hills beyond, far to the east, hiding the sea.

Time was pressing; she had taken too long already. The wind had chilled her. Clouds, looming up in the south-west, threatened another shower.

Julia walked back, scrambling down into the lee of the third ridge, looking for the entrance to the workings.

2

In the third century BC, the inhabitants of Maiden Castle had fortified their hilltop home by the building of wood and earth ramparts that entirely circled the two knolls on which the settlement had been made. Never a castle in the commonly understood sense, the ramparts had enclosed farming-land and a village, to which most of the inhabitants of ancient Wessex fled whenever hostile tribes invaded the region. In the twentieth century, by which time the earth walls had weathered to rounded, grassy slopes, such defences seemed inadequate, for they could be penetrated in a few minutes by even the most unambitious walker, but in pre-Roman Britain the ramparts and their closely defended gates were precaution enough against sling-shots and spears.

The site had been thoroughly excavated during the 1930s. Remains similar to those found in hill-forts all over southern England had been discovered, and the more interesting fragments placed on display in the Dorchester Museum. There had been a massacre of the villagers by Vespasian's legions in AD 43, and the most singular discovery in Maiden Castle was that of a primitive mass burial-ground, containing thousands of human bodies.

The archaeological workings had been covered before the Second World War, and from then until the early 1980s Maiden Castle had reverted to a former rôle: agricultural and pastoral land, walked over by casual visitor and sheep.

Maiden Castle had been selected as the site for the Wessex project for various reasons. It was partly because of its proximity to Dorchester, and road and rail connections to London, partly because of its height of 132 metres above sea-level, partly because of its commanding view across the Frome Valley, but especially because the Castle, of all the man-made constructions in the region, was the one most assured of permanence.

Julia Stretton had not visited the Castle while the underground laboratories were being tunnelled and equipped, and she had only a dim childhood memory of visiting the place with her parents, but she assumed that after the construction crews had left, and the surface had been tidied up, the outward appearance of the Castle had not been much changed. The car-park had been enlarged, and there was the entrance to the laboratories, but as far as possible the outside was untouched. The Duchy of Cornwall, the owners of the Castle, had insisted on that.

In the entrance to the laboratory – the only part open to the public – several glass cases held a selection of fragments unearthed during the tunnelling. The ancient Wessexmen buried tributes with their dead, and many cups and trinkets and pots had been found, as well as the inevitable macabre selection of bones. One almost complete skeleton was on show, the neck-bones neatly labelled where they had been shattered by a Roman arrowhead. A security-guard sat at a desk beside the case containing the skeleton, and as Julia passed him, holding out her identity-card, he nodded to her.

The elevator used by the medical teams was open, but Julia used the flight of concrete steps that went down around it. At the bottom, she walked along the main corridor, passing the rows of steel, white-painted lockers, and the many numbered doors.

She stopped at one room, knocked, then opened the door. As she had hoped, Marilyn James, one of the physiotherapists on the project, was there.

'Hello, Marilyn. I'm looking for John Eliot.'

'He's been looking for you. I think he's in the conference room.'

'I'm late. I was stuck in traffic.'

'I don't think it matters,' Marilyn said. 'We were just a bit worried in case there had been an accident. Did you have a good holiday?'

'So-so,' Julia said, thinking of Paul, thinking of the bitterness of the night before. 'It wasn't long enough to enjoy myself.'

It was cold in the tunnel, although it was supposed to be heated. Julia walked on, thinking about Paul again.

The conference room was at the very end of the main corridor, and Julia went straight in. Dr Eliot was here, sitting back in one of the armchairs, and reading a typewritten report. At the far end of the room, where the coffee-machine was, a group of five of the technicians sat at a table playing cards.

'Have I kept you waiting?' she said to Eliot.

'Come and sit down, Julia. Have you eaten today?'

'A slice of toast for breakfast,' she said. 'And I had a cup of coffee on the way down.'

'Nothing more? Good.'

Since the death of Carl Ridpath eighteen months before, John Eliot had been in charge of all projector functions at the Castle. He and Ridpath had worked in associated fields of neurhypnological research for several years, and it was partly as a result of a paper about neural conduction Eliot had published some fifteen years before that Ridpath developed his equipment. The fact that the neurhypnological projector bore Ridpath's name gave no indication of the debt he owed Eliot, one which he repeatedly affirmed in his lifetime, and yet it was as the 'Ridpath projector' that the equipment was now known, not only by those sections of the media which took an interest in such matters, but by the participants too.

During Ridpath's last illness Eliot had taken over the running of the project as if it had been his all along. Unlike Ridpath, though, who until the appearance of the cancer had enjoyed excellent health, Eliot suffered from a recurrent heart-murmur, and had never himself entered a projection, even for experimental purposes. He sometimes spoke to the participants about this, not enviously, but regretfully.

Now as Julia sat down beside him, he handed her a small pile of reports, including the one of her own she had filed a week before.

She settled down to concentrate on them, forcing thoughts of her private life out of her mind. This reading of reports was one of the more irksome duties to which she had to attend, but also one of the most crucial.

After this she asked for, and was granted, some time to herself, and she went to one of the private cubicles to study the file she had been compiling on David Harkman. The conversation with his ex-wife hadn't seemed to yield much at the time, but she went through the notes again, looking for anything that might add insights into his personality, however remotely.

Eliot came to the cubicle.

'This was sent down from Bincombe,' he said to her, and gave her an envelope. 'It arrived on Saturday.'

Julia glanced at the handwriting. 'Should I read it now?'

'It's up to you, of course. Do you know who it's from?'

'I don't think so.' But there was an old familiarity to it, an unpleasant association. 'Leave it here. I'll read it later.'

When Eliot had gone, she picked up the envelope and slit it hurriedly. She knew the handwriting: it was Paul Mason's.

Inside was a single sheet of paper, folded in half. She held it without opening it, logic struggling with curiosity.

She knew that concentration on her work was essential in the next hour, and that distraction would only hamper this. To read any kind of personal letter shortly before rejoining the projection was unwise, and one from Paul, who, with such unerring skill, could throw up so much emotional static in her, was especially risky. On the other hand, during yesterday's unpleasant scene with him she had not found out what was his connection with the Wessex project, and she was anxious to know. The letter, obviously written before the weekend, might have the answer.

At last she decided to read it, realizing that if she didn't the continuing curiosity would be as much a distraction as anything the letter might contain. As a compromise with herself, she resolved to practise the rote mnemonics afterwards, like an errant nun imposing twelve Hail Marys on herself.

The letter was short, and, to anyone not herself, apparently harmless. As soon as she had read it Julia put aside her file and went to take a shower.

Dear Julia,

I suppose you'll be as surprised to read this as I was to discover that our paths have crossed once more. I've been wondering what you've been up to recently, and how you've been keeping. Well, now I know.

I'm hoping to come down to visit Maiden Castle soon, so I hope you can get an evening off to have dinner with me. I'm still very fond of you, and would like to see you again. I'm sure we will have a lot to say to each other.

Paul

Julia soaped herself angrily in the shower. Paul's knack for touching on old wounds was amazing. 'Now I know' ... how much did he know? Why should he want to? Written by anyone else it was a mild platitude; written by Paul it reawakened all the paranoia of old. 'I'm sure we will have a lot to say to each other'; he'd written that before the weekend, before they discovered that what they had to say to each other was like the leftovers from a meal gone cold six years before, spiced up with many an afterthought.

And he had always been *fond* of her, like a possessive child is fond of a tormented puppy; he'd never used the word 'love', not once. Not even when they were closest. Not even to sign off a letter.

She left the shower, and dried herself, then sat naked on the edge of the wooden chair in the cubicle. She closed her eyes, and determinedly recited the mnemonics to herself, fulfilling the terms of her own compromise. This late in the projection, the mnemonics had lost much of their earlier use, but they still had the function of concentrating the mind.

Ideally, the minds of the participants should be as uncluttered with personal thoughts as was humanly possible. Personal identity continued, of course, on an unconscious level, but the maximum projective effect was achieved when the conscious mind was directed along the chosen course. In this case, Julia's main function was to establish contact with David Harkman, and the better she concentrated on that now the better the chance later of making that contact.

She glanced over her file on Harkman once again, then put on the simple surgical gown that had been left in the cubicle for her use. She folded up the rest of her clothes, and scribbled a note asking one of the staff to take them up to her room at Bincombe House.

Dr Eliot was waiting for her in the conference room.

'Don't forget to sign the release,' he said, pushing a printed form across to her. Julia signed it without reading it, knowing it was the standard permission form, allowing Eliot to hypnotize her and place her body inside the Ridpath.

'I'd like to see Harkman,' she said.

'We thought so. He's ready.'

She followed Eliot into the large, brightly lit room that the participants called, with conscious irony, the mortuary. It was more properly known as the projection hall, for it was here that the thirty-nine cabinets of the Ridpath projector were placed. In spite of the many electric lights beamed down on to the cabinets – necessary illumination for the constant medical attention the participants required – the hall was always cold, because it was air-conditioned by a refrigerant system, so that the effect of working by the cabinets was akin to sunbathing in an Arctic breeze. As Dr Eliot and one of the technicians slid Harkman's body out on the drawer of the cabinet, Julia wrapped her arms about her body, shivering.

Harkman lay as if dead. His body had been placed full-length along the surface of the drawer, with his head inwards. He was lying face-up, with his head and shoulders resting on the moulded supports so that his neck and spine made contact with the neural sensors implanted in the drawer. Seeing this, Julia felt a twinge of sympathetic pain in her own back, knowing the burning sensation she felt whenever she was taken from the projector.

Harkman had been inside the machine for almost two years without a break, and in that time his body had grown soft and flabby, in spite of the constant physiotherapy he received. His face was pale and waxen, as if embalmed, and his hair had grown long.

Julia stared impassively, watching his facial muscles twitch occasionally, and his hands, folded across his chest, tremble as if about to grasp at something. Beneath his lids, his eyes flickered like those of a man dreaming.

He *was* dreaming in a sense: a dream that had lasted nearly two years so far, a dream of a distant time and a strange society.

Dr Trowbridge, who was Eliot's chief assistant, came over to them from where he had been working at the far end of the hall.

'Is there anything wrong, Dr Eliot?'

'No ... Miss Stretton is familiarizing herself with Harkman's appearance.'

Trowbridge looked down at the face of the man in the drawer. 'Would photographs not give a more accurate impression? Harkman has put on so much weight.'

Julia said, still staring at the unconscious man: 'I suppose he could have wilfully changed his appearance.'

'Have any of the others?' Eliot said.

'Not as far as I know.'

'It's not consistent with his profile,' Eliot said. 'Everything we know about him underlines an inherent stability. There are no lapses. Harkman's personality is ideal for projection.'

'Perhaps too ideal,' Julia said, remembering his forceful arguments. She looked intently at the pale face, trying to imprint it on her memory, at the same time remembering how he had talked and acted before the projection began. This body was too like a dummy to imagine it alive and thinking. She said: 'I wonder if he was repressing some resentment against the others? Perhaps he felt we were somehow intruding, and on projecting he willed himself away from the rest of us.'

'It still isn't likely,' Eliot said. 'There's nothing in his preprojection notes to indicate that. It has to be a case of unconscious programming. We've had several minor cases of that.'

'And one major one, perhaps,' Julia said. She nodded to Trowbridge and the technician. 'You can put him back. I think I'm ready.'

They slid the drawer, and it closed with a sound of heavy, cushioned metal.

Eliot said to Trowbridge: 'I think we should cut back on his intra-venous feeding. I'll talk to you later.'

He took Julia's arm, and they went back through the side-tunnel to his surgery. As she followed him into the room, and he closed the door behind her, Julia thought momentarily of Paul. She remembered the row, and his letter, but she thought of them as unpleasant incidents in her experience, not as intrusions into her life. She felt a certain satisfaction that she had the strength at last to file him away into a cubby-hole of her conscious mind.

She went to sit in the deep chair in front of Eliot's littered desk, ready to accept his will.

Later, as she listened to Eliot speak to her of the Wessex projection, she wanted to look away, to see him with her peripheral vision, but she was unable to. Sitting before her, Eliot spoke calmly, repetitively, quietly, and soon she fell into a trance.

3

It was late afternoon in Dorchester, and the open-air cafés along Marine Boulevard were enjoying a busy trade as the tourists returned from the beaches. Inside the harbour, the whole extent of which could be seen by the people strolling along the Boulevard, the private yachts were marooned on the pebbles and mud of low tide, held upright by ropes and pontoons. A few men and women from the hired crews were on some of the boats, but most of the owners and their guests were ashore. When the tide was in, the private section of the harbour was a bustle of yachts coming and going, with visitors sitting on the decks enjoying the view and the sunshine, but for the moment those visitors still aboard their boats were concealed from public gaze beneath their gaily coloured canopies and festoons.

Outside the harbour, a small fleet of fishing boats was waiting for the tide.

Along the walls and quays that surrounded the harbour, and for the length of Marine Boulevard, hundreds of people milled about with an air of pleasurable languor. Beggar-musicians moved amongst them, collecting-bags swinging from the necks of their guitars, and along the part of the Boulevard overlooking the harbour were the licensed stalls and entertainers, the book and magazine stands, Sekker's Bar, and the store where tide-skimmers could be bought or hired and where the fashionable were always to be seen. It was in this part of town, at this time of day, that the visitors gathered.

The building of the English Regional Commission was situated in one of the sidestreets leading into Marine Boulevard, and it was from this that Donald Mander and Frederick Cro emerged.

They walked slowly through the crowd towards the harbour, Cro still wearing his jacket, but Mander carrying his over his arm.

They walked as far as the end of the quay, where they stopped to buy two *citrons pressés* at the soft-drinks bar.

From this position it became possible to see under the canopy of one of the yachts, and there, otherwise invisible from the harbour walls, were two young men and a woman. Although the men were dressed in beach-shorts and shirts, the young woman was naked. She sat quietly in a canvas chair, flipping through a magazine.

The Commission men both noticed her at the same time, but neither of them remarked on her. They were habitually guarded in what they said to each other, and by nature discreet with their reactions. Both men were bachelors in their fifties, and although they had worked in adjacent offices at the Regional Commission for more than twenty years they were still not on first-name terms.

When they had finished their drinks they walked slowly back down the quay.

Mander pointed towards the waiting fishing boats, most of which were grouped together in the deeper water about fifty metres from the harbour entrance. Several of the boats were lying low in the water, while their crews sat lazily in the warm sunlight on deck.

'There's been a good catch,' Mander said.

Cro nodded, and Mander smiled to himself. He knew that the other man detested seafood, and rarely ate in the local restaurants. One of the few facts Mander knew about Cro was that he lived on parcels of provisions, sent over by his parents, who were still alive and lived in relative affluence on the English mainland.

On the far side of the harbour, where the commercial work of the port was done, a steam crane emitted a loud hissing noise accompanied by a white jet of vapour. In a moment it trundled slowly along its rails to the regular berth of the hydrofoil service from the mainland. The boat was late this evening, and the carts of several tradesmen from the town stood waiting by.

Beyond, the bay was calm and blue.

The two men left the quay and walked into the crowd on

Marine Boulevard, heading for Sekker's Bar. They looked out of place in this leisurely part of town, more for their watchful manner than their clothes. The tourists stared as they sauntered in the warm air, caring only to notice and be noticed; Mander and Cro, though, glanced uneasily about them, minor public servants constantly on watch for minor details.

As they came near to the multi-coloured umbrellas over the tables of Sekker's Bar, Cro pointed towards one of the stalls of merchandise.

'The people from Maiden Castle,' he said. 'They're still here. I thought you were going to check their licence.'

'I did. There's nothing irregular.'

'Then it must be revoked. How did they get hold of one?'

'In the usual way,' Mander said. 'It was bought in the office.'

'We could find an ideological objection ...'

Mander shook his head, but not so the other would see. 'It's never as easy as that.'

The stall Cro had indicated would have seemed innocuous enough to eyes less instantly hostile. It was no larger than any of the others, and constructed along the same lines. Even the goods on offer were similar, at first sight, to those peddled from stalls all along the Boulevard. The wooden surface of the counter had been covered with a green woollen cloth, and spread out across this was a selection of hand-crafted goods: wooden bowls and candlesticks, ornamented chess-sets, brooches and armbands set with polished semi-precious stones, unglazed pottery; each item seemed well made and substantial, but with an appealing roughness to the finish that served only to emphasize the essential craft.

In this way the goods differed from those offered at the other stalls, for they sold inexpensive but uniform wares, mass-produced in cooperatives on the mainland. This individual quality was not lost on the tourists, for the stall was attracting more customers than most of the others.

Cro glanced disparagingly at the goods, and at the people selling them.

There were two women and a man behind the simple counter. One of the women sat upright on a stool at the back, but she was at ease and with her eyes closed. She wore the clothes that the Commission men had immediately recognized, the plain, dull-brown hand woven garments that were worn by the entire community at Maiden Castle. The man and the other woman were both younger, although the man – who was thin and pale, and had prematurely balding hair – was moving slowly, as if tired.

Mander and Cro lingered by the stall for a few moments, and although the young woman serving noticed their approach she gave no sign of recognition. Mander, who had often remarked to himself on her attractive figure, was hoping she might look his way again so that he could give her a secret reassuring smile, but she seemed determined to ignore them.

At last they walked on, and went up the steps to the patio of Sekker's Bar.

As they sat down at a vacant table, a distant explosion sounded across the bay, echoing from Purbeck Island in the south. This was the cannon mounted above Blandford Passage, which was fired twice a day to warn shipping and swimmers of the flood tide. At this hour of the day few people would be swimming, and apart from the fishing boats outside the harbour there were only one or two private yachts in sight. As usual, many people moved to the sea wall at the sound of the cannon, for a first sight of the tidal bore, but it would not be visible for several more minutes.

Cro said: 'How much do you know about the new man?'

'Harkman? As much as you.'

'I thought he'd been appointed to your department.'

Mander shook his head, but vaguely: an evasion, not a denial. 'He's working on some kind of research.'

'Is he English?'

'No, British. His mother defected from Scotland.' Mander looked across the Boulevard, and out to sea. 'I gather he's visited the States.'

Cro nodded as if he knew this already, but said: 'West or East?'

'Both, so far as I know. Look. I think that must be Nadja Morovin.'

A man and a young woman were strolling past Sekker's, arm in arm. The woman whom Mander had indicated, wore a wide-brimmed hat low over her face, but her sleeves were rolled up and her skirt was short, provocatively revealing the pallor of her plump limbs. The glamorous couple were affecting not to notice the fact that she was instantly recognizable, and as they walked slowly through the crowd they seemed not to realize that the people approaching them were stepping unobtrusively to one side. Behind them, people stared openly, and a short way away a young man – apparently a tourist from the States – was taking one photograph after another, using a powerful telephoto lens.

A few moments later, Mander and Cro lost sight of them as they went into the tide-skimmer shop.

'Isn't that the hydrofoil?' Mander said.

Cro looked out to sea again, then stood up for a better view, even though the patio at Sekker's gave one of the best panoramas in town. Several hundred people were now standing by the sea wall, waiting to see the tidal bore as it burst through Blandford Passage. From this distance, more than thirty kilometres, only the white crest of the wave could be seen with the naked eye, but recent tides had been high and the telescope renters along the front had been illegally increasing their prices.

Mander was pointing to the south of the Passage. From that direction, skimming along past Lawrence Island, came the hydrofoil. On the deepening blue of the presently calm waters of the bay it was the only sign of movement.

'The tide will be through any minute now,' Cro said. 'Do you suppose the pilot realizes?'

'He'll know,' Mander said.

A few seconds later, the people who had hired telescopes bent to their instruments, and the tidal wave appeared. Several of the tourists pointed seawards, pointing excitedly, and children were held aloft on the shoulders of their parents.

The waiter arrived to take their order, and Cro sat down.

'Is this . . . Mr Harkman on the hydrofoil?' he said, when two beers had been brought.

'I can't think why else it should be late,' Mander said, watching the other man for his reaction.

'I heard he wasn't rated above Regional Adviser. Would the boat be held for you or me?'

'It would depend on the circumstances.'

Well pleased with Cro's reaction, Mander sipped his beer.

Earlier in the day he had heard that the low-water berth at Pound-bury was going to be busy all day, obliging the hydrofoil to wait for the tide. He assumed Cro hadn't heard this, but decided against mentioning it because he liked Cro to have a few mysteries.

Cro took a mouthful of beer. He wiped his lips with his hand-kerchief, then stood up again.

Out in the bay the hydrofoil had slowed down, so that its hull had entered the water again. The boat had turned to face the flood-ing tide, and as Cro stepped down from Sekker's patio and crossed the Boulevard to the sea wall the first turbulence reached it. The boat yawed and pitched dramatically, but as soon as the first large waves were past it turned again towards Dorchester, and acceler-ated through the choppy water in the wake of the bore.

Still seated at the table, Mander looked at Cro with irrita-tion. The arrival of any high-level appointee brought inevitable conflicts within the office, as the hierarchy unwillingly accommo-dated the newcomer, but Harkman's appointment to Dorchester threatened the recent smooth state of office politics as surely as the twice-daily tides disrupted the calm waters of the bay.

It was the vagueness of Harkman's position at the Regional Commission that was the main problem. Mander had been told that Harkman was to be given access to whatever files or records he requested, and that Commissioner Borovitin's authorization would be channelled through his own office. As Mander's area of responsibility was Administration, this made sense, but he was still unsure of the nature of Harkman's intended research. Cro was displaying an unnatural amount of interest in the new man, so Mander suspected that he knew more than he was letting on. His questioning of Mander was probably less for his own infor-mation than to try to discover how much Mander knew.

Cro, a master at office manoeuvring, would be delighted to have someone working in his own department who had relative freedom of movement, as he would be certain to find some way of benefiting from it.

'Do you want another beer?' Mander said, when the other man returned to the table.

Cro looked at his wristwatch. 'I think we've time. The boat won't be in for another ten minutes.'

Mander took this as an acceptance, and summoned the waiter. In the bay, the flooding tidal wave from the north spread in a flattening semi-circle, the first turbulence subsiding. The rising tide still poured through Blandford Passage, and would continue to do so for another hour, but the initial violence of its arrival was past. In Dorchester Harbour the water-level, which all afternoon had risen only a metre or two, now came up quickly. The grounded pleasure-yachts lifted steadily, their hulls colliding gently with the supporting pontoons, and outside the harbour the waiting fishing boats started their engines and circled round, entering port one by one. By the time the last had tied up beside the fish-sheds the hydrofoil had arrived, and was nosing slowly towards its own berth. In the tourist part of the harbour not much had changed, except that those who idled on the decks were now in full view of those who strolled around the harbour; the commercial side of the port, by contrast, was bustling and noisy. Several of the boats had started to unload their cargoes of fish, and the tradesmen's carts and drays had moved forward to pick up the supplies brought from the mainland by the hydrofoil.

The horse-drawn Post Office van clattered through the crowds in Marine Boulevard, and turned down the ramp towards the hydrofoil berth.

Then Cro played a high card; perhaps it was a trump.

'I hear the man's an historian,' he said. 'Would that be so?'

'Possibly.'

Cro's most recent bureaucratic acquisition was supervision of the Commission's archives; it had been his triumph of the year before. If Harkman was an historian, he would certainly be working with Cro as a consequence.

As Mander finished his beer and stood up, he could already imagine the petty power-struggles of the weeks ahead.

He and Cro walked slowly across the Boulevard, and went towards the commercial side of the port.

By the time the first two passengers – an elderly couple from the States – had stepped ashore from the hydrofoil, Mander and Cro were waiting beside the fish-sheds, with a clear view of the landing stage.

More tourists stepped down from the boat, helped ashore

by the cabin stewards. Mander looked at each of them as they appeared, wondering what Harkman would look like. He was impressed in spite of himself, and irritated because of himself, by Cro's political advantage.

A figure dressed in a plain brown garment walked slowly past the two Commission men; it was the young woman who had been serving at the craft stall, the young woman from Maiden Castle. She stood a short distance in front of Cro and Mander, facing towards the hydrofoil.

Mander was distracted by her presence, as he always was when he happened to see her at the stall. From where he was waiting he could see her face in quarter-profile, and he could understand simultaneously why people like Cro thought of her and her community as a vague threat to the ordered existence of Soviet Wessex, and also why Cro and the others were wrong. At first glance the young woman seemed degenerate and wanton, giving off an aura of anarchy and irresponsibility: she had long, tousled hair, her dress was loose and immodest, and her legs and feet, clad in thin rope sandals, were dusty. But she also stood with poise and a certain elegance, her features were regular, and her eyes held a deep intelligence. In the same way, the other people from the Castle, who were occasionally seen about the town, behaved with a dignity and unobtrusiveness inconsistent with their primitive appearance, and the goods they sold were well made and distinctive.

Cro suddenly pointed towards someone who had just stepped down from the boat: 'That's our man. That's Harkman.'

'Are you sure?' Mander said, narrowing his eyes, but he knew Cro was right. The man was quite unlike anyone else on the quay. All the other passengers on the hydrofoil were obviously tourists or tradesmen; the former looked around uncertainly, seeking transport into town or help with their baggage, the latter immediately blended with the bustle around them.

Harkman, though, stood at the edge of the quay and looked appraisingly across the harbour towards the town. He seemed genuinely interested in what he saw, shading his eyes with his hand. Then he turned, looking away from the harbour towards the south, where Maiden Castle stood on its promontory overlooking the bay. To Mander he appeared to be about forty years old, dark-haired and lean; his bearing was relaxed and athletic, not at all that of the bookish historian Mander had imagined from what little he had heard about the man. Unlike the tourists, Harkman was unencumbered with luggage, but had with him just a small bag which was slung casually across his shoulders.

'He's not as young as I thought,' Cro said, eventually. 'The photo on file must be an old one.'

'Which photo?' Mander said, but Cro made no answer.

The young woman from Maiden Castle was watching Harkman too. She was standing quite close to him, making no effort to disguise her interest. When he turned to walk along the quay towards the town he passed her and they glanced at each other momentarily. She moved away to where the dock labourers were unloading crates of beer from the hold of the ship, and sat down on a stone bollard, staring out into the bay.

As Harkman passed the two Commission men he seemed to recognize them as colleagues, for he nodded to them briefly, but made no move to introduce himself.

Cro and Mander waited on the quay for a few minutes, by which time Harkman had vanished into the crowd in Marine Boulevard. On the minaret of the mosque that had been built for the visitors, the muezzin was calling the devout to prayer.

4

David Harkman breakfasted alone in the refectory of the Commission hostel. He assumed that the other people he saw were also employees of the Commission, but he made no attempt to introduce himself, and instead suffered their curious stares with an indifference affected out of self-defence. Friends in London had warned him of the protocol of the Regional Commissions, and that there would be a well-established order of precedence by which he would be introduced to his new colleagues. He had no intention of upsetting the balance of territorial claims within the office; his years at the Bureau of English Culture had made him wise in the ways of civil servants.

He cut short his uneasiness, and the curiosity of the others, by finishing his breakfast quickly, and with noncommittal nods to all in sight he left the hostel building and went for an exploratory stroll around the town.

It was a relief to be in Dorchester at last, after two years of waiting for the appointment to come through. Sometimes he had thought that Wessex Island was a part of the world as un-reachable from London as the Presidential Palace in Riyadh. It wasn't that his security-rating was less than impeccable; he had, after all, been given the temporary posting to Baltimore in the Western Emirate States, and had advised the Cultural Attaché in Rome for one very unexpected week a few years ago. Much more likely was the inevitable grinding slowness of the Party adminis-trative machine.

Not that Wessex was a place to which Party employees were freely transferred. With its mosques and casinos, and the thou-sands of idle-rich tourists from all over the States, Wessex Island was an area of some ideological embarrassment to the Party theorists.

Dorchester itself was the focus of this embarrassment for not only was it the nearest large town to the English mainland, but it was also the place to which most of the tourists came.

Only the fact that Wessex was physically distinct from the mainland made it acceptable to the Party; so long as travel was restricted in England, and permits to visit the international tour-ist zones of the island were granted only to foreign nationals and selected Party workers, the local inhabitants couldn't very well proclaim the evils of capitalism to the English populace at large. Or so the Party sophistry went; Harkman, like most people with a gram of intelligence or information, realized that the flood of Emirate dollars was a major contribution to the Westminster budget.

It was actually a concern for, and an interest in, the local popu-lation that had ostensibly brought Harkman to Wessex.

Ever since the catastrophic earthquakes and land subsidence of the previous century, what had formerly been south-west Eng-land had been separated from the mainland by the narrow but deep channel that was known as Blandford Passage. Wessexmen had been left to fend for themselves for many decades, until the Westminster government had realized the potential of the island as a tourist resort, since when it had been administered and developed and taxed in the same way as the other regions of England.

Harkman's interest, as a social historian, was in what had happened in Wessex during the years of isolation. There were still people alive on the island who remembered those days, and there were records scattered about – mainly in Dorchester, Plymouth and Truro – relating to conditions at the time, and Harkman intended to compile an exhaustive and definitive documentary account. It would probably take him many years, and he was prepared to treat it as his life's work.

This was his ostensible reason for the move to Dorchester, and it was the one which had obtained him his permission. But in his heart he knew that it was not the sole motive.

There was Wessex itself. From the day that he had conceived of the project, Harkman had felt that there was some indefinable insufficiency in his life. It wasn't just that his work at the Bureau of English Culture was unsatisfying – although in many respects it was – nor that he felt a sense of inadequacy about his life in London; more directly, it was an instinctive knowledge that Wessex was a spiritual and emotional home.

It had started with something he'd read about the community at Maiden Castle; it had interested him, and in trying to discover more about it he had sensed a growing involvement with the Castle and the island on which it stood. He simply hadn't understood it, and the need to understand had compelled him with more force than anything the intellectual challenge of his social research could muster.

So as he had arrived in Dorchester the previous evening, he had not only seen that day as the first on which his life's work began, but also as the last on which he had awakened with the feeling of separation from a place that had dominated his thoughts and actions for two years.

Then too, almost incidentally, there was the fact of the tidal bore through Blandford Passage.

Many years before, as a young man, he had had the chance to sample the terrors and excitements of wave-riding. He had had only three weeks in which to learn the elemental violence of the tidal wave, but it was a violence which, once experienced, always enthralled one.

Wave-riding was undeniably a young man's sport – and one for the rich – but over the years Harkman had kept himself in physical trim, and he'd been saving his wages all his life. He had the opportunity, the money and the will to ride the Blandford wave again, and he was determined that he wouldn't waste them.

It was a fine, bright morning in Dorchester, and Harkman relished the lightness and cleanness of the air, the decadence of the architecture, the narrowness of the streets. It was a town with a sunny hangover; the night-clubs and bars of Dorchester catered to the tastes of the visitors late into the night, and the shutters and louvred doors of the villas and apartment-blocks were closed against the freshness of the morning. Even so, there were many holidaymakers already about, strolling through the streets to do a little concessionary shopping before departing to one of the beaches outside town.

Impossible to believe that London was less than two hundred kilometres away!

When he reached the street where the Commission building was situated, Harkman made an instant decision and walked on past. He had an appointment to see Commissioner Borovitin, but there were still a few minutes in hand. He remembered having seen a skimmer-shop by the harbour when he landed the previous evening, and thought he would visit it.

He walked out of the narrow sidestreets into the bright sunlight of the Boulevard, and went down to the harbour. Here many yachts were moving in and out, for the tide was falling and in an hour or two it would be unnavigable. Harkman walked past the cafés and stalls on the Boulevard to the skimmer-shop, where, in a brightly coloured display, the various pieces of equipment needed for the sport were laid out.

Harkman looked first at the tide-skimmers themselves, of which several dozen were stacked under the awning outside the shop. These came in a variety of sizes and designs, and with a surprisingly wide range in prices. Harkman lifted one away from the stack, weighed it in his hands. He had forgotten how heavy a skimmer was, even unloaded! It seemed strong enough, and the painted finish was superb: bright flashes of red and yellow against a white background, polished to a high-gloss surface ... but there was something wrong with the balance, an instinctive feeling he had, something not quite perfect.

He leaned it back against the pile, selected another.

In a moment he walked into the interior of the shop, and looked around. There were several posters attached to one wall, depicting various incidents from the sport. One in particular attracted Harkman's attention: thirty or forty wave-riders standing on their boards in the calm of Blandford Passage, while the tidal wave roared towards them from behind, fifty metres or more in height. It was a superb photograph, catching in its frozen instant the very essence of the sport: the sheer violence of the tide-race, the elemental quality of man against the forces of nature.

Most of the stock was very high-priced: wet-suits were offered for just under ten thousand dollars, breathing-apparatus started at around fifteen thousand. Even the various books and instruction-manuals seemed to be priced above what one would expect to pay in London.

There were some assistants standing around in the shop – three young men with fashionably pale skin, and dressed in sweatshirts and loose, baggy shorts – but none of them seemed anxious for his custom, being involved in a conversation on the other side of the store. Harkman went outside again, and looked once more at the skimmers on sale.

The ideal craft had a combination of strength, balance and speed; the lower planes should be polished, the upper should be rough-grained enough for the rider's feet to gain a firm grip even when the skimmer was waterlogged. The engine-housing had to be flat and streamlined, the tanks distributed so that as the fuel was used up the balance of the craft was not disturbed. The whole craft, fully fuelled and with the engine installed, should be light enough for a strong man to carry, yet heavy enough to provide stability when the same man was standing on it in rough water. There was no perfect or standard tide-skimmer; the rider's demands of the best craft were as personal as the choice of a spouse.

Harkman sampled several more skimmers, taking them from the stack and balancing them as best he could in his hands. He looked in through the shop doorway, but the assistants continued to show no interest in him. He wished he could take one or two selected craft out on the water, to see how they handled.

He glanced at his wristwatch, and saw that he ought to return to the Commission. He took down one more tide-skimmer and held it in both hands above his head, but now each one felt like the one before it.

'Do you want to buy a skimmer?'

Harkman turned, thinking that one of the assistants had at last come forward, but the speaker was a young woman, standing in the shadow of the awning.

'I've been watching you,' she said. 'You don't look like the usual sort of buyer. Our skimmers are much cheaper.'

Harkman went across to her, and recognized her as the attractive but rather dishevelled young woman he'd seen on the quay the evening before.

'You sell skimmers too?' he said.

'We make them. They're hand-made, and can be finished exactly as you want them.'

'The problem is I don't really know what I want. It's been a long time since I did any wave-riding.'

'Then try a few. We've got a lot of samples.'

'Are they here?'

At that moment, two of the assistants came through the doorway of the shop and walked quickly across to them.

'You!' shouted one of them, jabbing the woman roughly on her shoulder. 'Get the hell out of here! We've told you before.'

She stepped back into the sunlight, and Harkman turned to face the man.

'We were just talk . . .'

'We know what she wants. Can we help you, sir?'

Harkman said: 'No.'

He turned his back on the two men, and followed the young woman. She was smiling.

'Did he hurt you?' he said.

'I'm used to it. What about our skimmers? Are you interested?'

'I'd like to see some, but I'm late for an appointment. Will you be here tomorrow?'

'I could be. That's our stall there.' She pointed to the craft-stall, overlooking the harbour. 'But we don't sell skimmers in the town, because we're not licensed for them. Why don't you come up to the Castle? You could see everything we have there.'

'You mean Maiden Castle?' Harkman said, and looked at once across the bay towards the green mound on the promontory.

'Yes.' She was about twenty-seven years old, Harkman supposed. He looked at her plain, unflattering smock, her tangled hair, her grimy legs and feet.

'I'll go to the Castle tomorrow,' he said. 'How will I find you?'

'Ask any of the others. I'm Julia.'

'Do you want my name?'

'I'll remember you,' she said, staring down at the boats in the harbour.

'I'm David Harkman,' he said, but she seemed not to be listening. She walked away from him, not looking back, and Harkman felt she had lost interest.

Then she said: 'I'll wait until you arrive,' but still she did not look back at him.

A large yacht had just berthed in the harbour, and a crowd was gathering by her stall.

5

The Commissioner in Dorchester was a man named Peter Borovitin. Russian name but English blood, back through three generations. Before leaving London, Harkman had found out what he could about the man, but it wasn't much. His reading of what he had learned was that Borovitin had risen in the Regional Service more on the strength of his family name than for any individual qualities within the Party. It suited the Soviet to administer the regions with native-born Englishmen, but Harkman had heard that at least a half of the Commissioners presently in service were Slav either in name or ancestry.

By repute, Borovitin was a good Commissioner, administering the Dorchester area of Wessex fairly and competently, if unimaginatively.

The interview in Borovitin's office – a sunny but bare room on the top floor of the Commission building, with a huge photograph of the Supreme President glaring down from the wall – was a brief one. Either Borovitin disliked Harkman, or he was not interested in him, but he seemed anxious to be finished.

After he had read Harkman's letter of introduction from the head of the Bureau, Borovitin stared heavily at him for at least a minute.

At last he said: 'What kind of research are you intending to do, Mr Harkman?'

'At first I want to do a lot of reading. Newspapers, local-government files, and so on. This will give me an insight into the way the island is run. Later I want to talk to local people. It will involve a certain amount of travelling.' Borovitin was still staring at him, so Harkman added: 'Is there likely to be any restriction on my movements, sir?'

'Not if you get my authorization first. Where are you going?'

Harkman knew if his project was to be done at all realistically, he would eventually have to visit every part of Wessex, but he also knew that unless he kept his early expectations modest he would find his movements strictly watched or controlled by the régime.

'I shall be staying in Dorchester for a few months at least,' he said. 'Perhaps next year I will need to visit Plymouth.'

Borovitin nodded, and Harkman felt that his approach had been correct. But then Borovitin said: 'I don't know what you expect to find in Dorchester.'

'There are the Commission archives, sir. Those will be a major source for my work. And I'd like to visit Maiden Castle.'

'Why?'

The response came so quickly that Harkman was taken off-guard.

He said: 'Is there any reason why I should not, sir?'

'No.' Borovitin was glancing over the introductory letter

again, as if the first time he read it he had missed something of relevance. 'I don't see why you need to go there.'

'It's historically of importance and interest.' Borovitin was staring at him again; suspicion or disinterest? Harkman went on:

'With the greatest respect, sir, I dare say that you have not worked in sociology. In the ancient past, Maiden Castle was a more important place than Dorchester. I believe that during the years Wessex was isolated from the rest of England Maiden Castle would have reverted to a rôle of great strategic and sociological importance.'

'You don't need my authorization to go there,' Borovitin said flatly.

This time Harkman stared back, aware that the Commissioner was not as disconcerted as he was by long silences. The reason he had offered for wanting to go to the Castle had been impromptu, but he felt he had produced an authentic-sounding reply. The fact was that he had to visit the Castle to fulfil some deeper, unspecified need, and he had no explanation for that.

And there was another reason now: to see the young woman, to buy a tide-skimmer.

'About the archives, sir,' he said in the end, no longer ill at ease under the Commissioner's bland scrutiny, but anxious to bring the interview to an end. 'Could I have your authority to inspect the Commission records?'

'You'll have to file a formal application. See Mander.'

'But I understood that the archives were under the jurisdiction of a Mr Cro. It was he who wrote to confirm my appointment.'

'All administrative functions are channelled through Mr Mander.'

A few minutes later, Harkman found the office that had been allocated to him for his use. Although it was quite large, and the previous occupant had cleared it out thoroughly, Harkman disliked the room immediately. It had only one window, and although it could be opened it was set high in the wall and only by standing on a chair could he see out. The effect of it was, as Harkman reflected as he tried it for the first time, that he could sit all day under the sterile glare of fluorescent strip-lights, and smell the fragrance of flowers, hear the buzzing of insects, and listen to the sounds of the holidaymakers walking in the narrow sunlit street outside.

Donald Mander came to see him, and Harkman's first impressions of the man were favourable. He was a florid-faced middle-aged man, with just a few wisps of hair feathering his pink, shiny head. He laughed a lot although Harkman guessed it was intended to put him at his ease – and had what appeared to be a noncommittal and cynical way of describing the office routines and personnel.

'Commissioner Borovitin tells me I must file an application for use of the archives through you.'

'That's right, yes.'

'Then could you take it that I have applied? I'd like to start as soon as possible.'

'You'll need a form, Harkman. I'll look one out for you, and send it down.'

Mander had brought a chair with him from the next office, and the swivel-joint was creaking as he changed his position.

'Couldn't I just have a note typed out?' Harkman said.

'It has to be on the proper form,' Mander said, and laughed. Harkman thought that anyone who found that idea funny must have been working too long in one place.

He said: 'I gather Mr Cro is in charge of the archives.'

'I'll introduce you to him later. Yes, the archives are his responsibility.'

From the mosque across the street, the muezzin called over the rooftops. The eerie, rising voice reminded Harkman of his short visit to the embassy in the Western States. It was the Muslim culture in North America that he had found the strangest of all strange things he had noticed in the trip. Five times daily the nation prostrated itself and prayed towards the east. It was as if the once independent America had to pay daily homage to a greater power than Allah, the power of oil-dollars, the power that had eventually absorbed a culture. This mosque in Dorchester, like the others in the main tourist centres of Wessex, was only a gesture to that power, but a reminder to the English, to the Wessexmen, of the alternatives to socialism.

'Perhaps I could meet Mr Cro?' Harkman said, wishing there was an alternative to this.

Mander swivelled in his chair again. 'Of course. And I'll show you round the building at the same time.'

The day passed slowly, and at the end of it Harkman was tired and irritable. The only positive thing he had to show for his day's efforts was that Cro had lent him a part of the index to the archives. As it was barely more than a list of numbers, it wasn't much better than nothing.

After leaving the Commission in the evening, and having declined an invitation to drinks with Mander and some of his colleagues, Harkman went for a long, solitary stroll around the town.

It was curious that the relaxed mood of the resort did not penetrate to the Commission offices. It was like one of the smaller administrative government offices in London that he had sometimes come up against; one was constantly reminded of form and manner and priorities, as if the Supreme President of the Soviet was expected at any moment.

Only in the front office, where there were public counters, was there any hint that Dorchester was the most fashionable resort in the country; here the large windows looked out across a tree-filled square, where there were two cafés and where several painters were at work. In the mornings the sun shone in, and all day there would be queues in the two carefully separated areas. In one, English nationals – Party employees, local residents and immigrant workers – came in and out to collect items of mail, to register for State employment funds, to buy licences for trade, and to submit to various other demands on their time and attention; at the other desk, States tourists could apply for visas to visit the English mainland, and their colourful clothes and relaxed manner made a noticeable contrast.

Harkman stood behind the counters for several minutes to watch this ordinary business of the Commission, but instead he had been distracted by the pervasive mood of leisure beyond the plate glass windows.

He walked out of the centre of town and went towards Poundbury Camp to the north, and stood for a long time watching the little yachts from Charminster across the inlet. Charminster, unlike its larger and more cosmopolitan neighbour, catered with its State-controlled hotels and villas for English families, who travelled to Wessex by a route that took them to the north coast of the island and passed nowhere near Dorchester.

Glancing back towards Dorchester, Harkman thought of the pictures he had seen of the town that had once stood on the same site. All the buildings of Old Dorchester had gone, and all their ancient associations with them. Those that had not been shaken down in the earthquakes had been flooded in the subsidence. The new Dorchester was a successful compromise between strength and amenity, between function and aesthetic. Although no tremors had been felt in the region for more than forty years the law required every building to be capable of withstanding an earth shock of 6 on the Richter Scale; equally, every new building had to blend with the planners' conception of a holiday centre. Accordingly, the reinforced steel and concrete shells of the buildings were faced with plaster and stucco and whitewash; the balconies and terraces overlooking the sea were integral parts of the tensioned skeletons, and yet were decorated with wrought-iron filigrees, and pinewood panels, and trailing abundant greenery; the windows were laminated, the roofs were prefabricated in one piece to appear as if tiled, and the streets, although charmingly narrow and cobbled, were straight enough and wide enough to allow emergency service vehicles access to any part of the town.

Even the mosque, whose dome and minarets dominated the town, would suffer only surface cracks should an earthquake strike.

In the distance, the Blandford cannon boomed, and Harkman sat down on the dry grass to wait for the tide to flood into the inlet. Here the water was always deeper than by Dorchester Harbour, and when the effect of the wave arrived twenty minutes later it was no more than about half a metre high. The little yachts were able to ride it out without difficulty, and across the water Harkman could hear the shrill, excited cries of children.

This was, in fact, not the wave at all, but the first ripple caused by the monstrous arrival of the main wave at Blandford Passage. But it was enough to remind Harkman of his intention to buy a skimmer the next day, and as more and more waves swept slowly down the inlet as the tide rose he was wondering if by the following evening he would have the nerve to make his first attempt at the Blandford wave.

That night, though, as he lay in his room at the Commission hostel, Harkman's thoughts were of Maiden Castle, and of a woman with evasive eyes.

6

Julia was woken by Greg's hands moving over her body. She lay with her back towards him, feeling him press himself against her. It was always like this in the mornings: Greg woke first, aroused, and before she was barely conscious he would want to make love. Each night, as sleep came on her, she would dread the morning, knowing the inevitability of his demands.

Still dreamy with sleep she tried to slip back, as if this alone would push him away from her.

Greg reached over her, put a hand under her cheek and turned her face towards his. He kissed her, and she felt his hot breath and moist lips on her mouth, his beard rasping on her cheek. She was limp, unresponsive; she could not even make her eyes open.

'Julia . . . kiss me,' he said hoarsely, but his mouth was against her ear now, and the words were a gassy, hissing intrusion. He thrust his hand through her legs from behind, and clutched at her sex. She turned towards him then, forcing him to take his hand away, and he put both his arms around her, kissing her voraciously. She stayed unresisting, and in a moment he pushed his way into her. She was dry and unaroused, and the gasp she gave he mistook for passion, and his movements became urgent and possessive. Through long habit she moved with him, but she felt nothing, only discomfort.

The pleasure of it was his alone; she could not remember the last time she had enjoyed sex with him.

By the time he had reached his panting, noisy climax she was fully awake, and she lay under his weight feeling tense and very aware of her own sexuality. She could feel him inside her, shrinking wetly, and she contracted her muscles against him, reaching for sensation ... but Greg, not noticing, pulled himself away from her without a word and lay beside her on his face, breathing deeply.

Every day it was the same! She responded to him, but too late, and when she was ready he was finished. She reached down and felt herself damp and warm, and the pressure of her hand brought an involuntary contraction of the muscles.

She looked at Greg beside her; he was not asleep, but his desire was exhausted. She would not stir him, would not try to. Greg made love his own way.

Julia waited for a few minutes longer, but Greg did not move again, so she slid out from beneath the rough sheet and walked across to the door of the hut. As she opened it, bright sunlight dazzled her.

She found a towel, wrapped it around the lower half of her body, then walked the short distance to the communal showers. The water was lukewarm and salt, but it refreshed her and flushed away the last remnants of her unfulfilled desire. By the time she returned, Greg had left the hut. She glanced around the dirty, untidy interior, wishing she had more will to clean the place up.

When she had had some food she went in search of Tom Benedict, who was one of the older members of the Castle community. She found him by one of the kilns, raking out the cinders from the fire-tray.

'Can I speak to you, Tom?'

He turned to look at her, and she saw that his eyes were red and watery, and that he held the rake in both hands, hunching a shoulder awkwardly. He let the rake go, and reached out a hand towards her.

'Julia. Help me up, will you?'

'Are you ill, Tom?'

She took his hand, and felt the large, bony knuckles bulging through his papery skin. His fingers were callused and dirty.

'I'm fine, Julia. I slept badly, that's all.'

He was standing now, but he did not release her hand. She

led him to the bench beside the kiln and they sat down. He was wheezing.

Julia had been busy at the stall for the last two or three weeks, because the influx of tourists was at its peak, and she had not seen much of Tom, except late in the evenings. Of all the people at the Castle, she probably knew more about Tom than anyone else because he had befriended her soon after his arrival. In the couple of years he had been at the Castle he had grown steadily more withdrawn, but she knew that he came from the mainland, that he had been happily married for many years, that he had a daughter who worked in Nottingham. There were two grandchildren, too. He had never directly explained why he had joined the Castle community, but from various things he said Julia understood that after the death of his wife he had had to live with his daughter, but had not got along well with her husband. Being older than most of the others at the Castle he had taken a long time to settle down, but he was now accepted by everyone. Several members of the community, Julia in particular, looked to him for guidance or advice.

'You shouldn't be working,' Julia said. 'What's happened to your arm?'

'I must have slept in a draught.' His weak eyes were looking into his lap as he said this.

'It's been hurting for some time, hasn't it?'

'Just a day or two.'

'Have you seen Allen?' He was the community doctor, but he was a remote and difficult man.

'I saw him.'

'No you didn't, Tom. I know you too well.'

'I'll see him today.'

'You ought to go into Dorchester. Go to the hospital.'

Julia stayed with Tom for half an hour, trying to persuade him to have medical treatment. It seemed to her that he was more frightened than obstinate, and Julia decided to speak to Allen herself, if Tom wouldn't do it.

Her problem, though, had been put out of her mind. She had approached Tom with the half-formed resolution to try to talk to him about Greg, about the misery of a loveless, passionless partner, and the stirrings of her body. She could not speak directly of these, of course, but even to talk about unspecified discontents would have been good enough.

Later, she went to the eastern end of the village to help out for a while with the children. Being on this edge of the village, and near the ramparts, the schoolhouse overlooked the sea. The community included about thirty children, and whenever Julia wasn't at the stall in Dorchester she went to help at the school.

Education at Maiden Castle only had the appearance of being casual; the classes were held in the open air whenever the weather allowed, and the attire of both teachers and pupils was informal, but ever since the Commission had sent inspectors to the Castle three years earlier, the content of the lessons had adhered to State doctrine. Children were educated at the Castle until the age of ten: after that they had to attend the State school in Dorchester.

Julia's assistance was generally confined to recreational activities, and on this particular morning she was given charge of a bunch of nine year olds, and organized them into two teams for football. Before long, she had become an active participant in the game, kicking the ball wildly whenever it was in reach, much to the amusement of the more ambitious children. Football was taken very seriously at Maiden Castle, and Julia's ineptitude revealed itself several times when puffing children whisked the ball away from her just as she was about to kick it.

After an hour of this she noticed that the impromptu match had a spectator: a man, standing alone, watching her.

She left the game at once, and went over to him. He was standing as she had seen him when he arrived on the hydrofoil: at ease and watchful, his jacket over his shoulder. He was grinning as she trotted towards him, and his frank look made her uncharacteristically self-conscious about her appearance. She was hot and untidy from running around, and wished she could brush her hair.

'I can wait,' he said. 'I was enjoying watching you.'

'No, I was only helping. You've come about the tide-skimmer.'

'I didn't think you'd remember.'

She had wanted to forget. As soon as she'd spoken to him at the skimmer-shop she had regretted it: Greg was possessive in ways other than sexual, and as soon as she had looked at this man she had recognized a response in herself, and a response in him.

'You're . . . David Harkman,' she said, hesitant with the name as if its use would convey some deeper significance to him, similar to the one it held for her.

'Yes. And you're Julia.'

He looked very cool. There was always a breeze on top of Maiden Castle however hot the sun, but she felt red-faced and sweaty in his company. She swept back the hair from her face.

'Did you come over in a boat?' she said.

'No, I walked around the shore. I wanted to take time from the office.'

'You work for the Commission.'

'I work in the building, but I'm not really on the staff.'

She was watching his face, sensing some recognition, a familiarity. There was no way they could have met before, no possibility of contact. And yet, the evening on the quay when he had arrived, yesterday by the skimmer-shop, now today . . . A nagging recognition of him. Even his name was no surprise. Harkman, Harkman . . . it was a part of her.

Trying to put the uncertainty aside, she said: 'Would you like to see some skimmers?'

'I'd like to try one or two, if that's possible.'

She glanced at his clothes. 'Is that how you normally dress for wave-riding?'

He laughed as he followed her along the edge of the sports field. 'I've brought a swimming costume.'

'We don't normally bother with those here.'

'So I see.'

During the summer months the people at the Castle normally wore very few clothes. Most of the children went entirely naked, and several adults too. In the workshops, clothes were worn for protection, but those who worked in the fields generally only wore a single garment. Julia wore her brown smock by habit, but only because she liked to have pockets. Walking next to David Harkman, she was aware of his machine-made clothes, the pressed trousers and polished shoes, the pale blue shirt. He looked unusual in the Castle surroundings, but the people they passed barely afforded him a glance.

They were walking towards the southern side of the Castle, where the encircling ramparts were laid in a more complex pattern than elsewhere. Julia led the way down into the first dip. They walked along the bottom of this for a short distance until they came to a break in the next wall. Here the ancient Wessexmen had had one of their gates, and it made walking through to the next dip a simple matter.

They came eventually to a recent construction: a large wooden building. It was open at the front, and looked down through another gap in the ramparts to an inlet of the bay below.

Julia walked inside, and at once they were assailed by the unique smells of the workshop: the heady, acidic cellulose paint, the fragrance of sawdust, of wood-glue. The paint-shop was in a separate part of the building, screened from the drifting, settling sawdust, but the paint smell was everywhere.

'Is Greg here?' Julia shouted to the group of men and women busy in the workshop, cutting and planing wood, sawing, sanding, hammering.

'In the paint-shop.'

At that moment Greg came out of the curtained area, wearing a white mask over his nose and mouth. When he saw Julia with Harkman he pulled the mask down, nodded to Harkman.

'Greg, this is David Harkman. He'd like to see some skimmers.'

'What sort of thing are you looking for, Harkman?'

'I don't know. I'd like to try a few.'

'Heavy? Light? What size engine?'

'I'm not sure. It's a long time since I did any wave-riding. What do you think?'

Greg looked him up and down. 'What do you weigh? About eighty kilos?'

'About that.'

'You'll need quite a large craft. If you're just getting back into riding, though, I wouldn't go for one with a big engine.'

'Have you got anything that might be right?'

'Let's have a look.'

Greg walked out of the workshop, and towards a smaller building at its side. Julia and Harkman followed. There were about two dozen completed craft in the shed, stacked one on top of the other.

'None of these has motors,' Greg said. 'But if you pick one out, I can get one fitted.'

For the next few minutes, Harkman and Greg took several of the skimmers from the stack, and carried them outside. Greg's advice was curt, and had a patronizing undertone that Julia had rarely heard in him. For all his unsatisfactory sexual demands, Greg was usually a generous and quiet man, and the only explanation was that he had detected something of her own awareness of Harkman's presence.

She watched as Harkman chose five of the skimmers. As he lifted each one to feel its balance she noticed that Greg was watching critically. He seemed ready to assume that Harkman was a complete novice.

'How much do you charge for one of these?'

Greg started to say: 'It depends . . .', but Julia interrupted.

'Find one you like first,' she said. 'They're all different prices.'

'Can I try these two?' Harkman said, indicating his choices.

'I'll get some motors,' Greg said, and walked back to the workshop. It took about half an hour for him and another man to install the engines, and explain the controls. The craft were carried down to a tiny beach beside the Castle ramparts.

As Harkman laid them out on the sand, Julia took Greg to one side.

'I can deal with him now,' she said.

'I think I'll stay around,' Greg said.

'He's my customer. I brought him up here.'

'Just a customer, is he? I don't like the way he was looking at you.'

'Greg, he's a Commission man. I want this sale for myself.' The young man looked critically again at Harkman, and Julia saw in his eyes the same possessive expression she saw when his jealousies were aroused. She hadn't been aware that Harkman had been looking at her in any certain way, and the information pleased her.

'Get the best price you can, then. If he's from the Commission he can afford the same prices as the government shop.'

'I run the stall, Greg. I know how to make a sale.' The young man still showed no sign of returning to the workshop. She added: 'I'll talk to you later.'

Greg hesitated a few moments longer, then, with one more wary look at Harkman, he clambered up the slope of the nearest rampart, and shortly was out of sight.

7

David Harkman leaned forward to take the balance, opened the skimmer's throttle, and felt the surge of acceleration beneath his feet. He throttled back at once, alarmed at the instant response of the engine. He guided the craft towards the shallow end of the inlet, and executed a wide, gentle turn. Facing towards the sea, he accelerated again, this time allowing the engine to take the craft as fast as it would go. The inlet, sheltered on one side by the bulk of the Castle and by a forested hill on the other, was as smooth as glass. The only thing that would tip him off the skimmer was his own inexperience.

As he passed the little beach where he had launched the skimmer, he looked for Julia to wave to her, but there was no sign of her. He reached the neck of the inlet and turned again, this time trying the standard skimmer-turn: flipping the board with his weight, turning it through a hundred and eighty degrees in not much more than its own length.

He started back with renewed confidence, and then he saw Julia. She was swimming, and he saw her arm wave from the water.

He liked the way the craft handled, and so he took it up and down the narrow creek three more times, acquiring confidence and regaining old skills each time. At last he took the skimmer to where Julia was swimming, and he slowed it, letting the engine idle.

She swam over to him. Her hair swept wetly back from her face, clinging to her head like the coat of an animal. As she rested her hands on the edge of the skimmer, he saw she was naked.

'You're as pale as the tourists!' she said, laughing, and splashed water up at his legs.

'I've been working in offices all my life,' he said, trying to keep his balance because she was deliberately wobbling him.

'Come and have a swim.'

'No, I want to try the other board.'

'I'll tip you in!'

He gunned the engine and swung away. When he was a short distance from her he turned and headed straight back, pulling up short a couple of metres away and sending a sheet of water spraying over her. Julia went under, and came up spitting water.

Laughing, Harkman accelerated away down the creek.

Julia was still swimming five minutes later, so he went back to the beach and dragged the second skimmer down to the water. It didn't take him more than one ride down the inlet to discover that this one, compared to the first, seemed slower and heavier.

He saw Julia standing in the shallows, up to her waist in the water, so he took the craft over to her.

'I'm going to take the first one,' he said, standing on the board and looking down at her. 'How much?'

She grinned sweetly at him, then tipped the skimmer with both hands. Harkman swung his arms wildly, and toppled backwards into the water. As soon as he had recovered his sense of direction he lunged at Julia, splashing water, trying to give her a second ducking . . . but she was wading out.

'Don't you want to swim?' he said, standing up with his hands on his hips.

'I've had enough. I was getting cold. I'll wait here.'

She picked up her discarded smock and began dabbing the water from her body with it. Harkman turned round and dived, and swam out to the deeper, greener water of the inlet, thinking it would have been a more interesting swim to be splashing around with a naked young woman. He floated on his back, and saw that Julia had put her smock on the sand, and was lying down beside it, waiting for him.

Five minutes later he walked up the beach, and Julia tossed him her smock. 'Here . . . you can dry yourself with this.'

He wiped his face and neck, and sat down beside her. 'I think I'll dry out in the sun.'

He lay back on the sand, aware of her nearness to him, aware of her nakedness.

'They're good skimmers,' he said, trying to keep his mind on other matters. Nudity was a commonplace in this part of Wessex: there was no invitation implied in her casual behaviour.

'I suppose so,' Julia said.

'Who designs them?'

'A couple of the men in the workshop.'

He wondered if she was aware of the tension he was feeling. They were talking in an off-hand, disinterested way, as if unwilling to confront each other with more direct statements. Or was it only he who felt it? She was lying back, supporting her weight on her elbows, and staring out across the inlet. Trying not to be too obvious about it, Harkman appraised her body, admired the neatness of her figure. Her skin was tanned all over to a mellow brown.

In an effort to persuade himself that he was not alone, Harkman wondered why Julia delayed here at the beach with him. If it was just a question of selling him the skimmer, the deal would be concluded now.

His clothes were piled near by, and he fumbled through the pockets of his jacket and found his cigarettes.

'Do you smoke?' he said.

'No thanks.'

He leaned back and inhaled smoke. The Castle heaped behind them, seeming to glow in the heat of the sun, radiating an ancient heat, an inner life. Was it just this that was affecting him? He had responded at last to the compulsion that had afflicted him in London, and he had visited the Castle. Yet it had been nothing, just as now, as he lay under the slope of its ramparts, it was nothing.

Julia was restless, and stared back up the rampart several times.

'Was that your boyfriend?' Harkman said in the end, breaking a silence that had endured for several minutes. 'The one in the paint-shop?'

'Greg? He's no one special.'

'I thought you were waiting for him to come back.'

'No . . . it's just . . .' She sat up, and turned round to face him. 'I shouldn't be here with you.'

'Do you want to put on your dress again?'

'It's not that. If Greg . . . or anybody came back, they'd wonder why I was still sitting here.'

'Well? Why are you?'

'I don't know.'

'Shall we close the deal?' Harkman said. 'I've brought the money with me.'

'No.' She put a hand on his. 'Please don't. Stay and talk to me.'

And there it was: for Harkman, a confirmation of his own feeling. Nothing specific, nothing he could put into words. No reasons, but a need to stay with her, a need to talk and make some kind of contact.

He said: 'When I arrived in Dorchester two days ago, I felt I recognized you. Do you know what I mean?'

She nodded. 'I knew your name. David Harkman . . . it was as if it was written in large letters all over you.'

'Was it?' he said, smiling.

'No . . . but I knew it. Have we met before?'

'I don't think so. I've never been to Wessex in my life.'

'I've only been here for about three years.' She spoke then of her past, as if to set out a sequence of events where their lives might have intersected. Harkman listened, but he knew that there was nowhere they could have seen each other: she had been brought up on a cooperative farm near Hereford, and lived there until three years ago. She'd never been to London, never even travelled further east than Malvern, where she had been to school.

Harkman thought of his own life, but didn't speak of it. He felt his age, realizing that he must be nearly fifteen years older than her . . . and that those fifteen years would take longer to tell than the story of her own whole life. And yet, in terms of events nothing much had happened: education, career, marriage, career, divorce, career . . . offices, government departments, reports written and published. Not much for more than forty years of life, but more than he wanted to describe to her.

'Then what is it?' she said. 'Why do I know you?'

'You really do feel it.'

She was looking at him directly, almost earnestly, and he re-membered the evasiveness of those same eyes when they had been talking outside the shop.

'I'm glad you said something,' Julia said. 'I thought it was only me.'

'I'll say it plainly: I'm attracted to you.'

A large fly buzzed around Julia's face, and she flicked a hand at it. Undeterred, it landed on her leg and walked up her thigh in quick, staccato movements. She knocked it away.

She said: 'I thought for a time that I ... It's difficult to say. Yesterday at the shop. Well, I thought it was one of those sexual things. You know, when you can't control it.'

'You're very attractive, Julia.'

'But it's not that, is it? Not just that.'

'I'm tempted to say yes,' he said. 'I wish it was only that, be-cause it would be simpler. It's there for me ... but that's not all.'

'I'd like my dress, please.'

He passed it to her without a word, and watched as she pulled it over her head. She stood up to shake it down over her legs, then sat beside him again.

'Did you get dressed because we were talking about sex?' he said.

'Yes.'

'Then I think we understand one another.' He had a sudden urge to touch her, and he reached out to take her hand, but she moved it away from him. He went on: 'I feel that we somehow possess each other, Julia. That we are linked in some way, and that it was inevitable we would meet. Do you know what I mean?'

'I think so.'

'I'd like a direct answer.'

She said: 'I'm not sure I can give you one.'

Harkman flicked away the end of his cigarette, and it cart-wheeled into the water and hissed. He lit another immediately.

'Am I offending you by talking about this?'

'No, but it's very difficult. I know what you mean, because I feel it too. As soon as I saw you I felt it.'

Harkman said: 'Julia, two years ago I was working at my office in London, when I suddenly felt a tremendous necessity to live and work here in Wessex. It obsessed me, I couldn't stop thinking about it. Eventually I applied for a transfer to Dorchester . . . and although it took two years for the permit to come through, I got here in the end. Now I'm here, and I still don't know why. It feels to me now, as I talk to you, that it was to meet you, or someone like you. But I know rationally that that's nonsense.'

He paused, remembering how he had fretted in London, waiting for the appointment to be confirmed.

'Go on.'

'That's about it. Except that now I've met you, it feels as if my reason for coming here was just a pretext.'

Julia said, unexpectedly: 'I think I understand. When I came to Maiden Castle for the first time, everything that had happened before seemed unreal.'

Harkman looked at her in surprise. 'Are you making that up?'

'No. I can remember my father and mother, and I can remember the farm, and schooldays . . . and all that. But at the same time I can hardly remember what it was really like.'

'Do you ever see your parents?'

'Sometimes. I think I saw them . . . recently. I'm not sure.'

'And you'd never go back to the farm?'

She shook her head. 'It would be impossible.'

'Do you know why?'

'Because I'm committed to the Castle.' She was looking away from him. 'No, it isn't just that. My place is here. I can't say why.'

'My place is with you,' Harkman said. 'I don't know why, either. I'll never leave Wessex.'

'What do you want, David?'

'I want you, Julia . . . and I want to know *why*.'

Looking directly at him, she said: 'If you had to settle for one, which would it be?'

And she looked away, just as she had done outside the skimmer-shop.

There was a noise above them, and Harkman turned. Greg

had appeared at the top of the nearest rampart, and was walking down towards them, Julia had seen him too.

Harkman said: 'Will you come to my room tonight? In Dorchester.'

'No, I can't. It's impossible.'

'Tomorrow, then.'

She shook her head, watching Greg come towards them, but said: 'I don't know where it is.'

She stood up, straightening her smock with guilty movements of her hands.

'The Commission hostel. Room 14.'

Greg scrambled down on to the sand, and walked towards them. Harkman turned to face him.

'I'd like this one,' he said.

Greg said: 'Two thousand dollars. Seven thousand extra for the engine.'

'Greg, that's not the usual price,' Julia said. Harkman looked at her, and, conscious of the double meaning, said: 'Well?'

Julia brushed the sand from her smock, keeping her face averted. 'We normally charge six thousand for the whole unit.'

Greg showed no response.

'That seems a fair price.' Harkman bent down and picked up his jacket.

'I'll deliver it myself,' Julia said. 'Tomorrow evening.'

As Harkman counted the money into Greg's hand, Julia was standing by the edge of the waves, staring out across the narrow inlet.

8

By mid-afternoon, Tom Benedict was plainly very ill, and Julia's intrigued day-dreams about David Harkman were interrupted as she arranged for Tom to be taken to the infirmary in the Castle village. Hannah and Mark, who ran the stall in Dorchester with her, were expecting her there for the evening trade, and she had to take time to send someone down with a message.

When she returned to the infirmary, Allen had already visited

Tom, and the old man was laid out as comfortably as possible in the cool, white-painted ward. He recognized Julia when she arrived, but soon afterwards fell asleep.

The Castle infirmary was run on an entirely voluntary basis, and had no proper medical facilities. It was simply a long, low hut, which was kept clean and ventilated, and contained sixteen beds where people suffering from minor ailments could be looked after. A few medical supplies were kept in a small room at one end, but any serious disease had to be treated in the Dorchester hospital.

Julia sought out one of the women who served occasional duties as a nurse.

'Where's Allen?' she said. 'What's he doing for Tom?'

'He said he needed rest. He's sent away to Dorchester, and someone's coming up this evening.'

'This evening! That might be too late. Did he say what was wrong?'

'No, Julia. Tom's old . . . it could be anything.'

Exasperated, Julia returned to the bedside and took Tom's tight-skinned hand in hers. The fingers were cold and stiff, and for a moment she thought he must have died while she was away from the bed. Then she saw a very slow, very shallow movement of his chest. She slipped his hand beneath the blanket and continued to hold it, trying to warm him.

It felt cold in the ward, because the windows were open and although there was only a slight breeze the sun never seemed to warm the infirmary. Julia swept back the thin white hair from the old man's brow, and felt that the skin there was also cool, not perspiring.

Julia felt closer to Tom than she could ever say; closer than she felt to her parents, closer than she felt to Greg . . . and yet it was neither a blood relationship nor a sexual one. There was an affinity there, an unspoken understanding.

There were approximately two hundred people in the Castle community, children included, but of these only a handful had any influence on her life or thoughts. She thought of the rest as pale shadows, lacking in personality, following where others led.

Allen, the doctor, was one such. He was unquestionably quali-
fied for medical practice, and in the treatment of minor ailments
and in diagnosing diseases he was excellent. But he seemed never
to act; anything that could not be treated with available medi-
cines was referred immediately to the hospital in Dorchester.
Perhaps it was right that this should be so . . . but Allen's personality was negative, unforthcoming.

Greg was another. In spite of the fact that she had slept with
him for months, and in spite of there having been a certain amount
of mutual interest at the start, Julia had never really grown to
know the young man. He was, to her, always the distant, effi-
cient craftsman who worked in the skimmer workshop, or the
inconsiderate, selfish and loveless man who used her body. In the
Castle community Greg seemed to be one of the more popular
people – and when Julia was not suffering his physical attentions
she found him amusing and pleasant company – but he too had
this paleness to his character that was a constant frustration to
her. Sometimes, when she was alone with him, Julia wanted to
shout at him or scream at him or wave her arms . . . anything to
elicit some kind of positive response.

There were the others, though, and they were here at the
Castle, and in Dorchester and the surrounding countryside.

There was Nathan Williams, who played a great part in organizing and shaping the community; some said he had been at
the Castle when the community was first formed. There was a
woman named Mary, who was one of the potters. There was
Rod, who worked on the fishing smack owned by the Castle.
There was Alicia, one of the teachers. There was Tom Benedict.

Sometimes, while she was working on the stall in Dorchester, Julia would see local people passing the harbour . . . and she
would detect that with them, too, there was this certain affinity.

For a long time she had felt it was a talent, an uncontrollable
clairvoyance. She had wondered if she had powers of telepathy,
or something similar, but there were never any other kinds of
manifestation. Just an empathic understanding, a recognition.

Ignoring it, as she had tried to do for some time, it became
less important, but meeting David Harkman had reminded her
that it was a real and inexplicable fact of her life. Although with

David there was another thing, a sexual charge, a physical desire, an emotional tension.

'Is that you, Julia?'

Tom spoke very weakly. His eyes hadn't opened. She squeezed his hand gently, under the blanket.

'I'm here, Tom. Don't worry. There's a doctor coming from Dorchester.'

'Don't let go . . .'

She looked around. She and Tom were alone in the infirmary: summer was a healthy time for the villagers. But she wished there were someone with them, a trained nurse . . . or Allen.

Through one of the windows she could see children running around, playing and calling to each other with shrill voices. School had finished for the day, evening would soon be here.

She never detected the affinity with any of the children, although she liked them, and the teachers at the school were always glad of her help. She saw the children as a milling, diminutive presence: noisy, quick-moving, demanding of time and energy. But as David Harkman had said of his career, and as she felt about her own past, the children were a fact, not something she had any feeling about.

One of the women in the village had given birth a few weeks before, and Julia had seen the mother and child soon afterwards. It had been like a classic portrait of healthy motherhood: the woman sitting up in bed in the infirmary, her hair tangled, a cardigan pinned around her shoulders. The child cried in her arms, pink and damp and very small. The mother's eyes were bright and tired, the bedclothes had been straightened over her. Nothing had gone wrong, no worries: mother and child doing well. Julia had never known a crisis for any of the village people; there were 'flu epidemics, and the children passed measles and mumps to one another . . . but she had never known anyone fall and break a leg, nor was there ever a pregnancy that went wrong, nor did anyone ever die violently. There was a graveyard at the western end of the Castle compound, but the few deaths that occurred happened quietly, unobtrusively.

It was a sheltered, undangerous place; the harsher realities of life seemed as if they were postponed.

Then, as if contradicting the thought, Tom groaned, and his head turned restlessly.

Tom was different, though, Tom recognized the affinity. He had always been at the front of the stage for her; a leading player, not a member of the chorus. This analogy had often occurred to her as if it would solve the puzzle, but all it ever did was underline the feeling.

Until she had spoken of it with David Harkman, she had never directly acknowledged the feeling to anyone else. Not to Nathan, or Mary . . . not even to Tom. But David Harkman had spoken of it himself, had pointed directly to it.

We are different, you and I, he had said. We are different, because we are the same.

The nursing woman appeared at the entrance to the ward, leading a small child by the hand. She walked slowly towards the bed and Julia turned anxiously towards her, but not releasing Tom's hand.

'Is the doctor coming?' she said.

'I told you, dear, he's on his way. They're probably busy in Dorchester, what with all the foreigners coming in.'

'Then will you try to find Allen?' Julia said. 'Tom's very ill. I don't know what to do.'

The woman reached past her, and touched the palm of her hand to the old man's brow.

'He's not feverish. He's just sleeping.'

'Look, please find Allen! I'm very worried.'

'I'll see where he is.'

The woman's child had been raising himself up and down on the end of the bed, falling across his stomach and laughing, uncaring that Tom's legs, which were directly under him, might be hurting. The woman took the child's hand again, and walked slowly towards the door. Julia wanted to urge her again to hurry, sensing somehow that things had reached a critical stage for Tom. His head was still moving slowly from side to side, and his eyes were open, but unseeing.

'Do you think he'd like some food?' The woman had paused by the door, looking back at her.

Julia turned towards her again. 'No. Get Allen . . . and please, for Tom's benefit, find him as soon – '

As she spoke, Julia felt Tom's hand move away from her own. Still facing the woman by the door, she reached further under the blanket, groping for him. She turned back to the bed, fearing the worst . . . but totally unprepared for what she saw.

The bed was empty.

The blanket was still crumpled over where he had lain, and the sheet beneath it bore a trace of the residual warmth of his old body, but Tom had vanished.

Julia gasped aloud and stood back, scraping her chair noisily.

'Tom! For God's sake, Tom!'

The nursing woman was watching her from the door. 'What's going on?'

'He's gone!'

Disbelieving, Julia threw back the blanket, as if the old man had somehow wriggled down under the bedclothes like a child playfully hiding. The blanket fell over the metal bed-end, humped on to the floor. The lower sheet still bore the impression of Tom's body.

'What are you doing in here, Julia? You know no one's here – '

Julia scrambled on to the bed, kneeling on it, leaning over to the far side, in the desperate inspired hope that Tom had fallen from the bed, that he was still there . . . but the floor was bare.

The woman had left the child by the door, and was striding towards her. As she reached the bed she seized Julia's arm, and pulled her round.

'If you were the one who had to make these beds . . .'

'Tom has vanished! He was here! I was holding his hand!'

'What are you talking about? There's no one here.'

Julia felt like screaming at the woman. She pointed in silent agony at the bed, its emptiness self-evident proof of what she was saying.

The woman pulled officiously at the blanket Julia had thrown back. 'These beds have to be kept ready. What are you doing here? Are you ill?'

The woman's words were meaningless. Julia moved back from the bed and stood before her, still trying to express the impossibility of what had happened.

'Tom! Tom Benedict! You saw him . . . he was here.'

The woman was scuffing her hand across the lower sheet, smoothing it out, as if erasing the last evidence of Tom's presence. In one last desperate attempt, Julia foolishly snatched away the pillow, as if Tom's frail body could somehow be concealed beneath it. The woman took it away from her, fluffed it with her hands and replaced it.

Julia stepped back, watching the nursing woman remake the bed. The child stood by the door, kicking the frame idly. The rest of the ward was bare, empty, quiet. It was beyond all reason: Tom could not slip away from her, vanish from the face of the earth!

Still uncomprehending, Julia turned again to the woman. 'Please! You saw Tom in this bed. He was dying! You felt his brow. You said he had no fever, and you were going to find Allen.'

At the mention of the doctor's name the woman looked at her. 'Allen? He's in Dorchester, I think. I haven't seen him all day.'

'But you did see Tom Benedict here?'

The woman shook her head slowly. 'Tom . . . Benedict? Who's that?'

'You know! Tom! Everyone knew him!'

The woman tucked the blanket under the mattress, smoothed it over with her hand, and then straightened.

'I'm sorry, Julia. I don't know what you're talking about. I find you all by yourself in here, wrecking the bed. What do you expect me to think? Are you saying someone's ill?'

Julia took a breath to say it all again, but suddenly realized that the woman genuinely had no idea what she was saying. The ward had an aseptic, unused feel to it: no one in the community had been ill for weeks.

'I'm sorry . . . I don't know what came over me.'

She walked slowly from the ward, past the child, and out into the sunlight. Children still played, a ball was being kicked around. One of the children ran from the crowd, crying. Two others followed, then went back to the game. In the distance, Julia could see the people working in the fields.

She waited outside the infirmary until the woman came out. She closed the door, looked curiously at Julia, then walked off towards the village.

Julia stayed by the infirmary, still unable to comprehend what had happened, still unwilling to leave the scene, as if by staying Tom would somehow return . . . the old grin on his face, confessing to a hoax.

She sat down on the grass, oblivious of all around her, and suddenly started to cry.

A little later she walked around the infirmary building, trying to see if there was some way Tom could have left the building without her noticing. There were two other doors, but they were both locked.

In the evening she spoke to Nathan Williams. 'Have you seen Tom?'

'Tom? Tom who?'

'Benedict. Tom Benedict.'

'Never heard of him.'

No one knew him. Later she found Allen, spoke to him.

'Did you treat Tom today?'

'I've been in Dorchester, Julia. Is he still ill? Who is it?'

'Tom . . .'

Then she found that she couldn't remember his surname. She ate a meal with a group of the others, trying to think of it . . . but by the time the meal was finished she could not even remember his first name.

She felt a sense of great loss, and an overwhelming sadness, and a sure knowledge that someone she had loved was no longer there.

Someone had died that day, or left the community. She wasn't sure which. Nor who it had been. It was very uncertain. Was it a man or woman . . . ?

By the time she lay down beside Greg that night, the feeling had become one of general sadness, not localized to any particular event or person.

She slept well, and when in the morning she was woken by Greg's insistent sexual advances she had no memory of what had happened the previous evening. Her sadness had gone, and as she lay with Greg thrusting himself into her she was thinking instead of David Harkman, and her intention to visit him in the evening. The intrigue and excitement were still there, and, because she was thinking of David, Greg's lovemaking for once did not leave her unsatisfied.

9

Before Greg left the hut to go to the workshop, Julia told him she was going to spend the day at the stall in Dorchester, and return in the late afternoon to collect the skimmer for David Harkman.

'Why don't you take it with you now?'

'The boat's going to be fully loaded,' she said. 'I've got to come back to the Castle this afternoon anyway. I can make a special journey.'

Greg looked at her suspiciously, and for a moment Julia thought he was going to say that he would deliver the skimmer to Harkman himself. She was prepared for that: although she had made up her mind about David Harkman, a residual doubt about the possible consequences would be appeased by the decision being made for her. Instead, Greg said nothing, and soon afterwards he went to the workshop.

When she was alone, Julia washed hurriedly, then went to find Mark and Hannah. Mark had already left for the town on foot, and Hannah was preparing the boat in which the Castle's wares were carried across to the town. It was a small dinghy, fitted with an old-fashioned petrol engine. It was the only motorized boat the Castle possessed – indeed, it was the only motorized vehicle of any kind – and it was moored overnight on a stretch of sand beneath the north-eastern ramparts of the Castle.

'I'll need the boat this evening, Hannah. I'll be returning to the Castle in the afternoon. Can you and Mark walk back this evening?'

Hannah was a quiet woman approaching middle age, and she nodded briefly.

Julia said: 'I'll walk over to Dorchester this morning. I've got a few things to do here first.'

Hannah nodded again, seeming to stare past her. Julia had found her a difficult person to get on with from the start, and the two women still hardly knew each other. Sometimes, two or three days would pass at the stall without their speaking to each other. It seemed not to matter.

Julia helped her launch the boat, and pushed it out into deeper water before Hannah started the engine.

She watched from the beach as the little boat chugged away, and then she walked back along the shore, beneath the northern ramparts. The skirt of her smock had got wet when she waded out into the sea, and so she took it off and laid it in the sunshine for a few minutes.

The warmth of the sun on her body reminded her of the day before, as she had lain on the sandy beach of the inlet, watching David Harkman swimming, and feeling the piquancy of sexual anticipation. That anticipation was still there. The prospect of the evening made her feel like she had when she was sixteen, when everything had been full of mystery and dangerous promise, when every young man on the farming cooperative had begun to look at her with new interest, and when she had started to explore the possibilities of that interest.

Those early experiences now felt remote and unreal; perhaps they had been changed in hindsight by the long months of sexual monotony with Greg, or perhaps the only real charge they had ever held was that of novelty.

Thinking of David Harkman, thinking of the intangible magnetism that drew them together, Julia felt an anticipatory moistness in her mouth, a tightness in her stomach: physical excitement, emotional arousal.

After a few minutes of such idle but pleasurable thoughts, Julia sat up and felt the skirt of her smock. It was still damp, but she felt like walking and so she pulled it on again.

She climbed the first rampart and stood for a while to stare out across the blue bay. The tide was high but ebbing, and dozens of pleasure craft were sailing on the calm water. There was a slight haze in the air, and the hills around Blandford Passage were invisible from the Castle. Sometimes Julia envied the rich tourists, for they could buy and enjoy this beautiful place and stay shielded from the less glamorous quotidian concerns of the local people. No one in this part of Wessex actually lived in poverty, but the villas and apartments and hotels that the visitors saw were a world away from local housing standards. The winter months in Wessex were hard for everybody, and when the tidal bore broke through the Passage in its midwinter fury it was as a reminder of the elemental forces that had shaped this region, not as a tourist attraction for the rich and idle.

The fact that Maiden Castle derived a substantial part of its income from supplying equipment for that attraction held a double irony for Julia. The first was implicit – for the Castle community could not survive without the sales of its skimmers – and the second was that it had brought David Harkman to her, and she thought of him as neither rich nor idle.

She turned and headed inland, walking along the crest of the first rampart. After a while she ran down the slope, and took a path that meandered over the meadows between the Castle and Dorchester, leading nowhere in particular but heading away from the sea. There was a favourite place of hers along here, a quiet hollow, a secret sanctuary.

The sea, however calm or windless, always scented the air at its shore; once inland, Julia felt its presence slipping away behind her, and the air seemed warmer, stiller, more dusty and laden with life. Insects flew and hummed, grass rustled, plants grew green and moist, and underfoot the soil was softer, browner. Julia walked slowly, feeling free and without worries.

She came at last to the place she was looking for: a mound of higher ground, overgrown with bracken. This was some distance from the Castle, although from one side of the low mound a part of the Castle could be seen through a break in the trees around the tiny hamlet of Clandon. Julia walked up the slope, pushing a way through the pathless bracken which grew, in places, as high as her shoulders. The ground was mossy, alive with all manner of tiny animals and insects. On the far side of the rise there was a natural break in the vegetation: the ground was stonier here, and the bracken grew less thickly.

Julia sat down, hugging her arms around her knees, and stared towards the south. She had never seen anyone from the Castle here. It was the one place she could come to and know she would be alone.

She sat and dreamed for about an hour, enjoying the warmth,

relishing the solitude. Later, she turned and walked back through the bracken, intending to take as long as possible to reach Dorchester, and then spend the rest of the day at the stall before taking the boat back to the Castle.

Unexpectedly, there came a sudden glint of dazzling light in her eyes, and she blinked and turned her head, as if trying to flick away a piece of grit. She looked around, trying to see the source of the light: it had come from her right, through the bracken.

She moved to one side, trying to peer across the thickly growing vegetation. There was nothing there, no movement, no sign of anything.

She walked on, but moving towards the right, as if to investigate it.

As she pushed aside a large growth of bracken she saw a gleam of white light travelling quickly and erratically across the stalks and leaves towards her. In an instant it found her, and again the brilliance of reflected sunlight dazzled her. She ducked away, and at once saw the source of the light: there was a young man crouching in the bracken about twenty metres away from her, holding a piece of glass in his hand.

He stood up as soon as he realized she had seen him.

'What are you doing?' she called to him, holding up her hand in case he played the light on her again.

'Watching you, m'dear.' A local accent and intonation, but her doubts were raised immediately by something she sensed in the voice, as if it were an assumed accent.

He was stepping towards her, brushing aside the bracken with his hands. She saw that he was dark-haired and good-looking, and with an easy walk and physique, but the smile on his face was vaguely sinister. She sensed danger, but then saw that he was dressed in a smock similar to her own, which meant that he was from the Castle. But she didn't know his face.

'Who are you?'

'Never mind who I am,' he said, and again there was a trace of the old Wessex lilt. 'I know you're Julia. That right?'

She nodded before she could stop herself. 'Are you from the Castle?'

'You could say that.'

'I've never seen you before.'

'I only just arrived, after a manner of speaking.'

He was standing before her now, not threatening her in any way but apparently amused at the sight of her. He was holding a mirror in his right hand, a small circle of polished and silvered glass, quite ordinary. He was playing with it as he stood there, turning it from side to side at shoulder height, and Julia glimpsed whirling reflections of bracken and sky and herself.

'What do you want?'

'Surely you know that, m'dear.'

Once again there was no suggestion of threat, but he seemed surprised that she did not know.

'I'm going back to the Castle,' she said, trying to move past him.

'So am I. We'll walk together.'

As he said this he stepped to one side, and the sun fell across his face. Once more the mirror caught the sun, and he flashed it at her so that the light went into her eyes.

She turned her face away. 'Don't do that, please!'

'Look into it, Julia.'

He held it towards her at eye-level. She wouldn't look at first, not wanting to be dazzled again, but this time he was holding it so that she could see a reflection of herself. His hand was steady, but the mirror was angled down very slightly so that she saw a reflection of her own chin and neck. Automatically, she stooped a little so that she could look into her own eyes.

'Hold still, Julia.'

She hardly heard what he said, because as she looked at her own eyes it was as if she was staring into a deep cavern. It frightened her and fascinated her, because the more obsessively she looked the deeper became the gaze of her own reflection.

She stepped back involuntarily, and blinked.

'Did you see yourself, Julia?'

'Please . . . I don't understand. What are you doing?'

He was still holding the mirror out to her, but she had moved away so that she was no longer transfixed by her own gaze. Then, in the mirror, she saw a second reflection. There was someone behind –

She turned, gasping aloud. Another man had come up behind her, silently through the bracken. He too was holding a mirror towards her, trying to make her see her own reflection.

Some dim awareness, a distant memory . . .

'No!' she said. 'Please!'

The first man was twirling his mirror again, catching the sun, making the brilliant rays flash about her head, whisk across her face.

She closed her eyes, trying to avoid the light, trying to rid herself of the terror that was in her.

The second man said: 'Julia, look into the mirror.'

He was standing beside the first man now, and they both had their mirrors held before her face. Although she was backing away, stumbling through the bracken, they were always in front of her, and soon it was inevitable that she –

Her gaze became locked with that of her reflected self. The same fright and fascination were there, drawing her in, holding her in the limbo of the illusory mirrored world. She became two-dimensional, spread across the plane between glass and silver. She felt a last, terrible compulsion to run, to hide, but it was too late and she was held in the mirror.

Later, she found herself walking back along the path she had followed, one man in front of her, the other behind. Her trance excluded all awareness of the things around her, except for the sight of the back of the man ahead, the sound of the man behind.

They came to Maiden Castle, and she walked with them up the slopes of the ramparts. They went over the first earthwork, then the second, then along the trough between second and third. There were a few people about, but Julia paid no attention to them, and they did not notice her.

At last they came to an artificial construction in the trough: a low, concrete building. It was open on one side, and they walked in. There was nothing here: rubble littered the floor, and the walls and ceiling were cracked. Daylight showed in many places. On the far side there was a flight of steps, leading down, and the first man led the way. They walked slowly and carefully, stepping over small heaps of broken plaster and concrete. The air was chill, and smelled of clay. At the bottom of the stairs it was dark, because an electric light-bulb attached to the wall had broken, but ahead was a long corridor, a tunnel, leading under the village of Maiden Castle, and this was well-lit.

They walked along the tunnel, and Julia saw that the floor was untidy with scraps of paper, broken glass, pools of water. Circular mirrors, lying as if discarded, winked up at her as she passed.

'In here, Julia.'

They walked into a long, low hall, chill and almost completely dark. Only one light-bulb burned, radiating a pool of light into a bright circle in the centre of the floor.

She felt numbness and fear, compounded by the sense of unwilling compliance with the men's will. The warmth of the sun, the breezes and brightness of the bay, the people in her life ... they were already long behind her, almost forgotten.

Along the length of one wall, barely visible in the gloom, there was a row of metal cabinets, grey-painted, dull-sheened. The second man, the one who walked behind, went across to these and walked along until he had found the one he was looking for. He put his hands on a steel handle, and pulled ... and a long shallow drawer appeared.

Julia walked towards it without being told.

The younger man, the dark-haired one with the Wessex voice, stood beside her.

'Don't you be frightened, Julia.'

She saw in him the affinity, the sense of recognition.

'What do you want me to do?'

'Take off your dress. Lie on the drawer.'

Talking had weakened the trance. She looked away from him, feeling a return of her sense of identity.

'No,' she said, but her voice was uncertain, trembling.

Watching her, he raised the little mirror again, and she shrank back from it, not wanting to see her own face. She felt the cold edge of the metal drawer against her hip.

'Take off your dress, Julia.'

'No, I won't.'

'I'll hold her down, Steve. You get it off.'

Before she could resist, Julia was pushed back against the drawer, and one of the men seized her from behind, his arm holding tightly across her shoulders. The other man snatched at the laces at the front, opening the dress, pulling it down. She struggled at first, but she was still under the partial influence of the mirror and in a few seconds she was naked.

'O.K., that's it.'

They turned her and pushed her down along the length of the drawer. The metal was cold against her flesh, and she resisted again ... but they were too strong and too determined. She felt their hands on her body, pulling her and holding her arms and legs. Her head was pushed down into a contoured support, and she felt a sharp pricking in her neck and back.

At once, she felt she had been paralysed.

The men released her, and together they pushed the drawer.

Julia slid backwards, into darkness.

As the drawer closed a brilliant light came on, and Julia saw that on the roof of the tiny cubicle, just above her, there was a round mirror, about half a metre in diameter. She saw in it a reflection of her naked body, supine on the drawer. For a moment of disorientation she felt as if she were standing before a mirror, staring at herself ... but then she saw the reflection of her own eyes, and the mirror held her absolutely, and she surrendered to it.

For a moment, the light inside the cabinet seemed to brighten, but then it dimmed rapidly.

10

Julia's return was instantaneous. As the lights inside the cabinet were extinguished, a bell began to ring and she felt the drawer sliding outwards again, of its own volition. Moments later, there was a cold draught blowing over her, and a woman spoke loudly.

'Dr Trowbridge! It's Miss Stretton.'

'Sedative please, nurse.'

Julia tried to open her eyes, but before she could do so she felt something damp and cold inside her elbow, and a needle pricked into her. She parted her eyelids weakly, and with filmy eyes saw Dr Trowbridge looking down at her.

'Don't try to say anything, Julia. It's all right. You're safe.'

She was lifted away from the drawer, and someone bathed her neck and shoulders with a liquid that stung, and smelt of iodine. Soon afterwards she was lifted on to a stretcher on a trolley, and tucked in beneath some blankets.

The trolley was pushed down a long corridor, fluorescent strips sliding down her vision like thin vertical windows to a brighter world; she thought for a moment that she was rising, as if in an elevator, but it was just the steady rolling of the trolley. Her perception was easily upset; for a time she closed her eyes and at once could imagine that the trolley was being pushed in the other direction, feet first, just as she had sometimes done as a child on train-journeys, as they hurtled through tunnels. As she opened her eyes, and saw the ceiling sliding above her, the alienating effect was the same; it was a jolt to return to reality.

She was about to try it again when the trolley halted. Metal gates were opened, and she was trundled into the compartment of a real elevator; it rose jerkily, a distant humming deep below, but she could not see the walls of the shaft, so she tried no experiments with perception.

At the top she was wheeled into the open air, and she felt cold wind and the spray of rain on her cheeks. A Land Rover was standing by, its engine running, and the two men who had been pushing her slid the trolley into the compartment at the back. Inside it was clean and warm, and rain drummed on the steel roof. The doors closed, and the vehicle pulled away. Through a window in the wall above her, Julia could see one of the shoulders of the Maiden Castle ramparts sliding by. The driver went slowly, taking the smoothest route.

There was a young woman sitting with her in the back of the Land Rover, and she was smiling at her.

'Welcome back.'

'Ma – Marilyn.' It was difficult to talk, because the drug was taking effect, and the blankets lay heavily across her chin.

'Don't talk, Julia. We're going to Bincombe House.'

She remembered then, her first real memory. Bincombe. The old country house used by the staff of the Wessex project. The familiarity of the memory made her want to cry. Marilyn reached over and clasped her hand.

The Land Rover lurched for the last time as it reached the car-park, and accelerated smoothly, crunching across the loose gravel. Julia wished she could sit up and see outside. Rain ran jerkily and diagonally down the window above her face, and as the Land Rover turned on to a paved road the metal bodywork of the vehicle began humming and droning in tune with the tyres.

She felt she was still in Wessex. The last events had happened only minutes before: the two young men with their mirrors, scaring her and wrenching her away from her life and her plans. She recognized them now: Andy and Steve, the two they knew as the retrievers, the ones who entered the projection to bring the participants back to reality . . . but inside the projection it was always the same, the lack of readiness, the sense of intrusion.

Marilyn, sitting across the compartment from her, continued to hold her hand, but was having to brace herself against the movements of the vehicle.

'It won't be long,' she said. 'We're nearly there.'

How long it took made no difference to Julia. It was always a relief to be back, the same shuddery instinctive relief one felt when reaching home after walking alone late at night. An irrational fear, a welcoming of the safety of the familiar. She knew she was back, knew she was herself again. This was the fifth time she had returned from Wessex, and this never changed. She embraced her memories as if they were long-forgotten friends.

The Land Rover slowed and turned, and Julia heard its wheels splashing through deep puddles. In a moment it halted, and the engine was turned off. She heard the driver's door open and close, boots scraped on grit, and the main doors at the back were opened. The driver called to someone and a second man appeared, presumably from within the house. Outside, wind and rain on her face again, the blankets lifting to allow a cold draught to blow on her, and then she was on a second trolley, wheeling down a corridor laid with soft, rubbery tiles. There was a good smell in the house: food and people and paintwork. Somewhere a telephone was ringing, and from behind a closed door she heard a radio playing. Two women passed the trolley, smiling down at her, and she saw that they were wearing ordinary clothes, jeans, woollen sweaters.

Julia's arms were folded across her stomach, and she raised them clear of the blanket. She lifted them and held them over her head, as if stretching after a long sleep, and luxuriated in the use of her muscles again. She let them drop immediately: she was weak and stiff, mentally exhausted.

They wheeled her into her room – the same old bed, the large window overlooking the grounds – and brought the trolley alongside the bed.

Marilyn had been following, and she came and stood beside her.

'I'll tell Dr Eliot you're here,' she said, and Julia nodded wearily.

She was lifted from the trolley to the bed, and the sheets were pulled over her. As Marilyn and the two attendants left the room, Julia breathed out loudly, a sigh, a great gasp of pleasure, and she lay against the soft pillow and closed her eyes. Whether or not Dr Eliot came to see her Julia did not know, because within a few seconds she had fallen into a deep and natural sleep.

She awoke to daylight, and the feel of her hair lying across her face. She moved instinctively to brush it aside, and at once a nurse, who had been waiting in an armchair on the other side of the room, crossed to the bed and leaned over her.

'Are you awake, Miss Stretton?' she said softly.

'Mmm.' Julia turned without opening her eyes, stretched, pulled the sheet around her shoulders again.

'Would you like a cup of tea?'

'Mmm.' She was still waking, still in the half-world between awareness and dreams. She heard the nurse speaking into a telephone, heard the clatter of the receiver as it was replaced. She wanted to sleep for ever.

'The doctor will come as soon as you've had your tea.'

She wasn't going to be allowed to drift back.

'Breakfast,' Julia said, and struggled up on the pillow. She looked blearily at the nurse. 'Can I have breakfast?'

'What would you like?'

'Something cooked. Bacon . . . lots of bacon. And eggs. And I'd like coffee, not tea.'

'You mustn't overdo things,' the nurse said.

'I'm not ill, I'm hungry. I haven't eaten for . . . how long was it this time?'

'Three weeks.'

'That's how hungry I am.'

Only three weeks. They had brought her back so soon! She had never before been in the projection for less than two months, and it was usually much longer. She should have been left alone, because there was always so much to accomplish. David Harkman . . . she remembered then that her retrieval had prevented her from seeing him in the evening, and in spite of the fact that her rational mind was in control, she felt again the sensations of curiosity and excitement that had so distracted her alter ego.

Although there was now, in addition, a sense of frustration.

The nurse had continued to look disapproving at Julia's request for breakfast, but nevertheless she had gone back to the telephone and was speaking to the kitchen.

Julia sat up in the bed, and arranged the pillow behind her. Many of her belongings were on the bedside table, and she picked up her hairbrush. It was impossible to wash the participants' hair while they were in the projection, and hers was always greasy and tangled after retrieval. She brushed it, hearing and feeling it crackle. It made her scalp feel good and fresh. She found a mirror and comb, and tidied herself up.

She looked calmly into the circular mirror, and saw the steady gaze of her own eyes. She stuck out her tongue; it was white and dry. Her pores were dirty: she would have a bath as soon as she got out of bed.

It felt good to be real again!

After she had eaten her breakfast, Dr Trowbridge came to see her. He examined her briefly, then got her to stand up and walk about the room.

'Any stiffness?'

'A little bit. Nothing unusual.'

'Is there any discomfort in the spine?'

'Some. I shouldn't care to carry anything heavy.'

He nodded. 'You can have a massage if you want it, but don't over-exert yourself for a day or two. Plenty of light exercise and fresh air would be good for you.'

Julia still felt that medical aftercare was over-solicitous on the project, but from the participants' point of view things had improved since the early days. On her first return, Julia had had to endure several days of tests and X-rays.

There was a bathroom attached to her room, and after Dr Trowbridge had left Julia took a leisurely bath. The sore patch on the back of her neck was sensitive to hot water, but she had a long, pleasurable wallow, and afterwards she dried her hair and put on a favourite dress. She looked through the window at the weather; it was not raining today, but a strong wind blew. She wondered idly about the date. The nurse said she had been gone for three weeks, so it must now be near the middle of August.

'Do you need me any more, Miss Stretton?' It was the nurse, looking round the door from outside.

'I don't think so. Dr Trowbridge has seen me.'

'Would you like me to arrange a massage for you?'

'Not at the moment. Perhaps this evening. By the way, what's the time?'

'About ten-fifteen.'

After the nurse had left, Julia found her wristwatch, set it to the time and shook it to make it work. It was always disorienting after a return. When she came to the house yesterday it must have been during the afternoon. How long had she slept? Sixteen hours? She felt refreshed for it, however long it had been.

A little while later, as Julia was sitting at the dressing-table making up her face, Marilyn came to the room.

'Are you feeling better, Julia?'

'Yes, fine.'

'You looked really ill yesterday. It was the first time I'd seen you come out of the mortuary.'

'I was just very tired. And drugged.'

Julia had seen participants immediately after they returned, and she was sufficiently vain to hope that no one she knew well would ever see her in that state. Looking into the dressing-table mirror, she judged that the damage had been repaired.

Marilyn said: 'There's a meeting this morning. At eleven. They want you to go.'

'Yes, of course. Listen, Marilyn, do you know why I was re-trieved so soon? The nurse said it was only three weeks.'

'Didn't Dr Eliot tell you?'

'I haven't seen him. Dr Trowbridge came.'

Marilyn said: 'It was because of Tom Benedict.'

Julia frowned, not understanding. Then she remembered: she hadn't thought of Tom since –

'What's happened to Tom?'

'He died, Julia. In the projector. He had a stroke, and it wasn't discovered until too late.'

Julia stared at her in genuine shock. The double memories created by the projector always confused and alarmed her after a return, because of the way realities seemed to overlap ... but this time it was as if she had to suffer the experience twice. She remembered Tom lying in the Castle infirmary and holding her hand, and she remembered that afterwards she had forgotten about him, his identity slipping from the grasp of her memory as surely as his hand had slipped from hers.

Then this: the return to her real life, with the forgetfulness re-maining until now.

'But Marilyn ... I didn't know!'

'There's to be an inquiry. You might have to go.'

'I didn't realize. You see, Marilyn, I was there! I was with him when he died!'

'In Wessex?'

'It was the strangest thing.' The memory was there in full now. 'I was holding his hand, he was ill. There was no doctor, no proper treatment. Then he vanished. He ceased to exist. And no one could remember him!'

She felt tears in her eyes, and she turned away and found a Kleenex.

'Tom was a friend of yours, wasn't he?' Marilyn said.

'A friend of my father's. It was Tom who got me this job. I wouldn't be here if it wasn't for him.' She blew her nose, then tucked the crumpled tissue into the sleeve of her dress. 'Of course, it makes sense now. I couldn't understand it when he van-ished! But it must have been when he died. He simply stopped projecting.'

When she was in Wessex she had no way of recognizing it, but whenever she returned she was intrigued by the way her deeper feelings found parallels. Tom Benedict had always been like one of her family; one of her earliest memories was of sitting on his lap when she was four, trying to catch soap-bubbles as he blew them. He and her father had known each other for years, and Tom, who had never married in spite of frequent urgings by his closest friends, often spent his holidays with the family. As she grew older, and made her own friends and left home, Julia had seen less of Tom, but his avuncular interest was always there in the background. Four years ago, while she was still in the two-year vacuum that had followed the break-up with Paul Mason, Tom had recommended her for a job with the Wessex Foundation. He was one of the trustees of the Foundation fund that financed the operation, and with his influence on the other trustees her appointment had gone through after the most cursory of interviews. She felt she had made her own way after that, and worked as hard and contributed as much as anyone else, but she and Tom had always been close. It was inevitable that when they were in the projector, in Wessex, there would be a similar harmony, and so it was. She had only seen Tom once since the beginning – seen him here in the real world, that is – and they had enjoyed their reminiscences of the future.

As he had been in his own life, Tom in Wessex had been wise, jolly, warm. It seemed a pitiless, lonely death, to die inside the projector, but his consciousness had been in Wessex, and he had known she was beside him.

Julia realized she had been silent for some time, and that Marilyn was watching her uncomfortably.

'Has Tom been buried yet?'

'No, the funeral's tomorrow. Will you go?'

'Of course. Have his relatives been told?'

Marilyn nodded. 'I believe your parents will be there.'

Julia thought about seeing them again: it would be very strange. Her memories of them were partly confused with those of her 'parents' in Wessex. Once, during a period of leave, she had telephoned her father and during the conversation she had asked him some question about the farming cooperative. He owned a large and prospering dairy-farm near Hereford, and to say the least he hadn't understood. She had made a weak joke to cover the slip; to explain would have taken far too long. Her parents had only the vaguest notion of what her work entailed.

It was a quarter to eleven.

Marilyn said: 'I suppose you had better go along to the meeting. I take it you haven't made a report yet?'

'I haven't had a chance.'

They went out into the corridor, and Julia said: 'By the way, I've found David Harkman. He's working at – '

'At the Regional Commission,' Marilyn said. 'Don Mander told us.'

'Is Don back too?'

'He wants to talk to you about David. He thinks you're up to something.'

Julia smiled at her memories.

She called in at the office on her way to the meeting, and picked up the mail that had accumulated over the last three weeks. There were about fifteen letters in all, and she sorted through them quickly. Most had been forwarded on from her flat in London, and most were bills. These she left with one of the secretaries; the Wessex participants all had their affairs looked after for them while they were inside the projector.

As she left the office a door on the opposite side of the corridor opened, and a man stepped out.

He said: 'Hello, Julia. I was told I would find you here.'

It was Paul Mason. The sight of him was so wholly unexpected that Julia froze in mid-step. She pressed herself back against the wall. Looking at him, seeing his confident, smiling face, Julia wanted to run. She felt a total compulsion to return to Maiden Castle at once, to bury herself in the future for ever.

11

Paul said: 'Aren't you pleased to see me?'

Everything that Julia had done since her return, and everything that she had thought about, was ejected from her mind by the sight of him as totally and efficiently as the memories of her own life were wiped out by the Ridpath projector. She saw Paul, only Paul, and all that he stood for in her past: the destruction of her pride, of her sense of identity, of her self-respect. In the same way that she had been morbidly obsessed with him after she had seen him during her last weekend in London, so he was now someone who by his very existence demanded, and received, her complete attention.

'Are you following me?' she said, and in so saying recognized in her own voice the sound of paranoia.

'What do you mean, Julia?' Was his innocent expression feigned?

'Look, Paul, I told you. We're finished. I don't want anything more to do with you.'

'So you keep saying.'

'Then what are you doing here?'

He smiled, and it was patronizingly reassuring. 'Not to see you, if that's what you think. We happen to work in the same job, that's all.'

Before she could stop herself, Julia said: 'You're not a member of the project!'

'I work for the trustees.'

Julia looked from side to side along the corridor. Marilyn had gone off to beg a lift back to the Castle, and was probably already out of the house. There was no one else in sight, but several doors along the corridor were open.

'We can't talk here,' Julia said. 'Someone will hear us.'

'You haven't got anything to hide, have you?'

Julia pushed past him and went into the room he had been in. It was an office, and the desk was cluttered with papers. She recognized what the papers were the instant she saw them: some of the many reports filed by members of the projection during their periods of return from Wessex. These reports were the raw material of the projection, from which the periodic findings presented to the trustees were compiled. To Julia, the fact that someone like Paul Mason could have access to them was the grossest imaginable breach of privacy.

Paul was standing by the door.

'If you want to talk to me,' Julia said, 'come in here.'

'You seem to be the one who wants to talk,' Paul said, but he came into the room and closed the door.

'Is this your room?' Julia said.

'It is for the moment. There's another room coming free this week, and I'll be moving into that.'

He meant Tom Benedict's room. Julia knew without having to be told.

With the door closed, Paul's manner changed. In the corridor he had had an air of amused formality, presumably because other people might have passed, but now that they were alone together Julia saw a more familiar Paul, one she recognized from the old days. In a particular sense this sudden change was a relief to her, for it confirmed her prejudices about him; there was always a doubt, when she was not with him, that she had imagined his destructive instincts.

Paul had walked round the desk, and was sitting behind it. He gave her a knowing look, then picked up two or three of the reports and held them for her to see.

'I'm interested in your dreamworld,' he said. 'It sounds pleasantly comforting.'

'Comforting?' she said. 'What do you mean?'

'It's just the sort of escape from reality you specialize in.' Paul was never content with an intrusion into privacy; he always had to pass comment sooner or later.

'Look, Paul, it's a real world.'

'But it is a fantasy, isn't it? You mould it to your own desires.'

'It's a scientific project.'

'It was intended to be. I've read your reports ... it's quite an idyllic little place you've worked out for yourself.'

Julia, simultaneously angry and embarrassed, felt again the urge to run from him, but she knew that this time she would have to face up to him. The charge that the project members were indulging themselves in a wish-fulfilment fantasy was one that had been made several times by the board of trustees. It was inevitable when the nature of the project was understood. Of necessity, any projection would reflect the unconscious desires of the participants, and thus become a congenial environment to them. For all that, though, the scientific nature of the work was paramount.

But for Paul to make this charge, and to make it to *her*, pitched it on an altogether different level.

'You know nothing about Wessex,' she said.

'I've read the reports. And I know you, Julia. Isn't it right up your street? Remember all those movies you used to see?'

'I don't know what you mean!' Julia said, but Paul smiled at her in a sly way, and she knew exactly what he meant.

There had been a time, about nine months before she left him, when she had felt she could go on no longer. She had been in one of her many secretarial jobs, bored and miserable, and in the evenings when she went back to the flat Paul was there to remind her of her failings and her faults, and the contempt he felt for her was only too clear. One evening, unable to face him, she'd rung him up and told him she had to work overtime . . . and went to the cinema instead. The two or three hours of relief had been sweet indeed, and the following evening she did the same. Over a period of three weeks she went alone to a cinema more often than she went home. And of course Paul had eventually found out. Trying to explain herself, trying to communicate her desperation, Julia had told him why, exactly why, but instead of sympathy she received only more contempt. From that day, 'going to the movies' had become another phrase in Paul's unique vocabulary of destructive criticism, a metaphor for her inadequacy to face up to the real world.

Paul never forgot; the vocabulary was still intact, and it spoke across the years she had been free of him.

'You've always run away,' Paul said. 'You even ran away from me.'

'It was all you deserved.'

'You used to say I was the most important person in your life. Remember?'

'I thought it for about a week.'

The first week. Those first deadly days when she had trusted and admired and loved him, or so she thought. The days when she had confided in him and talked frankly about herself, and at the same time was unknowingly sowing the seeds which would grow into the poisonous plants that he would be forever reaping.

'You can't run away again. You made the mistake once . . . but you know how you depend on me.'

Anger prevailed. 'My God, I don't need you! I've finished with you as completely as it's possible to be free of anyone. If I never see you again, I won't give a damn!'

'I seem to have heard that somewhere before.'

'This time it's final. I've got my own life.'

'Ah, yes. Your little escapist fantasy. How I admire you.'

Julia turned away from him, and went to the door, the fury trembling in her.

'Still running, Julia?'

As she turned the handle, she paused. Looking back at Paul she saw that he was at ease, and smiling. He'd always enjoyed peeling back the skin to expose her sensitive nerves, then picking at them with his fingernails.

'I don't need to run from you any more. You're nothing to me.'

'So I see. Then we'll test that in the projection.'

'What do you mean?'

'We'll see how your unconscious reacts to mine.'

She stared at him with a new horror. 'You're not going into the projection!'

'No, no, of course not. How could I have ever thought you would allow me to upset your life.'

Of all the various weapons at his disposal, sarcasm was the one most blunted by overuse.

Julia said: 'Paul, so help me I'll do everything in my power to make sure you go nowhere near the projector.'

He laughed as if to diminish the power she invoked. 'I suppose the trustees have no say in the matter. I'm answerable to them, not to you.'

'I'm a full participant. If I don't want you to join, I can stop you.'

'Against the majority vote of the others, naturally.'

There was a way . . . she knew there was a way.

'I can stop you, Paul,' she said again.

In the early days a tacit agreement had been reached by all the participants. The nature of the projection was so delicately determined by the unconscious minds of the participants that its balance could be upset by the reactions of one personality to another. From the start they had all agreed: no relationships outside the projection. No affairs, no forming of liaisons, no cliques. Personal animus would be resolved one way or another before the projection began, or one or both of the parties would resign. With the same delicacy as they had created the nuances of the projected world, the participants had achieved this somehow. They stayed of accord, they stayed of a mind . . . but outside the projection they lived their own lives, and met only to discuss the work.

Paul was waiting, smiling at her.

'There's a rule we abide by,' she said. 'I have only to tell the others what you are to me, and you'll be out.'

'So you would tell them you still fancy me?'

'No, you bastard. I'll tell them how much I loathe you. I'll tell them what you've done to me in the past, and I'll tell them what's happened today. I'll tell them anything . . . just to keep you out of Wessex.'

Paul's smile had vanished, but his eyes held the same expression they had held all along: a narrow, calculating look.

'I suppose that knife could be made to cut two ways,' he said.

'How?'

'It could be used on you as much as me.' He stood up quickly, alarming her, and she stepped back. Her hand was still on the door-knob, but she hadn't the strength to turn it. 'I've worked for a long time for an opportunity like this. I'm in this because it's my chance, and I'm going to take it. Nothing's going to get in my way, certainly not some frigid little bitch who's spent half her life blaming others for her own weakness. You can find somewhere else to hide. If it's between you and me, then it's going to be me.'

Julia said, summoning her last reserves of strength, knowing she could stand no more of this: 'I'm already established. You won't be allowed in.'

'Then we'll put it to the test. See what the others think. Who's going to tell them? You or me?'

Julia shook her head miserably.

Paul said: 'And while we're talking about that, shall we also mention your friendship with Benedict? Shall we tell them how you got your job?'

'No, Paul!'

'So we know what to tell the others. That's fine by me.'

Julia felt she was going to faint. In the last ten minutes every single one of her deepest and most intimate nightmares had come to pass. She had known Paul was ruthless, she had known he was ambitious; she knew everything and more about the chemistry of destruction that worked between them, but she had never realized that the three could combine to such spectacularly explosive effect. She let out an uncontrollable low moan of misery and despair, and turned away. Paul, sitting down behind his desk, was grinning again.

As she let herself out of the office, she heard him rustling through the personal reports that lay on his desk.

12

Although it was after one o'clock in the morning, the cafés and night-clubs of Dorchester were full, and the streets were thronged with people. It was a warm, stuffy night, a storm threatening. Music and voices competed on the patios of the cafés, and the open doors of the bars and night-clubs released a hot, aromatic radiance: music, body-heat, tobacco-smoke, glowing lights, like the open gates of a boilerhouse. People danced and sang and shouted, their faces shining, their thin clothes sticking to their bodies.

Only the sound of the sea, breaking against the concrete sea-wall, gave a cooling presence, a reminder of the wind.

Coloured lights were strung along the trees in Marine Boulevard, and these, with the golden, hissing glow of the gas-lamps against the sides of the buildings, cast an attractive multi-hued radiance over the passers-by.

David Harkman walked slowly down the Boulevard towards the harbour, his right arm resting lightly on Julia's shoulders. She held herself close to him, and her head rested against his chest; the nearness was a shadow of their earlier intimacy.

She seemed small against him, for his arm could pass right around her back. He felt very tender towards her, because she had been with him all evening, from the moment she knocked on the door of his hostel room. Their evening had been simple: they had gone to the harbour to move his new skimmer to the mooring he had rented earlier in the day, and after that they had eaten a meal at Sekker's Bar. From there they had returned to his room for the rest of the evening. They had been awkward with each other at first, neither of them wanting to talk about the strange link they both felt, but afterwards this mutual understanding had been acknowledged in an unspoken, physical way. Their lovemaking had been affectionate and passionate, exhausting them both.

Even so, as they walked in the humid night Harkman felt that the bond was weaker. It was not just that they had consummated the sexual desire, nor that mysteries had been dispelled. He had felt it as soon as she arrived: the intangible bond between them had been untied.

As they strolled along the Boulevard, Harkman realized that already the memory of their lovemaking had the same quality to it as those memories of his life before he had applied for the Dorchester posting. He remembered the fact of what they had done together, but the memory of it was remote.

Even as he thought this, Harkman knew that it was neither fair nor right. He had *felt* and *experienced*, had lived the moments.

He suspected and feared that it was a shortcoming in himself, an inability to feel, and he tried unsuccessfully to put it from his mind.

Julia was warm under his arm, and he could detect her heart beating against the side of his body. It was a clinical observation, like a test of reality.

When they reached the harbour, they went down the concrete

steps together, and he helped Julia into her boat. They kissed briefly, but with passion.

'Will you come again?'

'If you'd like me to,' she said.

'You know I would. But only if you want to.'

'I'll come ... tomorrow, I think.' She was standing unsteadily in the boat, holding his hands as he balanced on the edge of the steps. She said: 'David ... I do want to see you again.'

They kissed once more, then at last Julia settled herself at the back of the boat, started the engine and in a moment had steered away across the harbour. The water was black and calm, and the coloured lights hanging on the far side reflected back from the surface in perfect symmetry with themselves. As her boat churned up the water, the wake sent the colours flashing and colliding.

Harkman stood on the harbour wall at the top of the steps until he could hear the engine no more, then walked back through the town.

It was odd how memory seemed to detach itself from experience; already, the sight of Julia's boat heading out across the black, multi-coloured water seemed distant from himself. It was as if there were a false experience in memory, one given to him. It seemed that he had been walking alone through the Boulevard all evening and into the night, with entirely spurious memories appearing in sequence to supply the false experience.

Memory was created *by* events, surely?

It could not be the other way around.

He had said nothing of this dilemma to Julia, although he had been aware of reality reshaping itself behind him all evening.

The meal at Sekker's: a remarkably good seafood casserole, with wine from the north of France, it had been the most delicious meal Harkman had had since his arrival. Julia said she had never eaten at Sekker's before. Small incidents were memorable: the waiter who had given Julia a rose; the four musicians who had deafened everyone on the patio until being asked to leave by the head waiter; the uproarious party at the next table, with six States Americans dressed in Arab robes and singing campus chants. The meal had *happened*; his stomach could still feel its weight.

And yet, even as they left Sekker's, Harkman had had a nagging sense that the memory of it was false.

With Julia, too: as they'd made love Harkman had a sudden insight that her arrival in his bed was spontaneous, that she had always been there, and that the events leading up to the moment were there only in implanted memory.

Afterwards, the sex itself became a memory, the drained, relaxed hour that followed being in its turn the only reality.

And now, as he walked back towards the Commission hostel, Harkman thought of the whispered departure from the harbour, and the boat crossing the smooth black water, as events created by memory.

It was as if Julia had not been there, that she did not exist except as some palpable extension of his own imagination, which, like a childhood ghoul, had substance only as long as he concentrated on it.

He reached the hostel and made his way up to his room, careful not to meet any of his colleagues from the Commission. They all appeared to be in bed, for the building was silent.

He washed and undressed, and pulled back the crumpled covers of the bed. There, on the lower sheet, was a small damp patch of deeply intimate memory. Harkman stared at it thoughtfully, knowing that it was as real to him as all his other recollections of the evening; as real ... and as remote from memory.

As he lay naked in the bed, waiting for sleep, the patch of damp was against his back, cold and sticky.

13

Donald Mander was on the telephone to Wessex House in London. He had been brought back from Wessex a day before Julia Stretton and the others, and any signs of residual strain had passed. He felt rested and well, although the news of Tom Benedict's death had had a sobering effect on him. At fifty-four he was now the oldest member of the projection.

'... the inquiry will be held the day after tomorrow,' he was saying to Gerald Bonner, the trustees' legal adviser. 'Yes, after the funeral.'

Bonner was concerned about the possibility of adverse publicity following Tom's death. Although the Wessex project was not secret, after the initial interest shown at the inception of the projection, the media had turned its fickle ear to other matters and for most of the two years' life of the projection the work had gone on with what had become jealously guarded privacy and concentration.

'... no, there's no need for a post-mortem, apparently. Tom was technically under medical supervision. Yes, naturally we're being careful. The medical checks will be intensified before anyone goes back into the projection.'

He listened to Bonner talking about the possibility of a claim from Benedict's dependants, and how much that might cost.

'He wasn't married,' Mander said. 'But I'll see if anyone here knows about his family.'

Afterwards, Mander rang through to Maiden Castle and spoke to John Eliot, who had requested a meeting of participants this morning.

'We'll be ready to start in a few minutes,' he said.

Eliot confirmed that observation of all the participants had been stepped up. The only real cause for alarm was David Harkman; he was now the only participant who had never been brought back. The fact that he had been traced at last meant that it was only a matter of time, but for a human body to be held in suspension for more than two years could have any number of physiological side-effects. The two projection retrievers – Andrew Holder and Steve Carlsen – were in Wessex looking for him at the moment, but whether Harkman's long exposure to the future had weakened the mnemonics and the deep-hypnotic triggers was something nobody knew.

The retrievals were overlaid with elements of chance, and Mander himself couldn't help being amused at the way in which he had been retrieved this time.

Andy and Steve had presented themselves at the Commission, asking for a visa to visit France. The clerk on the desk had noticed the rough-sewn clothes – the unmistakable style of the Maiden

Castle community – and had stonewalled them for an hour. The two young men had persisted, until the clerk summoned Mander. Once they were in his office they produced their little mirrors, and he had followed them back to the Castle without any resistance.

It was always a haphazard operation. Neither the participants nor Steve and Andy had any real idea, while they were in their future personae, of why they should meet, and it was a credit to their own initiative and mnemonic training that they ever found the people they were looking for.

Like all the others, Donald Mander always felt an acute sense of frustration in the hours after being brought back. Once one had the perspective of one's real memories it was always so simple to see what could have been done as an alternative. But the future alter ego took over completely; personality and memory were left behind.

It was at the heart of the problem concerning Harkman: inside the projection he was motivated by the memories and personality of his alter ego.

By the time Mander had collected together his various notes, and the report he had typed up the night before, John Eliot had arrived from the Castle, and they met in the hall downstairs.

'Have you seen Paul Mason yet?' Eliot said, as they walked slowly down the corridor to the lounge they used for the meetings.

'I spoke to him briefly last night after I'd seen you. I didn't find out much about him.'

'He's got a good degree. Durham University. He did a spell in journalism, but for the last five years he's been in commerce. Technically, he's just what we need to replace Tom. He worked with a property research group, planning capital outlay.'

'But do you really think he'll fit in?' Mander said, expressing the one doubt that could never be allayed by Eliot's talk of qualifications and experience. Yesterday evening, he and Eliot had had a long, private argument, Mander voicing what he imagined would be the objection of all the other participants: that no one new could join the projection this late in its existence and not bring drastic changes to its shape.

'Whether he fits in or not, you'll have to prepare yourself for him. The trustees are adamant about him joining. But I don't see any problems. He's a very personable young man, and he's certainly grasped the principle of projection quickly.'

'I gather he's coming to this meeting.'

'That's right. I thought he should meet one or two of the others.' They had reached the door, and Eliot pushed it open. 'After you.'

Because the projection was weakened by the removal of participants, it was held that at any one time no more than five people should be out of the projector, and with Tom Benedict's death this number had been reduced to four.

At the moment, in addition to Don Mander himself, Colin Willment had been brought back, as he was due for a period of leave. Mary Rickard had been retrieved also, at the request of her family, but she was expected to stay out of the projection for only a few days. In addition, Julia Stretton had been retrieved for further discussions about David Harkman, and the situation arising out of Tom's death.

When Mander and Eliot walked into the lounge, Colin and Mary were waiting for them. Julia had still not arrived.

Mander nodded to them with the slightly wary expression he found himself adopting whenever he met fellow participants outside the projection.

Apart from himself, Mary Rickard was the most senior member present. She was a biochemist from Bristol University, and had been with the projection from its earliest days. A shrewd judge of character, and a forceful theoretician about the nature of the projection, Mary had gained the respect of the others in the early, planning days, but since then, because of her inadvertently secondary rôle in Wessex, her manner had mellowed somewhat. Mary's future alter ego was a member of the Maiden Castle craft community, and neither she nor Mander had any recollection of their ever meeting in Wessex.

Colin Willment was the project's economist, and had been missing, for a time, in the way that Harkman had been missing. He had been traced eventually to the commercial dock at Poundbury, where his alter ego worked as a stevedore.

While they waited for the others to arrive, Mander and Eliot poured themselves coffee from the electric percolator that the staff at Bincombe provided.

Mary Rickard said: 'Don, I'd like to go to Tom's funeral. Will that be possible?'

'Yes, of course. I imagine Julia will want to go too.'

'Has she been retrieved?' Mary said.

'Yesterday. She should be here. Does anyone know where she is?'

John Eliot said: 'Trowbridge examined her this morning. She knows about the meeting . . . she should be here.'

As Mander and Eliot found chairs, Julia walked into the room. Mander's first thought was that she was still recovering from the after-effects of retrieval: she looked pale and drawn, and seemed very tense. She said hello to the others, then went to the side-board to pour herself a cup of coffee. He noticed that her hands were shaking, and that as she spooned sugar into her cup she spilled a lot of it into the saucer.

Watching her, Mander was reminded of the many times he had seen her future persona at the stall in Dorchester. His own alter ego was a mildly lecherous one, and purposely passed the stall during his evening strolls. The first time he had met Julia outside the projection, he had explained to her that his frequent winks and knowing smiles were obviously a symptom of the subliminal recognition that members of the projection often experienced between each other in Wessex.

To the amused embarrassment of his real self, the Wessex Mander's lechery had continued afterwards, and showed no sign of abating. Once she had caught him standing on tiptoe to peep down the front of her dress as she leaned forward . . . and the look she had given him then had not been one of projective recognition.

As Julia sat down, John Eliot said: 'I'm afraid we have quite a lot of work to get through this morning, but first we must estab-lish who will be returning to the projection this week. Mary, you have to go up to London?'

Mary nodded; her house had been occupied by squatters, and there was a court-order to apply for. She said: 'I'll probably be away for a couple of days.'

'The problem is,' Eliot said, 'that Andy and Steve are likely to be retrieving David Harkman very soon. That will mean another three will be leaving the projection. Julia, I take it you could go back in the next two or three days? And you too, Don?'

They both confirmed this, Julia staring away from them, looking through the window and across the grounds.

'And you, Colin? You're due for leave.'

Colin said: 'I'll take it if I have to ... but if I'm needed I'll go back in tomorrow.'

'You're all eager to stay. Sometimes I think you're happier in Wessex than you are here.'

No one said anything to that, and Mander, glancing round the group, saw something of the bond between them, the bond that tied them inside the projection. This was rarely discussed when they were in these meetings, but speaking in private he had found that his own experience was typical: Wessex had become the ideal retreat, a place where there was no danger, where the whims of the unconscious were satisfied. Life had a hypnotic quality of peace and security, an ordered languor; it was a restful, secure place. Even the climate was good.

Most of the participants came from or presently lived in the cities; at least half came from London. Life today in the cities was far from pleasant. Housing was in increasingly short supply, leading to the almost automatic occupation by squatters of any property left unoccupied for more than a day; exactly what had happened to Mary Rickard, in fact. Also, with the phenomenal cost of any kind of heating or fuel, the recurring food-shortages and consequent black-markets, the daily life of the average city-dweller, according to what remained of the responsible press, was approaching the level of urban savagery. All this compounded with the ever-increasing incidence of violent crime and the terrorist attacks, made anywhere more than twenty miles from a city a place of temporary escape.

Wessex, tourist island in an imagined future, became the ultimate escapist fantasy, a bolt-hole from reality.

Mander knew that none of the participants would admit to this, for it coloured in garish poster-paint a response which was for him, and for those with whom he had discussed it, a delicate watercolour of an experience.

The attraction Wessex held for him was a subtle affair; he knew that his own alter ego was discontented with his job, and had been for many years, and there was a routine dullness to life in the Regional Commission that he had not had to endure since an office-job he had taken during one university vacation thirty-five years ago. Even so, Mander always felt restless when he was out of the projection, hungered for the return.

Eliot said: 'There's one other matter of great importance, and that's the effect on the projection of Tom Benedict's tragic death.'

Mander glanced at the others and saw that they looked as uncomfortable about it as he felt. On the one hand there was the human tragedy of the death, but on the other the projection would have to go on. The majority of the participants, in other words those presently inside the projection, would have no knowledge of what had happened.

'Tom was very centralist,' Colin Willment said. 'I was in the projection until yesterday, and I'm not aware of any change that followed.'

'I think we all appreciate that,' Eliot said. 'The real problem is with the trustees. You all know that there have been various suggestions from London that the projection has now outlived its usefulness, and that it must be run down soon. I know that when they heard the news about Tom, the first reaction was that this was as good a reason as any to close it now.'

'But was Tom's death directly caused by being inside the projector?' Mary said.

'I don't think so. I shall be giving evidence at the inquiry, and as the senior doctor on the project, my opinion is that it was death from natural causes.'

'And you've said this to the trustees?' Mary said.

'Of course. That was their first reaction, as I said. On later consideration, it seemed to them that the projection could continue, but at the same time it would be possible to correct some of what they see as its present shortcomings.'

Eliot looked briefly at Mander as he said this. It was a sensitive area to tread, for the participants were fiercely jealous of their creation.

Eliot went on: 'You've heard the criticism before ... the belief held by some of the trustees that in certain ways the projection has become an end in itself.'

Looking at Mary Rickard and the others, Mander again saw his own thoughts reflected. It was a charge against which they were more or less defenceless. In the early days the reports the participants had made had reflected the spirit of the projection: that they were discovering a society, and speculating about the way it was run. As time passed, though, and as the participants became more deeply embedded in that society, their reports had gradually become more factual in tone, relating the future society to *itself* rather than to the present. Expressed in a different way, it meant that the participants were treating the projection as a real world, rather than one which was a conscious extrapolation from their own.

But this was inevitable and always had been, although no one had realized it at the time. Because Wessex was created in part by the unconscious, it became real for the period of the projection.

The trustees, who had budget considerations always in mind, had not been getting the results they were seeking.

It was a daring and imaginative conception: to postulate a future society so far ahead of the present day that the contemporary concerns and problems of the world would have been solved, one way or another. There would be no famine, because the projection created a world with plenty of food. There would be no threat of worldwide war, because the projection imagined a stable world political situation. The population explosion would be contained, because the projection decided that would be so. The use of technology and fossil fuels would have stabilized, because the projection created a world where this was achieved.

The projection itself created the ends; the participants, by moving within that society, would discover the means by which they had been achieved ... and this was the purpose of the projection.

Two years since the projection began, the processes of the solutions were still not understood. Wessex in the early years of the twenty-second century, and the place it occupied in the world as a whole, was imagined and understood in the finest detail, but only the barest hints of how the stability had been achieved were capable of being passed back to the Foundation that funded the research.

'Some of you will be aware,' Eliot said, 'that the trustees have employed a Mr Paul Mason to replace Tom Benedict. I gather that Mr Mason was appointed two or three months ago, to assist the trustees in assessing the worth of the project's findings, but after the news of Tom's death it was suggested that Mason should replace him. They believe that he has the necessary qualities to direct our work more towards obtaining the information they require.'

Mander said: 'Do the trustees realize the effect a newcomer might have on the projection?'

'You mean in possible changes to the projected society?' Eliot, cast in the unlikely rôle of apologist for the trustees, seemed uneasy. 'I believe so. Mason is quite clearly a man of formidable intelligence, and has spent the last few weeks familiarizing himself not only with the original program, but also with the reports that have been filed. I've spent a lot of time with him myself, and his grasp of what we are doing is remarkable. I believe that any changes that might happen as a result of his joining the projection would be slight. No more, in fact, than those caused by Tom's death.'

'But Tom's projective part was very much a consensus one,' Mary Rickard said.

'How do you know that Mason's is not?' Eliot said. 'I'd like you to meet him this morning. He's waiting outside. You can make up your own minds about him.'

'And if we do not think him suitable?' Mander said.

'Then, presumably, the trustees would expect the projection to be closed in the next few weeks.'

'So we shall have no real choice,' Mary said.

'I think you'll find that Mason isn't as much of a threat as you think. He seems committed to the projection.'

Again, Mander saw Mary Rickard and Colin Willment catching his eye. He knew their doubts without being told, for they were the same as his own. No one could be 'committed' to the projection without entering it. It could not be experienced by sampling the reports, nor understood by reading the program. It had to be lived in to be felt . . . and only then was a commitment formed.

But the projection was an intensely private world; any newcomer, however sympathetic, would be an intruder. Paul Mason would not be welcomed until he had made the world reflect his own personality . . . and no one in the projection would willingly allow him to do that.

Mander said: 'I suppose we should meet Mr Mason.'

'May I bring him in then?' Eliot looked at the others for their approval. 'Good. I'll go and find him.'

Eliot left the room, and as soon as the door was closed Mander turned to the others.

'What do we do?' he said.

Colin shrugged. 'We're tied. We have to accept him.'

Mary Rickard said: 'We're being blackmailed. If we accept him, he'll affect the projection. If we reject him, the projection will be closed.'

'So what do you think?'

'We'll have to accept him.'

'Julia? What about you?'

Throughout the discussion Julia had sat silently in her armchair. She looked pale and fragile, and the coffee she had poured herself was untouched.

'Are you feeling unwell, Julia?' Mary said.

'No . . . I'm all right.'

Just then, Eliot came back into the room, and following him was a tall, smartly dressed young man, clearly at his ease.

Mander stood up, walked across to him and extended his hand. 'Mr Mason. Good to see you again.' He turned towards the others. 'I'd like you to meet your new colleagues. Mrs. Rickard, Miss Stretton, Mr Willment . . .'

Paul Mason shook hands with them all, one by one, and Colin Willment rocked the percolator to see if there was any coffee left.

14

Julia felt better as soon as Paul came into the room. So obsessed had she been with the short, fraught conversation in Paul's office that she barely heard what John Eliot and Don Mander had been saying. Only at the end, when Eliot had been out of the room, had she realized that Mary and Colin had their own reasons for not wanting Paul in the projection.

Then Paul came in, and the unseen threat that had been lurking outside became a visible antagonist, and thus less fearful.

'How do you do, Miss Stretton?' he had said, for all the world as if they were total strangers ... and the menace he presented became containable. The introduction had been a time when he could have revealed that they knew each other, but he had let the chance slip by, and played a part instead.

He had the trustees behind him; he didn't have to force a confrontation with her to join the projection.

She sat back in her armchair, trying to steady her breathing, and she watched Paul.

She had had the strength once to defy him, and she must do it again.

He was sitting forward, listening and talking to Mander and Eliot. He had an intent, interested expression on his face ... the one he reserved for polite company, when he wanted to make an impression and be liked by those around him. She had not seen the expression for years, but she recognized it instantly. It reminded her of the time –

The recollection was like a physical blow, and she felt herself reddening as if a hand had raked across her face. The memory had been buried in the past, but Paul's presence dug it out as easily as if it had lain on the surface for all that time.

It had been soon after she started living with him in London, long before the final rows. Some instinct for self-preservation had surfaced; it was only an instinct, then, because she was too heavily influenced by him to rationalize her miseries, and she believed what he told her about herself. Trying to express her uncertainties she had started a diary, a secret, honest diary, the sort that was never meant to be read, not even by its author. She'd written about herself, about her dreams, about her ambitions, about her sexual fantasies; they all poured out in an ungrammatical, unpunctuated gush of abbreviated words, like a scream from the unconscious. The diary was always locked away, pointedly, punctiliously, but it was Paul's flat and he had keys for everything. A few weeks after she'd begun the diary they had gone to dinner at the house of a magazine-editor Paul was then trying to impress. He'd sat at the dinner-table with this expression on his face, polite interest, an openness to other people's ideas ... and then, after the editor had related an anecdote, Paul had answered by quoting aloud something she had scribbled in her diary the night before. It had to be deliberate, but it was done so that it sounded in context like something he'd made up himself; he even laughed at himself for saying it, apologized for triviality.

Then he smiled at her, seeming to seek her approval, but saying with his eyes what she was to learn a hundred times over in the months ahead: I possess you and control you. There is nothing of yours I cannot touch or colour. There is nothing of yours you may call your own.

And as Paul listened to the others he sometimes looked towards her, and his eyes were saying the same.

Don Mander at least seemed to have accepted that Paul would join the projection, although it was noticeable to Julia how quiet Colin and Mary were keeping.

Mander was saying: '... because the Ridpath operates on the unconscious as well as the conscious mind, our original program had to conform to a realistic consensus view of what this future might actually be like. If there were any deep doubts in the minds of the participants, they had to be allayed before we began.'

Julia remembered the early days, when the interminable planning discussions were going on. Sometimes for weeks on end it seemed that an impasse had been reached, that there would be a minority of dissenters to every proposal put forward.

'I'm interested in the notion of communist control,' Paul said. 'Surely this would have seemed unlikely? Is it really possible that Britain could ever accept state socialism?'

'We felt it was,' Eliot said. 'Remember, it's not Britain as a whole that's being considered. One important feature is the assumption that Scotland will eventually break away from the union, and keep control of the oil-deposits in the North Sea. We've also assumed a different economic rôle for the oil itself; the natural deposits become state reserves, like gold. The oil left in the ground would be worth more than that taken out and used. Without this kind of commodity asset, England by itself would have no economic strength. It would be ripe for takeover.'

'But why the eastern bloc, Dr Eliot?'

There was a reason for everything, Julia thought. In spite of herself and her intense feelings, she was being beguiled by Paul's reasonable manner. He was, after all, only asking the sort of questions anyone might. It occurred to her, for approximately the thousandth time in her life, that it might be only she who ever saw the bad side of Paul, that her prejudice was unfair.

She realized that the coffee she had poured herself had gone cold, so she went to the sideboard and took a fresh cup. Mary glanced at her as she walked back to her chair; both she and Colin were as quiet as Julia. Colin, affecting disinterest, was sprawling back across the sofa.

Julia had always liked this room, with its blackened beams and its huge Portland stone fireplace. Someone famous had lived here during the nineteenth century, and the house was listed as a monument to preserve it for future generations. But Julia had walked across these downs one day – one day in Wessex – and the house had no longer been here. She had been saddened when she realized it after retrieval, and lying in her room at the other end of the house she'd remembered the future when the place was gone. Bincombe House was warm with age, full of glad memories of other centuries. The sort of tensions that Paul created had no place here.

She tried to concentrate on what Eliot and Mander were explaining to Paul, hoping to come to terms with the new situation by involving herself in it more.

Mander was talking about the political shape of the twenty-second century, as conceived in the projection: the Muslim-dominated Emirate States that half the world would comprise, and which would include both Americas, most of Africa, the Middle East, southern Europe. The communist bloc that made up most of the rest: northern Europe, England, Iceland, Scandinavia, most of Asia including India. A few countries still independent of both: Canada, Scotland, Switzerland, Eire, Australia. No Third World, unless you counted southern Africa, which called itself independent.

Part of the scenario had concentrated on energy resources. Oil would not be refined on such a universal scale: there would be petrol, but only for the very rich, or for reserved uses. Coal and hydro-electrics would still generate electricity, but there would be much more use of local resources: solar energy in the tropics; wood burning; geothermal drilling; wave and tidal power.

Julia had worked with the energy-resources team for a while. There was known to be some oil beneath Dorset, and, to a much more exploitable degree, a deep layer of hot rocks.

Don Mander was telling Paul of the geophysical nature of this speculated future world, and for the first time Julia heard her name mentioned. Paul glanced at her: he was still playing his part, for he nodded politely.

Geothermal drilling had so far only been tried on a small scale, and with limited success. Julia, working with the other people, had reached the conclusion that if the particular deposit of rocks five miles beneath the Frome Valley was exploited for its energy content, then several dangers would appear. The main one of these was that the rocks would cool when water was injected to tap the heat. This would probably result in seismic activity. The Wessex project included a seismologist – Kieran Santesson, who was presently inside the projection – and he had calculated that in an otherwise stable seismic zone, large earthquakes and widespread subsidence could occur. In an early test-run of the Ridpath, results indicated that certain parts of Dorset could sink as much as two hundred and fifty feet, thus effectively cutting off the West Country from the mainland.

This notion, that Wessex could become an island, had appealed to everyone in the project, and it had immediately become a dominant image in the program.

Eliot was saying: '... you see, Mason, the conscious shape of the projection can be predetermined. What we cannot control is the unconscious nature of the landscape, nor the rôles played by the alter egos.'

This had been Don Mander's province during the planning. Mander, one of the two psychologists on the project, had described the projection as a psychodrama of the mind, and for Julia the term had had sinister undertones, as if a clinical experiment was to take place. She had not been alone in this reaction. Many of the participants had had their doubts from the beginning; there was something almost indecent about the idea of pooling one's unconscious mind with comparative strangers. No one could rape the mind of anyone else, though, for the effect of the Ridpath was to blend the unconscious, to produce a kind of collective dream.

The unconscious produced its illogicalities, especially in the way it treated the lives of the alter egos. The participants took rôles that reflected not their training or qualifications, but some deeper wish. Mander became a bureaucrat, Mary a potter; Kieran – the seismologist – worked as a chef in one of the waterfront restaurants; Colin Willment was a labourer in the docks. To one extent or another these could be traced to the real lives of the participants: Mary Rickard did pottery for relaxation, Colin often spoke of his frustrations about the purely theoretical nature of his work as an economist, Kieran was known to be an excellent cook.

The landscape, too, reflected the unconscious. It had its idiosyncrasies and illogicalities – the climate was either dramatically good or dramatically bad, the days seemed longer, the hills seemed higher and the valleys deeper – but it was still a recognizable version of the true Dorset.

Someone had remarked at the beginning that the collective unconscious would produce archetypal horrors, nightmare images, dreamlike situations. It had been a semi-facetious remark, but many had taken it seriously. Unlike the dream-state, though, the Wessex of the group mind was controllable. There was constant correction stemming from reason, sanity, experience; the conscious mind could override the unconscious. The nightmare fantasies did not appear.

But the dreamlike quality was always there, and they all shared it. The participants had grown used to each other. Wessex had been shaped, and it belonged to those who had shaped it. An outsider trying to interfere with it presented a threat which acted on the deepest levels of identity, memory and mind.

When that outsider was someone like Paul, who, even when Julia disregarded her private feelings, was by his own account self-seeking and ambitious, the unconscious quality of the projection would be inevitably affected.

She was trying to be rational, trying to argue with herself. There was always a chance that if Paul entered the projection the results would not be as bad as she feared. He was intelligent enough, after all, and from his manner he seemed prepared to cooperate, to blend his will with that of the others.

She wondered what had been happening to him in the last six years. There must have been another woman in that time, perhaps several women. He had not mentioned them to her, either today or during her last weekend in London. Perhaps there was someone he was involved with now. Could it be just Julia's own paranoid imaginings that he was still motivated to control and dominate her? Had that scarring, devastating affair been simply a product of youth, and they had both matured since?

And when the worst happened, what then? When Paul entered the projection, and they were there together in Wessex, was it possible that the old differences would be forgotten, along with their memories of the real world?

It was a possibility. Many of the participants had written about this in the personal sections of their reports. They found that the identity assumed by their alter egos lacked the cares of their real lives.

Thinking of this, Julia remembered Greg. He did not exist in reality: he was not a member of the projection.

Greg was one of the people of Wessex, imagined into being by the group unconscious. To use Don Mander's psychodrama analogy, Greg was one of the thousands of unscripted supporting rôles, the auxiliary egos. Most of these were in the background, like extras in a film . . . but sometimes the participants gave minor speaking parts to these players. Julia's unconscious had written a script for Greg, one that had a direct bearing on some inner need of her own. Greg became a physical lover, an incubus of the mind.

But the unconscious played its tricks: Greg was an unsatisfactory sexual partner.

In her own reports Julia had described the fact of the sexual relationship with Greg, but she had never detailed the way he almost invariably left her unsatisfied. In this, her reports were less than complete, but, realizing that the nature of the relationship with Greg would reveal a very personal and intimate inadequacy, Julia felt justified in omitting this.

It was all directly relevant to Paul Mason.

She had long ago come to the conclusion that Paul's destructive, poisonous attitude to her came from an inner need of his own, a compensation for some physical failing.

If Paul still felt this failing, and he entered the projection, then it was almost certain that he too would find himself in some imagined, unconscious relationship with an auxiliary ego of his own. Perhaps he would learn from this, as she had learned from Greg.

It was a pious hope, but still a hope . . . and when, a few minutes later, the discussion was interrupted by the lunch-bell, Julia felt calmer about the prospects than she had since she met Paul that morning.

15

David Harkman had set his alarm-clock for six-thirty in the morning, and in spite of his late night was awake in seconds. The previous day, knowing that Julia was going to deliver his new skimmer, he had made enquiries about the times of the tides. There was usually only one tidal bore a day which could be ridden, and as the time of the tides moved forward about half an hour every day the evening flood was now too close to nightfall to be safe. Today's tidal wave suitable for riders was due to appear at about eight forty-five in the morning, and Harkman was eager to try his skill.

He dressed hurriedly, putting on a pair of swimming trunks beneath his trousers, and left the Commission hostel.

Dorchester had a grey, dismal appearance. The humid weather of the day before had broken, and a heavy, wetting drizzle drifted across the town, making the buildings look dank and cheerless. It was difficult to imagine that Marine Boulevard, in this deadening early-morning light, could have been the scene of colourful revelry only a few hours before. The lights were off, the bars and cafés were shuttered.

There were only a few people about, and most of those, like himself, were heading for the harbour.

He went first to the skimmer-shop, which adjusted its opening hours to those of the tides. At this time of day the management knew its customers and their needs exactly, and there was no sign of the careless indifference that Harkman had seen on his first visit. As he went into the shop an assistant came forward, and within twenty minutes Harkman was equipped with the necessary rubber wet-suit and breathing-apparatus.

At low tide the harbour was unnavigable, and the Child Okeford launch was waiting in the deeper water against the outside of the harbour wall. There were already more than two dozen people sitting on the benches on the forward deck, many of them wearing their shiny black wet-suits, like so many seals clustered on a rock.

The rear part of the boat was filled with the riders' equipment: the skimmers were stacked on special wooden racks, so that one did not rest on another, and there were several piles of clothing, wet-suits and breathing and flotation-apparatus.

Harkman went down the concrete steps to the two men standing by the rail of the launch, paid his fare and dumped his newly bought gear on the deck.

There were several boys from the town standing around – such occasions inevitably brought them out to watch – and Harkman got two of them to help him remove his skimmer from its mooring, and carry it to a place on one of the racks. After this, he went to the forward deck and waited with the others for the launch to depart.

The drizzle persisted, soaking his clothes and slicking his hair over his forehead. Sitting in the crowd, Harkman reflected that the idea of wearing a wet-suit was not such a bad one after all.

Most of the other riders were men, but there was also a small group of women sitting together. They looked muscular and masculine in the padded rubber suits, and Harkman tried to imagine what Julia's slim body would look like in one. The thought of her immediately reminded him of the unusual sense of false memory he had felt the previous night – indeed, the recollection itself had the same abstract quality that had so disconcerted him – and he looked away from the women, and stared into the harbour at the rows of private yachts, dripping and melancholy at their moorings.

At last the craft nosed slowly away from the harbour wall, seeking the deeper water. The craft was flat-bottomed, but even so it bumped and scraped on the pebbly sea-bed. As soon as they were out of the shallows, the captain lowered the keel, and the engine accelerated the launch towards the east.

Harkman watched the coast as they roared past, seeing the broad flat beaches that during the days attracted so many visitors.

The journey to Blandford Passage took more than half an hour, and it was after eight o'clock when the launch moved slowly into the harbour at Child Okeford. There was a slight delay during disembarkation as Okeford was on mainland England and the visas of the overseas visitors had to be checked.

Here, in Blandford Passage itself, was the narrowest gap between England and Wessex Island. During the seismic disturbances of the previous century, the valley of the River Stour had been transformed from a shallow pass through the North Dorset Downs into a deep, narrow chasm, bounded on each side by crumbling chalk cliffs. To the north lay the wide Somerset Sea, which stretched from the Quantock Hills on Wessex Island to the Mendip Hills in England, and opened out into what had been the Bristol Channel. This triangular sea, whose southerly funnel was the pass over the remains of Blandford Forum, took the effect of the rising tide an hour before the sheltered waters of Dorchester

Bay, which opened into the English Channel far to the east. Twice every day, as the level of the Somerset Sea rose, a tidal bore moved towards the south. Between the Quantocks and the Mendips its presence was imperceptible; as it passed the Wessex coastal town of Crewkerne it could be clearly seen as a wave of water some two or three metres high; as it reached Child Okeford, at the head of the narrow Passage, it was rarely less than twenty metres high, and in the seasonal spring tides had been known to reach fifty metres or more.

When the wind blew from the south-east the wave became a deadly rolling breaker, bursting out of the Passage in a spectacular cascade of foaming surf. It was this unique phenomenon that had first attracted visitors to the region, and it was this that had been the cause of the development of tourism on Wessex and the mainland.

Child Okeford, set high on the safety of Hambledon Hill, had become the centre for wave-riders, although it was Dorchester that attracted the visitors, with its night-life and beaches, its casino and mosque.

When Harkman left the launch, and had unloaded his equipment with the help of stewards, he went to the nearby pavilion to change. The wave-riders were obliged to follow many safety regulations, not the least of which was that all riders had to be out of Child Okeford harbour fifteen minutes before the wave arrived. This was so that the boom could be lowered over the harbour entrance, to prevent a potentially catastrophic inflooding of water as the wave passed. In any event, the riders needed to be ready in the centre of the Passage, well before the wave arrived.

Harkman struggled into his new wet-suit, pulling it on over his swimming trunks. The assistant in the shop had measured him for fit, but even so it felt tighter than it should. The Party had introduced new safety measures for riders, and there was more padding inside the suit than in the one he had worn when wave-riding in his youth. When he had finally got it on he went outside, needing help with the breathing-apparatus. This had to be checked by a steward to ensure it conformed to the regulations, and he was asked if this was to be his first ride; in that case he would have needed to have an approved supervisor following him, at an extra cost of ten thousand dollars.

The skimmer's engine started smoothly, and after a few seconds to allow it to warm up, Harkman stepped down on to the broad surface of the craft, balanced himself, then accelerated smoothly across the harbour. As he passed through into the open Passage he saw that there were already some thirty or more riders ahead of him, with others following; it was more crowded than he would have liked, but still manageable.

While riding out he tried a few more practice turns, executing each without the ignominy of a fall. It was one thing to practise in the sheltered water of a creek by Maiden Castle, it was another to do it with the Okeford stewards watching from the shore.

He remembered his first fall, while learning to ride a skimmer. The throttle of the engine had remained open, and the little craft had skipped off into the wide stretches of the Somerset Sea on its own. Three days had passed before an army helicopter had spotted and retrieved it.

Another memory: flat and cool in the mind. Had it really happened?

A rider passed him, going in the same direction.

'Thirty metres!' he shouted, but with the noise of the engine, and the helmet of his suit covering his head, Harkman barely heard him.

'*What?*' he shouted back, but the other rider had gone on. A little later, another rider passed the same information. This time Harkman heard him and, entering into the spirit, shouted it to another when he got the chance. Someone must have had a wave-height estimate from the stewards.

He looked towards the north, but there was as yet no discernible sign of the bore. Harkman remembered from the years before that distances were often deceptive, and that the only reliable guide was to watch the walls of the chasm for the signs of the swell.

His muscles were tense, so in the few minutes he had left he went through the rote of his old training, flexing his arms and legs, trying to make his body as supple as possible. He couldn't help but be tense with expectation; in the past he had suffered many falls on the wave, and he knew too well the violence of the breaker.

The safest position for an uncertain rider was in the centre of the channel, but it was there that most of the riders congregated. Harkman liked freedom of manoeuvre, and so he moved to the Wessex side, knowing that if the wave was higher than he could safely ride, the smoothness of the cliffs on that side would keep the surface of the swell relatively stable while he moved back to the centre.

In the distance there was a loud explosion: the cannon fired to warn shipping, but the sound which, by tradition, started the riders jockeying to and fro in anticipation of the wave. Harkman glanced again towards the north, and this time he saw the wave as a dark line across the smooth sea. It was already nearer and higher than he had expected. He turned the skimmer round in one last practice flip, still not entirely at ease with the new equipment, but knowing that at this late stage there was no avoiding the wave.

Moments later there came the sound of breaking water, and Harkman saw the swell creaming against the base of the cliff.

He opened the throttle and moved sideways, away from the cliff and towards the centre of the channel; after a few metres he flipped round, went back again. Then he felt the swell lifting him, so he accelerated forward and across the wave, staying in front of it but feeling the board tipping up from behind. The wave was rising quickly, as it raced into the constricted width of the Passage.

After a few seconds Harkman saw that he was moving perilously close to other riders, and so he did a standard reversal flip, turning in the skimmer's own length and moving back the other way. He was still racing away from the wave, but gradually it was catching up with him so that he was riding on its forward face.

For the moment the wave was unbroken, except where it rushed against the wall of the cliff, and here it roared and rebounded in white fury. Harkman flipped the board again, moving back towards the centre, and as he did so he found he was looking directly across the breadth of the wave, a terrifying mound of rising water, rushing through the Passage. Many of the riders at the centre had reached the crest too soon, and were leaning forward on their skimmers, racing their engines to keep abreast of the speed of the wave. Many fell or slipped back, were lost to sight behind the ever-rising wave.

Harkman was about halfway up the wave now, still racing forwards to avoid the crest, but zig-zagging broadly to time it as accurately as possible.

He flipped back, away from the other riders, but found at once that the wave had taken him much further into the Passage than he had thought, and that the cliff wall was only a few metres from him. Badly shocked, he flipped again, and with a quick movement of his hand turned on his air-supply.

The mouth of the Passage was ahead: a rocky, jagged pass into the open waters of the bay. It was less than a hundred metres away. Now was the time to reach the crest!

He throttled the engine back, and allowed the skimmer to ride diagonally up the wave. The gradient was steep, and already in places white spume was blowing up from the crest. Harkman was unpractised: he reached the crest too soon, before the wave had started to curl, and for an instant he slipped behind. He gunned the engine to its maximum, and regained the crest.

The wave had reached the mouth of the Passage, and it curled.

Harkman saw for an instant the spectacle that only riders of the wave ever saw: the calm stretch of the bay, grey under the cloudy sky, reaching from Dorchester in the west to the distant hills of Bournemouth in the east; the island of Purbeck was a black mound ahead.

As the wave curled the crest thinned and shot Harkman forward. He slid forward and down, falling through to the shimmering slope of rising water beneath. The practised wave-rider would anticipate, would try to land on the slope, and accelerate down the wave to safety before it crashed on top of him. But Harkman was taken unawares, and the skimmer landed tail-first. For an instant he thought he had recovered balance, but the skimmer was turning to one side ... and the dark tunnel of the immense pipeline wave was closing above him.

He closed his eyes, and forced his limbs to relax.

He was thrown from the board with a violence that almost

knocked him senseless, and then he was in a black bedlam of noise and pressure and gigantic currents, tearing him up, down, sideways.

The wave was collapsing, bursting into Dorchester Bay in a swathe of white foam that stretched for more than a kilometre. Harkman, inside the turmoil of raging water, plunged by the weight of the wave to the depths of the bay, was crushed and turned and wrenched. He made himself breathe steadily through his mask, tried not to resist the pressures on his body, knowing that the violence would subside in the end.

At last it did and Harkman surfaced, his head surrounded by the brilliant yellow of the flotation bags that he inflated from his air-supply the instant he saw the sky.

Half an hour later, the stewards' launch from Winterbourne found him, and he was plucked out of the water. Only seven other riders had made it as far as the bay, and as the launch ploughed back through the now navigable tidal flood towards Child Oke-ford, Harkman learned from the regular riders that the wave had been satisfactory, but not as big as usual.

Harkman was shivering, but it was not from cold, for the clouds had cleared at last and the sun was shining hotly.

As soon as he got back to Dorchester, he went to see Julia at the stall, and they arranged to meet again in the evening. He was so exhilarated by his ride that it was impossible to work, and spent the day in his office restlessly.

During the afternoon he heard that his skimmer had been re-covered undamaged from the bay, and that there was a salvage fee to pay.

16

Marilyn had come back from the Castle for lunch, and Julia shared a table with her. She was glad of the break from the emotional stresses of the hour before. She saw Paul sharing a table with Eliot and Mander at the far end of the room, and Paul had his back towards her. It was as if someone had turned an electric fire away from her, so that the radiance was directed elsewhere.

The dining-room was in the old part of Bincombe House, and it was a high, stately room with small leaded windows. Relics of the past were attached to the walls: crossed pikestaffs, old shields, axes. In two glass cases were assortments of coins and pottery taken from archaeological digs in the grounds, and half of one wall was covered by an ancient brocade, protected by transparent plastic sheeting.

Marilyn filled her in on the gossip and news that had accumulated while she had been inside the projector. The gossip didn't interest Julia much – living with two separate identities of her own provided her with enough involvements without wondering about the private lives of others – but she always asked about it, because Marilyn was funny when she gossiped.

The news was more involving, and more depressing. Ever since the British troops had withdrawn from Northern Ireland, the Loyalist extremists had thrown in their lot with paramilitary Scottish independence groups, and for the last two years an intense urban bombing campaign had been conducted in English cities. For two of the three weeks Julia had been inside the projection there had been a lull, but on the day the Scottish Assembly had been surrounded by British troops – to protect the elected representatives, according to Westminster – two major bus-bombs had been set off, one in London, one in Bristol. At the same time, a bomb had exploded inside a rush-hour London Underground train. The casualties had been frightful. Public transport in every English city had come to a standstill as a result. There was other news too: another war in the Middle East, a dollar crisis, a royal pregnancy.

Julia listened with a feeling of growing detachment; the projection did that for her, and she knew that the others felt it too. Although they were sometimes accused of running away from the real world, the fact was that once they had lived in Wessex the participants became distanced from real life, and there was no need to hide from something insubstantial.

In another sense, though, Julia welcomed Marilyn's talk about matters outside, because it took her mind off Paul. She was feeling stronger about that, and as Marilyn chatted on Paul's malign presence faded.

After lunch they reassembled in the lounge, and they were helping themselves to more coffee when John Eliot was called away to the telephone. While they waited, Paul offered her a cigarette, and she refused it. Others were present; still no sign passed between them that they were anything other than recent acquaintances.

When Eliot came back he seemed preoccupied, and poured himself a coffee from the sideboard without saying anything.

Then, as he sat down, he said: 'That was Trowbridge at the Castle. Andy and Steve have just come back from Wessex.'

'Did they locate Harkman?' Don Mander said.

'Apparently, yes. But they couldn't retrieve him.'

'Did something go wrong?'

'I've only had a partial account, because they're still recovering. But from what I gather, Harkman didn't respond to the mirrors.'

'But that's impossible,' Mander said. 'Are they sure?'

'It's what they said.'

The little circular mirrors that Andy and Steve used were the only known way of retrieving anyone from Wessex. It was a system Ridpath and Eliot had worked out between them: because of the loss of real identity within the projection, the participants would need an independent post-hypnotic trigger to make them abandon the unconscious world. They had decided on the use of mirrors. Nowhere in Wessex – and, for all they knew, nowhere in the whole imagined future world – was there another circular mirror. Square mirrors, rectangular mirrors, oval mirrors . . . but none circular. The only ones in existence were at Maiden Castle.

'Do you think it's possible that Harkman has become resistant?' Mander said.

'That's what it seems,' Eliot said. 'Apparently, Steve found him at the stall in Dorchester. He tried to sell him a mirror, but when he held it out Harkman simply said "no thanks", and Steve left it at that. I gather you were there too, Julia.'

That took her by surprise. 'You mean at the stall?'

'Steve said you took the mirror from him, and threw it away. Then there was an argument, about the sort of goods that the stall should sell.'

Julia smiled; her alter ego had firm ideas about that sort of thing.

'When was this?' Mander said.

'This morning.'

When the participants had first discovered that their alter egos lived on in Wessex *after* retrieval there had been considerable confusion, especially in the minds of those people still projecting. How could the future identity continue to have substance without the projected personality? The answer was that during the period of return, the alter ego existed in the unconscious minds of the others; it became an auxiliary ego for the duration, projected by those who were in closest contact in the future world.

While the participant was outside the projector, it was of course impossible to discover what the alter ego was doing, but on rejoining the projection there would be full memories of the interim period.

Julia was aware that when she went back to Wessex she would know exactly what the imagined Julia had done in the meantime; she would know because it would seem to be a part of her experience.

On the evening of the day she had been retrieved she had been intending to meet David Harkman in Dorchester. She wondered if they had met as planned.

In the same way that she had a double, and sometimes contradictory, image of herself and her own future persona, so Julia had conflicting feelings about David Harkman. As she was here, living her real life in the real world, Harkman was just another member of the projection, if one in an unusual situation. But her memory of Harkman's alter ego was altogether different: warm, intrigued, excited, deeply personal.

If she had been seen in Dorchester with David Harkman it could mean only one thing: that her ego was being projected by him. He was relating closely to her, she had reached his unconscious mind. Just as the participants projected auxiliary egos to satisfy some unconscious longing, so Harkman was projecting an image of her in her absence.

This realization stirred a profound response in Julia; as Wessex had become an unconscious refuge for all the participants, so

David Harkman had become a personal one for her. She felt again the call of the future, but this time it was one emanating from a particular source.

Her reports already omitted the personal dissatisfactions of her life with Greg; there was no reason why she should report the satisfactions she felt with someone else. It would be something no one need ever discover, an area of her life she could exclude from everyone.

She noticed that Paul was staring at her across the room, and she looked straight back at him. David Harkman had become a source of strength; he was one thing that Paul could never tamper with!

Lost in her own thoughts, Julia was paying little attention to what was going on around her. The purpose of a meeting like this was usually for the various participants to talk about their latest experiences in Wessex. Although written reports were always filed, verbal exchanges were considered to be of equal importance for being informal. A process known as conscious assimilation was supposed to take place: unexplained gaps in the projected world's structure, as seen from one person's point of view, could sometimes be filled by another's observations.

Colin Willment was speaking at the moment, describing the last few weeks in Wessex. Normally, Julia would listen to the others' reports with interest, but today her mind was elsewhere.

It was still Paul who was distracting her. It frightened her to think that he might have more emotional trapdoors to open under her, but she was calmer now, better able to cope.

For the moment there was equilibrium. Paul was to join the projection, and she had inner strengths to draw on.

Colin finished his verbal report in a few minutes, and Mary Rickard followed. Julia knew her turn would come, and so she thought more directly about what she would say. She wanted nothing inadvertent to slip out, especially about David, nothing that would give Paul any more information about her part in the projection than he already had.

Part of the difficulty was that Don, Mary and Colin were present. How much should be stated, how much remain private?

Julia wondered if her interest in David's alter ego was already known to them. Matters of this sort trickled through into the consciousness. She knew, for instance, that Colin Willment was 'married' in Wessex, just as he was married in reality. She knew also, although she had never been told, that his projected wife was quite different from his real wife.

It was something she understood on an instinctive level, and one she felt honour-bound not to explore further.

So although the other participants would already have an inkling that something was developing between her and Harkman, Julia saw no reason to talk about it. If it was being assimilated on an unconscious level, why accelerate the process by drawing attention to it now?

She waited while Mary talked, not listening to her but organizing her thoughts and memories. Paul was still watching.

Then John Eliot said: 'Julia, since we're interested in David Harkman at the moment, and you were trying to locate him, perhaps you could report next.'

She hadn't realized that Mary had finished. She sat forward in her chair, trying to look as if she had been following what she had said.

'Miss Stretton,' Eliot said to Paul, 'is the geologist in the team.'

'Yes, I know,' Paul said. 'We're old friends.'

It came so unexpectedly, and was said in such an off-hand manner, that for a moment or two Julia hardly realized that Paul had thrown the hand-grenade whose pin he had removed that morning. But she had had time to recover from that surprise, and as the bomb landed she was able to pick it up and toss it back.

'Well, hardly old friends,' she said, and affected a light laugh. 'It seems we were at university together. Quite a coincidence really.'

Mary, sitting next to Julia, said unexpectedly: 'Mr Mason, you know there's a rule we have in the project? We discourage relationships outside the projection.'

'Mary, you're embarrassing Julia,' Don Mander said.

'Not at all,' Julia said, suddenly aware that Mary at least had revealed where her loyalties lay. 'We're almost strangers to each other. I didn't recognize Mr Mason until he introduced himself.'

Eliot, who had been looking from Paul to Julia, seemed relieved by the casual tone of her answer.

'Go on, Julia . . . tell us about David Harkman.'

'There's not much to tell.' She was trying to avoid thinking of the consequences of what had just happened. Paul had tried to carry out his threat, and it had failed. Would he try again? What would he do next?

'I think I'd been in the projection a fortnight before Harkman appeared,' she said, talking, making words. 'You know that the stall is on the harbour, and one evening . . .'

She was talking too quickly, trying to get her story out. The censor she had invoked stayed in place, but she was embellishing her report with too many irrelevant details. She didn't want to seem as if thrown off-balance by Paul, or anyone, and it was a relief to speak of the thing she knew best. By the time she had been talking for about five minutes she was more in control of herself, and kept her story factual and to the point. She described meeting Harkman outside the skimmer-shop, and the next day when he visited the Castle. She described where Harkman was known to be living and working, where the retrievers would have their best chance of finding him. After this, she talked about Tom Benedict, and what had happened to him.

If the others were aware of the tension she felt they did not show it. They listened with interest, asking occasional questions.

But Paul was silent, sitting opposite her. He was leaning back in his chair, with his legs crossed, and all the time she was talking his hard eyes never once turned away from her.

17

The meeting lasted all day. In the evening, as they walked along the corridor to the dining-room, Paul fell in beside her. John Eliot and Mander were a few yards ahead of them; Mary and Colin walked a few paces behind.

Paul said: 'I want a word with you.'

She stared ahead, trying not to acknowledge him.

Each table was set for four, and Julia headed for the one she had used at lunchtime. Paul followed, and sat at the same table.

John Eliot saw this, and came over to them.

'I expect you two have a lot in common,' he said, smiling at Julia.

'Old college days,' Paul said. 'Which year did you take your finals, Miss Stretton?'

As Eliot went over to sit at another table with Mander, Julia said softly: 'You can drop the pretence, Paul. I'm going to tell them.'

'What? Everything? You wouldn't dare.'

'Everything they need to know. I'm not the only one who doesn't want you here.'

'Tell them whatever you like. Suits me. Are you going to tell them about the money?'

'What money?' Julia said at once.

'The fifty quid you owe me.'

'I don't know what you mean.' A movement by the door caught her eye, and she turned away from him, her face reddening. It was Marilyn, and Julia waved to her to come to the table.

Julia went through the motions of introducing her to Paul, but inside she felt a deep, familiar dread. She knew which fifty pounds Paul meant, but it didn't matter. Not now.

Paul said to Marilyn: 'You've just saved Julia from an old debt. She owes me fifty pounds.'

Marilyn laughed. 'I thought you two had only just met!'

'He's joking,' Julia said, and forced a laugh of her own.

One day they'd had a row. Why it was that day and that row didn't matter . . . it was just one of dozens. Paul had won an office sweep, and he had come in from work brandishing the winnings. He was talking big in those days, wanted to set up on his own. Julia – it felt like a different Julia now – had spent the day job-hunting, was tired and bitter. An argument had started, the row developed. At the end, Julia had snatched the money from where he'd put it, stormed out of the flat. Stupidly, stupidly, she lost her purse, and with it went the money and her door-key. Afterwards, he would only let her in after she wept and knelt outside the door, and he'd pushed her on the bed and possessed her violently. There was a parting shot, there always was with Paul: the worst fifty quid's worth he'd had. That week.

Later he told the story for laughs, changing the facts to suit his own vanity. He always told the story in her presence, always got his laugh. After that, whenever money was mentioned, any money, he always somehow equated it with sex.

The surface of the dining-table was deep-grained, dark-polished wood, and Julia stared at the rush place-mat in front of her, shifting it with her fingers and making the cutlery tinkle. Paul was talking in a friendly way to Marilyn, the fifty pounds wasn't being mentioned.

She had never paid it back, never got round to it. She was always broke in the old days, and since then, since leaving Paul, she had put it out of her mind. She could pay it back now, pay it back twenty times and hardly miss it . . . but that wasn't the point. If she offered it to him he would refuse it; if she didn't he would never let her forget. But of course it wasn't the money itself. It had become a symbolic debt, the repayment that was due for walking out on him.

But then, as had happened during the afternoon, Julia felt her spirits rallying.

The debt was one she did not acknowledge; the money was irrelevant, and if she had ever done one thing in her life she never regretted it was leaving Paul.

While the first course was being served, Julia noticed Paul eyeing Marilyn's body.

She was bigger, more bosomy than Julia, and this evening she was wearing a skinny-thin sweater without a bra. Paul would like that, Paul had a thing about breasts. Even in that he had tried to make her feel inadequate; he used to point out other women to her, and complain that she was too thin and round-shouldered.

Her spirits were still high: it suddenly occurred to her that the only remaining vulnerabilities were petty and unimportant. A small sum of money, her bust-measurement: were these *all* that Paul could threaten her with?

Her sardonic amusement must have revealed itself on her face, because Marilyn suddenly looked away from Paul and grinned at her.

'Do you feel like going out for a drink this evening?' she said to her.

Julia shook her head. 'No . . . I'd better stay in. I've got to write my report tonight.'

Paul said nothing, but Julia saw him looking towards her. He was wearing a broad, false smile, and he winked lewdly at her. Marilyn, looking round for some butter, didn't see. It seemed to be a pointless thing to do.

Julia said very little during the meal, and as soon as she had had her dessert she excused herself from the table.

She went across to John Eliot, who was still eating.

'Dr Eliot, I'd like to rejoin the projection as soon as possible. Can it be tomorrow evening?'

'You'll be going to Tom's funeral?'

'Of course.'

'I'm not sure. You've only just been retrieved. We really should leave it for three days.'

'What's the hurry, Julia?' Don Mander said.

'No hurry. I feel I'm wasting time here, and the projection is weak at the moment. Even Andy and Steve are out.'

Eliot said: 'We'll need a written report from you, and – '

'I'm going to my room to do it now. Look, I'm perfectly fit. I've got a feeling I'm the only person who can get David Harkman back, and I want to try. We've wasted all day talking, and the one thing we should be worrying about is David. How can he have developed resistance to the mirrors?'

'We were just discussing that. Don thinks that Steve must have made a mistake.'

'Then that's what we've got to find out,' Julia said. 'When will he and Andy be ready for another try?'

'In two or three days.'

'I want to be in Wessex before then. You made him my responsibility.'

She turned away from their table before they could answer. Paul and Marilyn were at their table, and she walked past them quickly. She saw Marilyn turn, but she didn't look back. Her room had been cleaned during the day, and the mess she had made in the bathroom had been tidied up. It was cold, so she lit the gas-fire then sat on the floor in front of it, staring at the orange-glowing radiants. Her nails had grown while she was inside the projector, and so she found her scissors and file and began reshaping them, deliberately not thinking about the day.

When the room had warmed she cleared a space on the table, then set up her portable typewriter and a light.

She worked for two hours, trying to present an objective account of all she had seen and done in Wessex. The verbal accounts were useful, but their effectiveness was limited to those people who heard them. The written reports were the only way of communicating with the other participants.

And that reminded her that she had her own reading to do: several reports would have accumulated in the last three weeks. She would have to go over to Salisbury in the morning for the funeral, and she would see if she could travel in Marilyn's car, and read them on the way.

In her report she described David Harkman's projected appearance in detail; they knew where he was for the moment, but there was never any certainty they wouldn't lose him again. The description was important. She remembered the pallid, waxen David Harkman she had seen in the mortuary before she went to Wessex last time, and the difference she had seen in the man she met. Pale, yes, but from working in offices, not from the weird half-life of the projector. She thought of the slim, muscular body riding the skimmer, and the easy, athletic walk across the quay.

She also described the disappearance of Tom Benedict in as much detail as she could recall; this was difficult, because the amnesia she had suffered directly afterwards had made the incident vague. She remembered his hand holding hers under the sheet, she remembered the cool white ward, and the officious woman with the child.

There were the same omissions in this written report as she had made in the afternoon. Feelings, mostly, and hopes. She wrote about the affinity she had detected with David Harkman, and with Tom Benedict, the sense of recognition when Andy had held the mirror before her eyes ... but this was well known to them all. What she omitted were the things that mattered to her, that were as private to her as the whole projection was to them all. Moments like those few seconds on the quayside when she had seen David Harkman walking towards her, and she'd caught her breath and felt her nipples hardening under the coarse fabric of her dress. Or down at the creek when she had agreed to go to David's room, with Greg a short distance away ... and she had *seen* Greg falter in his stride, she had *made* Greg look away until she could agree.

To write of Wessex was to be reminded of it, even if for her it was only a partial account. It was always like this. In the hours following a return, one's real life intersected with the projection, and memories became confused.

Wessex became an obsession, a waking dream, a constant yearning.

It had given her the first real function in life, and Wessex had become her first reality.

All that went before Wessex seemed like a half-hearted rehearsal for an improvised play. Wessex was the play, and it dominated her personality as a strong character will dominate a good actor.

Only Paul, and all that he stood for, had as powerful an influence on her. And that had been a destructive, selfish influence; it was right that she should put it behind her.

Wessex was real, and it seduced her, in the same way that Paul had once seduced her. It grew around her, adapting to her personality. It was an unconscious wish come true, an extension of her own identity that totally embraced her; the perfect lover.

She stared at the sheet of typewritten paper, thinking how the words only described the surface-qualities of the experience. It was true what John Eliot had said that morning; the reports were no longer observations of anything functional to the project. Now the true experiences were held back, recycled through the unconscious to the further enrichment of the projection.

Like a genuine and deeply felt relationship, the fundamental truths need never be stated.

Julia decided she had finished her report, so she turned the last sheet out of the typewriter and separated it from the carbon-copy. She read it through, making a few small corrections, then laid it aside.

It was still fairly early in the evening, and she wondered for a moment if she should look for the others. They had probably gone into Dorchester for a drink. But Paul would be with them, and anyway the months inside the projection had taken away her taste for alcohol and cigarettes.

She tidied the desk, then went into the bathroom and undressed and washed. Afterwards, wearing her dressing-gown, she sat again on the mat in front of the gas-fire and stared blankly into the flames. She wished she had a pack of cards; she felt like a game of patience.

Then the door opened and closed, and Paul was there.

18

Julia said: 'Paul, go away.'

He walked across the room, sat down in the armchair. 'I thought I'd drop in to say goodnight. We haven't had much chance to talk today.'

'I've nothing to say to you. I told you this morning: I've finished with you for good. I'm happy now.'

'So you say. That isn't what John Eliot says about you.'

A trout snaps at bait without knowing what it is; Julia recognized it, couldn't resist it. 'What do you mean?'

'He thinks you're over-tired. Been projecting too long. He wants you to take long leave.'

'Paul, you're lying.' She closed her eyes, turned her face away. 'For God's sake, get out!'

She heard him tap a cigarette against the side of a packet, then a match struck. When she looked back at him he was holding the match vertically so that the flame burned high. He blew it out with a long funnel of smoke, then flicked the match with his nail so that the black end flew away. He always did that, and she wondered how many thousands of times he had done it in the six years she hadn't seen him.

'Do you have an ashtray?' he said, curling the match in his fingers.

'I don't smoke.'

He dropped the match on the carpet. 'Such will-power. You used to smoke more than me.'

'Paul, I don't know what you're doing in here, nor what you

want, but it isn't going to work. I don't want you here, I don't want you in the project, I never want to see you again!'

'The same old paranoia,' he said. 'I'm handy to have around, aren't I? Without me you'd have no one to blame for your short-comings.'

She moved so that she turned her back towards him. Where were the inner strengths she had found during the day? Had they been a delusion?

'If you don't get out of here in the next five seconds, I'm going to call the others.'

'Supposing they could hear you,' he said. 'And what would happen then? We have our showdown? O.K., if that's what you want. We'll tell them that we are, after all, old and intimate friends, and that you're having doubts about the work. I'll say that I agree you're over-tired, and after all didn't I live with you long enough to know you better than I know myself? You look pale and haggard, Julia. Perhaps you should have a holiday?'

'So you do want me out of the project!'

'Only if you force me.'

She said nothing, staring at the carpet.

'Turn round so I can see you, Julia.'

'Why?'

'I can always tell what you're thinking when I see your face.'

She didn't move, and in a moment heard him leave his chair. She braced herself against his touch, but he walked past her, flicking ash towards the gas-fire as he did so. He sat on the bed, facing her.

'Why do you want to get into the project so badly?' she said.

'I told you: it's the finest opportunity of my career.'

'You self-seeking bastard!'

'And you're in it for totally unselfish reasons, I suppose?'

'I'm involved because I believe in it.'

'Then for once we agree,' Paul said. 'There's only one Ridpath projector, and I want to use it.'

'I, I, I. Never mind the others.'

'I'm needed because I've got something that none of you have. An objective and intelligent viewpoint.'

She glared up at him. 'Are you trying to say – ?'

'The word was objective. I was hired by the trustees because the projection is subjective and indulgent. They're paying for results, and that means new ideas.'

'Which you have, presumably.'

'I have one idea.'

'What is it?'

Paul had his calculating grin again. 'If I told you it would become your idea, wouldn't it? Let's just say that your little world has one omission so obvious I'm surprised no one thought of it before. I intend to rectify it.'

'You're going to change the projection!'

'Not at all. I know how dear it is to you. After all, we mustn't *ever* change the projection.'

'Paul, you're interfering in something you don't understand!'

'I understand only too well.' Paul's voice had changed from false reasonableness to genuine harshness. 'It's a fantasy-world for emotionally immature academics. All this talk of psychodrama! What we're talking about is failure, inadequacy! Look at you, you little slut. Incapable of enjoying sex in real life, you have to dream up some half-wit mechanic to screw you every night.'

'You've been reading my reports!'

'I'm not obsessed with you. I've read them all. Not just yours.'

She felt a surge of hysterical rage, and she scrambled to her feet, reaching out for him. She raised her hand to hit him, but he caught it and twisted her wrist painfully. She tore herself away, kicked out at him, then threw herself face-down across the armchair and began to sob.

Paul waited. He finished his cigarette, ground it out in the grate, then lit another.

'I'd like to meet this guy you've conjured up. I can see him now. Well-hung, and as stupid as – '

'Paul, *shut up!*' Sobbing, she tried to cover her ears. 'Go away!'

'And of course he fucks you better than I ever could. I'll bet he's everything you said I wasn't.'

She closed her mind to the voice, the intrusive, damaging presence. He always talked dirty to anger her, because he knew she couldn't stand it.

He had made her think of Greg, and after this the young man in Wessex, whom everybody liked, whose only fault was that he didn't know how to satisfy her, seemed safe and gentle and reassuring.

She began to calm down, and realized that Paul had stopped talking. She lay where she was, sprawled across the floor with her head and chest in the seat of the armchair, breathing deeply to steady herself, trying to restore order to the chaos of her emotions.

The projection used mental techniques; the mnemonics trained the mind, taught discipline and self-control. The experience of the projection itself had a similar effect: it taught one the power of the unconscious mind, the way to use the conscious.

She thought: it's Greg! Paul cannot come to terms with the fact that my unconscious has created Greg!

But not David Harkman . . . no mention of David. He doesn't know, because no one knows.

David was the strength with which she could resist him. Once in her life she had defied Paul by leaving him, and suddenly she realized that she had, quite unwittingly, done it again. His ego could not accept the notion that her Wessex lover might be better in bed than he was.

She raised her face from the cushion, and wiped her eyes on her sleeve. As she turned back to face Paul she discovered that as she had sprawled into the chair her shortie dressing-gown had ridden up, exposing her.

Paul, sitting on the bed, watched as she tried to cover herself. 'I've seen it all before, Julia.'

'You can say what you like. I don't care what you look at, I don't care what you think happens in Wessex, and I don't even care if you go there and see for yourself. I just want you to get out of my room, otherwise I'll bring everyone in the house here.'

She said the words calmly and factually, for once expressing her true and total feelings.

Paul stared silently for a moment, and then stood up. As he did so, Julia realized that his watching of her exposed body had been more callous than she could have imagined, for as he turned she saw that he was noticeably aroused.

He took off the jacket of his suit, and hung it on the hook on the door.

'Don't get any ideas, Paul.'

'I came to say goodnight, remember? You know what that means. We were always good together.'

'Paul, I'll scream if you come near me!'

But she didn't scream, even then. A paralysis held her, the old familiar paralysis. Paul stepped quickly to her, and put his hand across her mouth, pressing his thumb and fingers into her cheeks. It was the first time he had deliberately touched her, and as if this released a long-coiled spring, she struggled violently to escape. His hand swiped against the side of her head, half stunning her. He moved behind her, still pressing his hand across her mouth, pulling her head back.

'You like me rough, you little bitch. Well, you're going to enjoy this more than ever . . .'

With his free hand he reached down and tore at the front of her gown. One button tore away, the other pulled the fabric with it, hanging on threads. The gown fell open and his hand snatched at her breast, twisting and pulling at the nipple. She tried to gasp, but he was choking her. He released her mouth for an instant, but before she could draw breath he had clamped his arm across her throat, making her gag. She could feel him pressing himself against her back, could feel the hardness of his arousal pushing into her buttocks.

She tried to scream, had no breath. She was clawing at his arm with her hands, kicking backwards . . . *anything* to get him to release her!

He was fumbling with his trousers now, and she knew that this was the only moment when she had a chance of freedom. With all her strength she forced her body down, leaning forwards. His arm pulled back, throttling her. She straightened, but then, using her last resource of strength, forced herself forward again.

His arm weakened, and she stumbled away.

She turned to face him, one half of her gown torn from her body, hanging down. Paul stood before her, his penis jutting from the front of his trousers.

'Don't move!' she said, and her bruised throat made her cough painfully. 'Not one inch nearer!'

Paul, red in the face and breathing heavily, took a step towards her.

Julia saw the nail-scissors on the floor by the gas-fire, and snatched them up.

Holding one of the tiny blades out like a knife, Julia said: 'Paul, I'll kill you.' He took another step, and she said: 'I mean it!'

'You like me rough,' he said for the second time, but now it was without menace, almost pleadingly.

'Get out.' She was more terrified than she had ever been in her life.

They stared in glaring silence, like two animals cornered by each other, but then Paul relaxed.

He reached down into the front of his trousers, straightened himself up, zipped the fly. He walked slowly to the door, took down his jacket.

Julia watched his every movement.

When he had put on his jacket he swept back the hair from his face, and opened the door.

'I'm sorry, Miss Stretton,' he said loudly, into the corridor. 'I thought you were playing hard to get.'

As the door slammed behind him, Julia dropped the scissors, and fell across the bed and sobbed uncontrollably.

Half an hour later, she went to the door, turned the lock, then went to have a bath. She had a purple bruise across her throat, and there were scratches on her cheek where his fingernails had raked her. Her right breast was swollen and sore. She felt soiled, dirtied.

But later, as she lay awake in the dark, trying for sleep, she realized that Paul could not threaten her again. She could match him psychologically. She *knew* him now as she had never known him before, and she could contain the knowledge.

And she felt, without fear, that Paul had the same knowledge of her.

19

While they were driving back from the funeral in Salisbury, Julia read the other reports as she had planned. Her heart and mind weren't in them though, and she skimmed them, hoping to glean the necessary information with her eyes alone. Funerals always dispirited her, and the windswept grounds of the crematorium, with the processions of hearses leaving and arriving every few minutes, had seemed like the setting for a continuous, organized tragedy, staged scrupulously and tastefully.

Afterwards there had been the other ordeal: the nice cup of tea with her parents. Her father looked awkward and large in his dark suit, and her mother, tearful during the service, transferred her grief for Tom to nagging concern for Julia. 'You don't look as if you get any fresh air, dear', and 'I hope they're feeding you well', and 'Do you ever hear from that nice boy you used to see in London?' I'm very busy, Mum, and I'm happy, and yet isn't it sad about Tom, and I get all the fresh air I want, and I think we ought to be getting back pretty soon.

Marilyn had gone with her to the tea-shop, and pretended not to listen to the conversation.

There had been no sign of Paul in the morning, but she did not even feel relief. If she had any feelings left about Paul, they were fatalistic ones. He might yet try to take revenge, but she was ready for anything. She was prepared to take the silk scarf from her throat, to show what it presently concealed, and bare her bruised breast if it would be enough to convince the others that it was Paul who was a threat to the projection, not her.

Marilyn had sensed that something climactic had happened the previous evening, but Julia had sidestepped her questions. When the participants returned from Wessex they were often in an upset state for hours afterwards, and Marilyn had grown accustomed to it. Although she was not directly involved with the projection, Marilyn had grown to know the participants, and had sometimes remarked to Julia on the way it was changing them.

'How has it changed me?' Julia had once asked her.

'For the better,' was the answer, but it was a laughing one and Marilyn had said no more.

As they drove out of Dorchester, and crossed the Frome Valley towards Maiden Castle and Bincombe House beyond, Julia looked at the bleak, wind-blown scenery, trying to see it with her Wessex eyes, to see the calm, blue bay, dotted with boats. The southern side of Dorchester was ugly, with the post-war council houses of Victoria Park lining the hills. There was no sign of their existence in Wessex, evidence of the participants' unconscious consensus of distaste.

The main road passed Maiden Castle, which loomed up on its hill to their right. Glancing at it, Julia said: 'Marilyn, do you know any reason why I shouldn't go back into the projection today?'

'You know it isn't anything to do with me.'

'Yes, but I wondered if you'd heard anything.'

'About you?'

'Not specially,' Julia said. 'But I returned only the day before yesterday, and someone was saying that after Tom's death the periods outside the projector should be longer.'

'The only thing I've heard is that the medical examinations are going to be more rigorous.'

'I'd heard that too.'

Before they had left for Salisbury in the morning, Don Mander had called a brief meeting. It was urgent that at least two people should rejoin the projection, as there was now a total of seven participants out, although Steve and Andy were not counted as full projecting members. Colin Willment had gone on to London after the funeral, although it was likely he would be back in a day or two. Don Mander himself was undecided whether or not to take leave. Mary and Julia had offered themselves for an immediate return, although Mary needed at least one day to herself in London.

Of Paul Mason, nothing had been said.

When they reached Bincombe House, Julia went to her room and began to go through her clothes, wondering if she would need them in the next few days. There were a few that needed laundering, and she put them aside for the staff to deal with. She now had more clothes here than she had at her flat in London, but she never needed more than a few. She had brought most of them down with her the last time she came from London; now she was thinking she might take some of them back.

On the way down to Salisbury she had stopped for a snack with Marilyn, but hadn't eaten since . . . not even tea-cakes or scones in the afternoon, much to her parents' surprise.

She was hungry now, and if she was rejoining the projection she should stay that way. She wanted to see John Eliot or Mander, and see what they wanted her to do. In spite of her new equanimity about Paul, his barb about her needing long leave still clung to her.

She went downstairs, but there was no one about. She stood indecisively by the fireplace in the lounge for ten minutes, wondering where Paul had been during the day. Marilyn had told her on the way back from the funeral that he was staying at the Antelope Hotel in Dorchester, so that accounted for why she hadn't seen him in Bincombe during the morning, but she had fully expected him to be there when they got back.

Upstairs, she found Mary Rickard packing a suitcase.

'I hope your house is going to be all right,' Julia said. 'What are you going to do about it?'

'I'll have to take out a court-order tomorrow, then give power of attorney to my ex-husband. It should be quite straightforward, because the house used to be in his name anyway.'

'When do you hope to be back here?'

'The day after tomorrow,' Mary said. 'I wasn't expecting to see you . . . I thought you were back in Wessex.'

'I'm still waiting to hear from John Eliot.'

'From what I know, he's waiting for you. He told me you were rejoining immediately after the funeral.'

'So I'm going back!'

Julia felt a pleasant sense of relief, and also a thrill of excitement. Wessex was still there for her.

'Mary, what do you think of Paul Mason?'

'He seems a pleasant young man.'

As she said this, Mary was folding a skirt and she did not look at Julia.

'Come on Mary. I'd like to know.'

'He's a friend of yours, isn't he?'

'Did he tell you that?'

'No . . . but you said you were at university together.'

'We were there at the same time,' Julia said. 'I remember him vaguely.'

'So you say, dear. It doesn't matter to me. I noticed the way he was watching you.'

For a moment Julia was tempted to tell her what had happened last night, but she had long been in the habit of not confiding in other members of the projection – consciously, at least – and she knew Mary less well than most.

'I did go out with him once or twice.'

'I said it doesn't matter. In spite of what I said today, I was never one who believed we should treat each other as if we weren't human. Anyway, I happen to know that before the projection began there was at least one affaire going on. It doesn't seem to have made much difference.'

Julia said, with interest: 'Who was it between?'

'A man and a woman,' Mary said, with a smile. 'It was finished without blood or tears, as far as I know. So if you once had something going with Paul Mason, and you don't want to talk about it, then that's your business.'

'You still haven't told me what you think of him.'

Mary closed the suitcase lid, and sat down on the edge of her bed. She had large, soft features, kind eyes.

'I'll tell you, Julia, because that does matter to me. I think he's a dangerous and self-centred man. I think he will harm the projection, and there's nothing we can do about it.'

She was speaking quietly, calmly. Mary rarely exaggerated: her reports were always exemplary of precise observation, telling images.

Julia said: 'Do you know anything about him?'

'Nothing I can't see with my own eyes. And nothing I can't work out for myself. The trustees have hired him because he's just the kind of sharp young man they think the projection needs.

But they don't realize what a malevolent ambition could do.'

'I thought Don Mander and John Eliot liked him.'

'Eliot likes him, Don doesn't. It doesn't matter what the participants think, anyway. The trustees want their money's worth, and they think a slick young operator with a background in gutter journalism and property speculation will get that for them. I suppose it's our own fault, ultimately. The trustees have always been out of touch with the projection. Julia, Wessex is *real* for me. I don't want it changed.'

Julia remembered Paul in her room; the calculating grin before he tried to rape her.

'Mary, last night ... I spoke to Paul Mason. He was talking about what he was going to do with the projection.'

'What did he say?'

'Nothing specific. But he dropped a large hint, said there was an obvious omission in the projection.'

'I heard him talking to John Eliot,' Mary said. 'He was asking how the projection equipment was used in Wessex. Eliot said it was used to retrieve the participants, and Paul asked him if it could be used for anything else. Do you suppose this is the same thing?'

'It might be. What did Eliot say?'

'He said, of course, that it couldn't. That's all I heard.'

Julia said: 'He's up to something. Mary, what's it going to be?'

'We'll find out eventually. But we have a consolation.'

'What's that?'

'We know the projection better than he does. It's ours, and we can keep it ours. There are thirty-eight of us, Julia, and only one of him. No one can change the projection alone ... Wessex is too deeply embedded now.'

Julia thought of Paul, the ambitious graduate who claimed that no job was too big for him and his talents, and had been right. Paul the career-climber, the rat-race smoothie. She knew Paul would have the will.

Mary said: 'If we succumb to Paul he'll do what he wants. Our only hope is to be united with ourselves.'

'But only four of us know about Paul! And Colin's on leave, and you're going back to London.'

'I've already talked to Colin. He feels the same as us. He's entitled to his leave, but he'll be coming back as soon as he can. Maybe in a day or two. I'll be back in two days' time. As for the others . . . they'll have to be told as they're retrieved. Although if Paul makes changes, they'll see what's happening for themselves while they're in Wessex.'

Mary stood up, and took her coat down from the door.

'I want to catch the last train,' she said. 'And I'll have to ring for a taxi.'

Julia watched as Mary checked that the suitcase was firmly closed, then glanced about the room to make sure she hadn't forgotten anything. Julia followed her out of the room, and they went downstairs together. Don Mander was waiting for them in the hall.

Julia caught Mary's arm as they turned on the stairs, holding her back before Don saw them. She had suddenly realized that after Mary left she and Don would be the only two active participants at Bincombe. The thought frightened her, and made her understand how Mary had become an unexpected ally against Paul. Don Mander she didn't trust; he seemed altogether too ready to accept the trustees' appointment of Paul.

'Mary,' she said softly, 'can't we do something to stop Paul?'

'I think not, dear. He joined the projection this afternoon.'

'Then it's too late.'

'To do anything here, yes. But we'll be in Wessex.'

Julia followed her down to the hall, and waited with Mary until the taxi arrived from Dorchester. When the car had driven away, Julia went up to her room, tidied her things, put away her clothes. She was thirsty, so she drank a little water from the toothbrush glass in the bathroom, then went downstairs again and talked to Don Mander. She was to return to Wessex that evening; there was no special brief for her, except to keep in contact with David Harkman; John Eliot and his staff were waiting for her at Maiden Castle.

Later, as Julia refreshed the mnemonics in her mind, she was thinking of David, remembering how, when oppressed by Paul, the thought of him had strengthened her.

Once Wessex itself had been the unacknowledged refuge from Paul; now there was only David, and Paul did not know.

20

It was suffocatingly warm in David Harkman's office, and he sat with his jacket off and his tie undone. Even though the window was wide open, there was no draught to speak of, and the sounds of the tourists walking in the cobbled street outside were a continual distraction.

He was reading through the minutes of the Culture and Arts Committee, the body in the Commission theoretically responsible for subsidies to local drama workshops, art-galleries, playwrights, libraries and musical societies. Very little money was ever approved for direct sponsorship of the arts, because most of the Committee's allocation seemed to be spent on administrative expenses. It made depressing reading, and the page of Harkman's notebook, on which he had started to jot down observations, was still almost blank.

He picked up the internal telephone, and dialled a number.

'Is that Mr Mander?'

'Speaking.'

'David Harkman. Has the Commissioner had a chance to approve my application?'

'Mr Borovitin has been engaged all day, Harkman. Will you try again in the morning?'

'I've been waiting for two days already. I can't start work until I have access to the archives.'

'Call me again tomorrow.'

Harkman had grown accustomed to the bureaucratic delays of Westminster, and had learned how to take short cuts when it was necessary, but he had not expected to come up against similar habitual obstructiveness here. Civil servants were probably the same all over the world, but the departmental mind was dissonant with the idyllic atmosphere of Dorchester.

Harkman closed the Culture and Arts file, and leaned back in his chair, staring irritably at the opposite wall. He was blocked in every way. The work he was paid to do couldn't be started properly. Julia was busy during the days, and even wave-riding was excluded from him. High tide came just too late now, at a time when he was supposed to be at his desk. The exhilaration of his ride of the day before was still in him, but his next day off wasn't for another week, and it would be only towards the end of the week following that the wave would arrive late enough in the afternoon for him to take the time off.

It was at moments like this, when his external drives were temporarily thwarted, that Harkman felt his inner compulsion the strongest. It was what he had talked to Julia about, that morning at the Castle: the unaccountable urge to be in Wessex, to live and work in Dorchester. But it was not only Dorchester and Wessex, because he was here and the urge had been satisfied.

Maiden Castle was the focus. He was obsessed and dominated by it. He could not walk the streets of the town without looking frequently to the south-west, he could not conceive of Dorchester without the Castle beside it, he could not feel at ease unless he knew in which direction it lay from where he was. Just as the States tourists prostrated themselves five times daily towards Mecca, so Harkman paid frequent instinctive homage to the low, rounded hill-fort overlooking the bay.

Dwelling again on these matters renewed his frustration at the bureaucratic delay. As the days passed, Harkman realized that his own work would have to be set aside until he had investigated whatever records there were about Maiden Castle and its community.

On an impulse, Harkman hurried out of his office, determined to go directly to the Castle, as if this alone would dispel the compulsion, but before he was halfway along the corridor that led to the front office he had changed his mind. He had already been to the Castle, and it had not satisfied the urge.

He walked on, with less resolution than before. He passed through the front office and saw the usual line of States tourists, waiting patiently to apply for English visas.

As soon as he entered Marine Boulevard, Harkman looked towards the south-west, like the needle of a compass swinging towards the north. He could see the Castle across the bay: the day was sunny and humid, but in the sky beyond the Castle dark clouds were lowering. A weird light seemed to surround the hilltop, a glowing golden green, sunlight on storm; Harkman could almost detect the thermal of rising heat, like the hypnotic power of the Castle had over him, an invisible but detectable radiation, mystical and elemental.

A high tide in the morning made it impossible for him to ride the Blandford wave, but it meant that the harbour was open all during the rest of the day, and when Harkman reached the stall he found it crowded with visitors.

He managed to catch Julia's attention.

'Can you get away?' he said.

'Not until later. We're too busy.'

As she spoke, an argument broke out between two of the customers over which of them had picked up a fragile crystal vase first. The two men squabbled in a fast North American dialect, rich in Arabic words, incomprehensible to the English.

'Five o'clock?' Harkman said.

'All right. If this has quietened down.'

She turned away from him, and took the vase gently from the man who was clutching it. Harkman watched as she deftly intervened in the argument, clearly favouring one of the two, yet appeasing the other with a combination of flattery and the production of a slightly more expensive piece of merchandise. She spoke in English, and this itself had a calming effect. Harkman waited until both sales had been made, and then he walked away through the crowd of strolling tourists and went to the far end of the quay, overlooking the entrance to the harbour. He sat down on the paving-stones, feeling the sun's warmth through the fabric of his suit, a reminder of the long timeless summer, and his incongruous preoccupations in this tourist centre.

Many private cruisers were taking advantage of the tide, and the harbour remained busy until well after five. Harkman waited until half-past before walking back to the stall.

Julia looked tired, but she seemed pleased to see him, and as soon as she had spoken to the other two people behind the stall she left with him.

'What would you like to do?' he said, as they walked up the hill away from the shore, and towards the wild heaths that spread for miles around the town.

'Be with you,' she said. 'Alone.'

What they had together was still a novelty, and no habits had formed. They walked quickly, although the air was hot and humid, until they found a sheltered dell away from the path, and there they made love. The newness, the freshness of what they had gave them the excitement of recent encounter, the sense of mutual conquest.

Harkman felt relaxed and tender, and when Julia had pulled on her loose-fitting dress again he hugged her against him, and they lay back in the long grass together.

'Julia, I love you.'

Her face was turned towards him, and she stretched up to kiss his neck beneath his ear.

'I love you too, David.'

Last night they had said the same words again and again, a dozen times in an hour, and each time it had seemed fresh and original, the feeling belied by the inadequacy of the words. This evening it was as if they said them for the first time.

Because he had spent much of the afternoon pondering on the intangible compulsion of the Castle, Harkman had allowed himself to overlook the feeling of displaced memory that Julia aroused in him. He had felt it again as they met, and he felt it now as she lay in his arms. If he held her tightly he could diminish it, but nothing could dispel it entirely.

It was not that Julia gave only a part of herself to him, nor that she was distant or unaffectionate, because the first tendernesses came from her, the first loving kisses. She was in every way as dependent on him as he was on her, and in the manner of responses or of gestures, or of physical commitment, she satisfied him utterly.

He possessed Julia in every conceivable way bar their permanently living together, but he did not *experience* her. He remembered her into existence.

The thundercloud Harkman had seen earlier was blacker than before, but seemed no closer. A breeze had sprung up from the sea, and as it moved through the long grass it made a soothing, sweeping sound, at variance with the calm which tradition laid before the storm. They had heard the rumbling of thunder all afternoon, but the storm did not seem likely to strike for an hour or more.

Harkman, holding Julia, felt the stillness of fulfilment, felt the breeze of disconcerting compulsions, awaited the onset of what was to come.

She moved in his arms, and turned to lie on her back beside him, her head resting on his arm. She stared up at the sky. If the storm did not break beforehand there were about two hours until sunset, the time when they both knew she would return to Maiden Castle.

This temporary, borrowed aspect of their affaire had begun to have a corroding effect on Harkman.

He said, in a while: 'Julia, I want you to leave the Castle. Come and live with me in Dorchester. We can find somewhere.'

'No. It's impossible!'

The readiness, and finality, of her answer came as a shock to him.

'What do you mean?' he said.

'I can't leave the community.'

'Is it more important?'

She turned to face him and laid her hand on his chest, stroking him. Her touch suddenly felt alien, unwelcome.

'Don't let's argue about it,' she said.

'Argue? It's too important for an argument! Do you love me?'

'Of course.'

'Then there's no question. Julia, I love you so much I couldn't –'

'David, it's no good. I simply can't leave the Castle now.'

'Now? But later?'

'I don't think so,' she said.

There was one matter that Harkman had never raised with her, preferring to imagine the best than know the worst, but there could be no more avoiding it. He had to know.

'There's someone else,' he said. 'Another man.'

She said, very quietly: 'Of course.'

'Then who – ?'

'But it isn't that, David. I'd leave him for you. Surely you know that?'

'Who is it?'

'You haven't met him. His name wouldn't mean anything to you.' She sat up and faced him, looking down seriously at him. The breeze played with her hair, and behind her the storm-cloud loomed. 'Don't question me about him. If it was just that I'd leave today.'

Harkman, still burned by the fires of possessiveness and jealousy, barely heard this.

He said: 'But I have met him. The man with the beard . . . at the workshop. Greg, wasn't it?'

She laughed dismissively, but there was strain in the sound.

'It's not Greg. I told you, you haven't met him.'

'He was acting very strangely that day.'

She shook her head firmly. 'Greg's always like that. It was because you were from the Commission. He wanted to make you pay more.'

'Then who is it?'

'Someone else. You haven't met him, probably never will. It doesn't matter who he is.'

'It does to me.'

It occurred to him then that Julia might be lying. There had been that unmistakable expression on Greg's face, that morning at the Castle, the expression which seemed to plant territorial fences around Julia whenever he looked at her.

'David, please don't go on asking about it. I love you, surely you know that?'

'Then come and live with me.'

'I can't.'

Again, the finality.

'Give me one reason, apart from this other man, why you will not.'

She said nothing for a long time, so long in fact that Harkman thought she was going to avoid the question by maintaining the silence. But at last she said: 'I can't leave the Castle because I live and work there.'

'You work in Dorchester.'

She said: 'I'm not going back to the stall again. I've finished there.'

'You haven't told me this before.'

'You haven't given me a chance. I was going to tell you later. From tomorrow I shall be at the Castle all the time.'

'Then I could live with you there?'

'No, David . . .'

'So we come back to this other man, whose name you won't tell me.'

'I suppose so,' she said.

Harkman felt disappointed, angry, hurt. For a moment he thought he had seen a way round the problem, but it returned to source.

'What is it? Are you in love with him?'

Her eyes widened, not in affected innocence but in a surprise that seemed genuine.

'Oh no, David. I love you.'

'You live with him . . . is it because of the sex?'

'It used to be. Not now. He repels me. *Really*. That side of it is finished, but I need more time to work it out. I've only known you for five days . . .'

He had to allow her that. What they had was profound, but it was certainly recent. For him there was a feeling of rightness about it that rose above the conventions, and in that moment of hope he had thought there was a way: he had been prepared to leave his work to live with her, to become one of the community at the Castle. The idea still appealed to him, because of its simplicity, but he knew too that if it came to a decision – here, on this heath, in this instant – he'd want more time to think about it.

Wasn't Julia only asking the same?

But the vagueness of her relationship with the other man, or at least the vagueness of how she presented it to him, was as potentially hurtful to him as the pain a hidden weapon could inflict. He was nervous of it, watchful for it, uncertain of how it might be used against him.

'Will you try to work it out, Julia? Can you?'

'I think so. Give me time.'

'Tell me you love me.'

'I do, I do,' she said, and leant forward to kiss him on the lips, but as soon as the kiss was finished she drew away again.

'David, it's not just this other man. If I told you the rest, would it be between us alone? Completely confidential?'

'You know it would.'

'I mean the Commission. You know there are several people there who are set against the Castle, and because you work at the Commission, I'm . . . well, unsure.'

'I'm only attached to the place because of the archives,' he said at once. 'I'm not a civil servant, and I confide in no one there.'

She was staring at him very closely, and he felt uneasy under the intensity of her gaze.

'We're doing something at the Castle that no one at the Commission knows about. It's not illegal . . . but if Commissioner Borovitin or one of his deputies found out there'd be so much interference that the work would become impossible.'

'Then it must be illegal.'

'No . . . secret. There's a distinction.'

'It wouldn't seem much of a difference to Borovitin.'

'That's it precisely.' She was sitting away from him now. Her legs were crossed, but she leaned forward towards him earnestly. 'All that you saw at the Castle the other day, the craftwork, the skimmers, they're cover for something else. Most of the people at the Castle are scientists and academics, drawn from all parts of England. They have a common ideal, and the Castle is the only place they can pursue it.'

'Don't they have ideals in universities any more?'

'The universities are State-controlled. The only research that's possible is under the management of politicians and bureaucrats. What we're interested in is social and economic research, free of political pressure. The facilities for that exist at the Castle, and that is why the community was established.'

'You said "we",' Harkman said.

'I'm one of them. Our real work at the Castle is just about to start, and I'm going to be heavily involved in a few days' time. When it's finished, things will be different.'

He did not see why this should prevent him from living with her at the Castle, but then he did. There was always the other man. He stared back at her in silence, feeling that something he valued above all else had been taken away from him.

Apparently thinking that what she said was insufficient to convince him, Julia leaned forward again, placed her hand on his wrist.

'It's utterly serious, David. I'm not asking much of you, except patience. The results of this project could ultimately affect everyone in England, and I have to commit myself to that. You should understand: you have your own work.'

'It doesn't come between you and me.'

'It does so long as you're attached to the Commission.'

Harkman said: 'What is this project at the Castle?'

'Obviously I can't tell you. It's . . . a little like your work, except that your research is with the past.'

'And yours is with the future.' He meant it ironically, but she reacted at once by taking away her hand and staring into her lap.

'It's a new kind of sociological research,' she said. 'A different way of seeing the present.' She turned her head, glanced back at the storm-cloud in the distance. 'I've probably said too much. But do you understand how important it is?'

He looked back at her, trying to betray nothing. 'I understand that I won't see you. That you live with someone else. That your work is more important to you than I am. That all this has happened in the last few minutes.'

'There's something else, David. Stronger than any of those.'

'What's that?'

'I love you. I wouldn't say it if I didn't mean it. I love you more than anyone I have ever known.'

He shook his head, and said nothing.

Julia drew away, and stood up. She looked about her: the grass of the heath waved in the breeze.

'What is it?' David sat up, propping himself on an elbow. 'Is someone there?'

'Please wait . . . just for a minute.'

Before he could answer she moved away from him, walking quickly up the slope of the little hollow where they had been lying, and went across the heath towards the west. The great cumulonimbus which straddled the horizon, blue-black at its base, a soaring white anvil at its peak, seemed about to obscure the sun, for it spread laterally and hugely towards it. Julia walked in front of the sun, and for a moment he was dazzled by it. He saw her pause, raise her hands to her face, lower her head.

He thought she was crying, but nothing in her mood had warned of that . . . and as he watched he saw that she was motionless, as if meditating or waiting. Then she raised her head and looked towards the south, to where the mound of Maiden Castle breasted its hill.

She seemed to be waiting, and so he waited with her, aware above all else of the juxtaposition of the three: the Castle and Julia and himself. There was some incontestable link between them, and yet it was something that also threatened to divide them. In those moments, while Julia stood on the grassy edge of the hollow, profiled against the turbulent sky, Harkman tried to understand everything that had been said in the last few minutes. Unexpectedly, the explanation came from the enigma that had dogged him since the first night.

What he had heard from her had not actually been said: he had *remembered* it into his experience.

The only reality was the young woman in the sun, black and wary against the sky. The sensation was more marked now than Harkman had ever known it. It was all illusory, remembered by him, remembered for him; not real.

Had they talked of love, of another man, of a scientific project?

He knew they had and he knew they hadn't. The contradiction was ultimate. Reality began at this instant, at every instant, and the past became false.

Then Julia turned towards him, hurrying back, skipping in the grass.

'David!' she called. 'David, I'm here!'

He stood up as she ran towards him, because he recognized something in her at last, something he had been seeking. She rushed towards him, and went into his arms, kissing him, holding him.

'David,' she said breathlessly, kissing his face. 'Oh I love you!'

He looked into her eyes, and it was there. The intangible; the life; the reality.

Harkman felt her in his arms and in his heart. The sensation that memory created her was gone. Julia was there, and she was real, and total. She had returned to him.

But as he embraced her, the darkening shoulders of Maiden Castle stood behind her, calling her back.

21

They hurried, because the sun had gone in behind the encroaching cloud, and the storm was almost upon them. No rain had yet fallen, but the breeze had died and the countryside lay humid and silent in anticipation.

The path divided by the stretch of shore known locally as Victoria Beach, and as she and David embraced Julia noticed that the sand was still crowded with tourists, apparently unheeding of the imminent downpour. Foreign tourists never seemed to learn the vagaries of English weather, and she knew that in a few minutes they would all be scurrying for cover, exclaiming about the unannounced storm. After she had left David, and was walking back to the Castle, she allowed more charitably that they were probably waiting until the last possible moment before returning to town; sea-bathing was impossible almost everywhere else in the world, because of industrial pollution, and one of the undeniable attractions of Wessex was its clean sea.

She was trying not to think of what had passed between her and David, because she had presented the truth to him and he had found it unpalatable. Looking at the visitors on the beach, as she walked quickly towards the Castle, she felt a deep and vague sadness about David, and she wished her function here was as simple as that of the tourists.

It had always been like this, though. She should not have allowed herself the luxury of David Harkman. There had always been the monotony of the detailed preparations at the Castle, the need for concentration and absorption in her work.

(Then: a ghost. Another summer, another life. David at the stall, then arriving at the Castle one morning, trying out the skimmers as she lazed on the beach of the inlet. Five days ago . . .

or never? When had she ever had the time to spend like that?)

She had reached the first of the Castle's ramparts as this spectral memory struck her, and she paused reflexively. Like the recollection of a dream it had momentary conviction, but unlike the breaking of a dream the memory remained in her mind for her to explore.

There was a duality: on the one hand a complete certainty that for the last few months, all through the long summer, she and the others had been absorbed in their preparations in the tunnels beneath the Castle; on the other, a faint but quite distinct memory of a different kind of summer, the stall, the harbour, the crowds of tourists . . . and Greg.

David had talked of Greg, thinking that he and she were lovers, but she denied it. Of course she denied it: Greg was nothing to her.

The fainter memory placed Greg beside her, possessing her. There was a brilliant flash of lightning, and Julia turned sharply, expecting the crack of thunder to come on cue, a momentous natural event to celebrate a momentous realization . . . but thunder did not sound.

She glanced up the wall of the rampart, seeing the cloud massing above. It was almost on top of her, and the nearness to it had changed the colour from its earlier blue-black to a sickly yellowish grey. She looked towards the west, from where the storm was approaching, and saw that already the landscape had disappeared in a grey mist; the rain was almost upon her.

She hurried on, going up the path across the side of the first rampart, following its curving, dipping course towards the second. She was running, suddenly frightened of the might of the storm.

She had intended to go to the house she shared with Paul, but that was too far away on the other side of the village. Her fear of the storm became panicky, a terror of being struck by lightning in the open spaces at the top of the Castle, so she left the path and ran down the slope towards the entrance to the underground passages. Several people from the village were crowded into the doorway, looking apprehensively at the sky.

Thunder rolled and rumbled, and the rain started: heavy drops hissing down on to the sun-baked earth. Within seconds the rain had become a deluge, water and ice combined, sluicing down in a vicious torrent. The hailstones stung her shoulders and neck and legs, scattered on the ground before her as she ran with the wind. Her hair and dress had plastered wetly to her body in the first few moments of the downpour.

She reached the shelter at last, panting and frightened. She expected, without thinking, that the crowd of people would step back to let her in, but they seemed not to have noticed her, and she stood in front of them in the driving rain. Lightning flashed again, and thunder cracked immediately afterwards. She pushed against the people, forcing them to move back, and at last she was out of the worst of the rain.

The people clustering in the entrance to the shelter continued to pay no attention to her, even though she was pressed against at least three of them. She knew none of them, except by sight: they were mostly farmers, or artisans from the craft workshops. None of them was involved with the real work of the community.

Angrily, she pressed against them, forcing a passage, and they moved reluctantly aside, complaining to each other – but not directly at her – about her persistence.

When she broke free of the press of bodies she was well inside the bare, unlit construction, standing under the cracked concrete roof. For the first time she noticed that Greg had been among the people blocking the entrance, but he had not acknowledged her. He, like the others, was peering out at the spectacular weather from the safety of the shelter.

Outside, there was another brilliant white flash of lightning, accompanied by a deafening crash of thunder.

Julia turned away, and walked across the rubble-littered floor towards the narrow staircase at the back. She pinched the damp fabric between thumb and forefinger of each hand, and lifted it away from her thighs, then went quickly down the stairs. The tunnels and cells of the laboratories were about fifteen metres below the surface, and before she had reached the bottom of the stairs the storm had become inaudible. Here, in the depths of Maiden Castle, they could not be touched by the elements.

John Eliot's room was empty, as she had expected, so she went on down to the end of the corridor and entered the conference room.

This was the only place in the whole underground system that was heated, and by common consent it had become the centre of all the preparatory activity. Here, in contrast with the other rooms, they had made a more than minimal effort to furnish it comfortably, bringing down from the village many chairs and tables. Several of the Castle's better craft products had been placed ornamentally on view, and many hundreds of books were stacked on shelves along one of the walls.

About fifteen of the chosen participants were in the conference room, as well as Dr Eliot and some of his staff. Marilyn was there, and as soon as she saw Julia she waved to her. She was sitting at the large table at the far end of the room, listening in to one of the interminable policy-discussions.

John Eliot noticed her, left the discussion and came over to her.

'Where have you been?' he said. 'We were waiting for you.'

'I was caught in the storm,' she said, realizing that Eliot probably had no knowledge of the weather. Neither he nor any of the staff ever seemed to leave the underground passages.

'So I noticed,' Eliot said, glancing at her rain-soaked dress. 'Do you want to change?'

'I'll do it later. It's still raining out. I can keep warm here.'

'There's more reading for you. Will you do it on your own, or are you going to join the discussion?'

'What's it about this evening?' Julia said.

'The election of a new member. At the moment opinion seems to be split.'

'Who is it to be?'

'A man called Donald Mander. He's a Commission official. He'd make an excellent administrator.'

'Someone from the Commission?' Julia said, frowning. 'That's an unusual step.'

'So some of us think. Others think it would be worth the risk.'

She stared at Eliot blankly, thinking of David. If they could seriously consider a government official for the project then they could hardly object to David. Her negative answer to David's simple, understandable request had hurt him bitterly ... but then she had not seen a way. But now, perhaps she could suggest ...

No, there was Paul. Always Paul.

'Is Paul here?'

'He's in the mortuary at the moment,' Eliot said. 'He'll be back later.'

'What does Paul think about Mander?'

'He's for him.'

'So am I,' Julia said.

'Do you know him?'

'I've seen him about Dorchester. I don't know much about him, but he used to smile at me when I was at the stall.'

'I didn't know you were vain, Julia.'

'I'm not. I've a feeling about Mander. That's been enough for the rest of us, hasn't it?'

Eliot nodded, but vaguely. Julia and the others had tried to explain about the intangible sense of recognition, but Eliot claimed he never experienced it. It had now become the fundamental criterion by which people were invited to join the project. Julia herself knew the intangible well enough, because it was the same with David.

The same, but *different* with David.

'Are you going to speak up in Mander's favour?' Eliot said, looking towards the table, where the arguments had continued as they had been speaking.

'No need. He'll be accepted in the end. You can put me down for an "aye", if you like. Where's the reading I have to do?'

Julia looked around for somewhere to sit, while Eliot went to the shelves to find a book. In the warm air of the conference room her wet clothes did not feel too uncomfortable. She found a chair near one of the heaters, thinking that she could steam quietly by herself until dry. She tossed back her hair, wondering if she could borrow a brush or a comb from Marilyn.

She looked to see who was already here. She recognized Rod, Nathan, Alicia and Clark from the Castle community; she knew each of these well, as they had been in Wessex for many months. There were several other people at the table, people she recognized from other conferences, to whom she had been introduced but whose names she had since forgotten. They were all from Dorchester or its environs. One man worked on a farm near Cerne Abbas; two of the women came from villages on the southern shore of the bay. All had social or academic qualifications, all were living double lives to facilitate their work here. It was a strange contrivance, and she was glad that because she was already a member of the Castle community she did not have to resort to elaborate deceptions to come here.

Eliot returned with the book, opening it at the pages he had selected.

'This is the passage to read,' he said.

The book was an old work, describing the geological substrata of the Wessex region before the seismic upheavals of the previous century. The idea, Eliot explained, was to work out a theory by which the present land subsidence could be seen as but a temporary phase in geophysical evolution, so that a return to something like the former circumstances could be envisaged.

Julia took the book with mixed feelings: geology was her subject, so there would be no difficulty with technical language – which made her work harder in other faculties – but at the same time it meant she would have to cover old ground, in an almost literal sense. What had thrilled her during her studies had been the *present* geological structure of this region, one which on a geological scale had been shaped only yesterday.

Old theories, old facts, had to be learned; the present had to be unlearned.

Nevertheless, in spite of these misgivings, she soon became interested in the book, and was still reading half an hour later when Paul Mason walked into the room.

Everyone noticed his arrival: he was that sort of man. As the director of this project he commanded immediate respect and attention. All the work, all the eventual functions of the project, were his. He had worked for several years to bring these people together: he was an idealist with an achieved ideal, and he inspired the others.

As he walked across the room he saw Julia, and gave her one of his secret smiles, the sort he reserved for her alone. She responded automatically, feeling, as she always did, the instinctive and selfish pride of ownership.

She shared Paul with no one: she was his woman.

That look he gave her spoke of the things no one here could ever intrude into: the secret life, the private man. Only she was allowed this insight into the other Paul, and it was allowed because of their intimate understanding of each other.

Deep inside her, a spectral memory flared like a match-flame in a darkened cellar ... and a spectral version of herself recoiled in horror.

As Paul sat down at the table with the others, Julia stared with unfocused eyes at the floor, her spectral identity struggling for release. She thought of David, she thought of his love, she thought of hers.

Soon, she began to tremble.

22

The heavy thunderstorm had brought a break in the weather, and six days later it was cool, windy and squally in Dorchester. David Harkman's frustration continued: he had not seen Julia since the afternoon on the heath, and discreet enquiries, mainly of the two Castle people working behind the stall, got him nowhere. They appeared to know nothing of her, and were surprised that he should be interested.

He was still being blocked by Mander's apparent reluctance to let him at the archives, and on the fourth day he had left the Commission in a rage and travelled up to Child Okeford to ride the Blandford wave. This too had left him unsatisfied; the tide was unseasonally low, and the wave had been crowded with inept amateurs. Swerving to avoid a group of riders, Harkman had slipped behind the crest of the wave, making the whole expedition futile and irritating.

Futility and irritation were two feelings he was well acquainted with, and Harkman had little doubt whence they grew.

It was a cruel irony that within a few minutes of Julia's apparent return to him – his knowledge that the intangible was there again – she had left him. And in spite of what she told him, Harkman remained convinced that she had left him for some other man.

His response was human and straightforward: he suffered an abiding and wounding jealousy.

On the sixth morning he enquired again about the matter of the archives, and once more Mander told him that Commissioner Borovitin was 'considering' his request. Harkman, enraged again, left the Commission offices and for want of anything better to do strolled along the sea-front, watching the holidaymakers with a mixture of boredom and envy. He walked the length of the Boulevard, past the skimmer-shop and all the stalls, past Sekker's Bar, and along the road that led to Victoria Beach.

Two peddlers approached him, holding out some of their wares. At first he didn't see what they were offering, noticing instead that they were wearing Castle clothes.

'Will you look at a mirror, sir?' said one of the two, and held a little circular piece of glass before his eyes.

Harkman saw a crazy, flashing reflection of himself, but then he pushed past them and walked on. The mirror was a cheap bauble, a common ornament. It was the second time peddlers had tried to sell him one.

Victoria Beach was as crowded as usual, in spite of the cool weather. Many of the visitors lay on the sand, presenting their naked bodies to the cloudy sky, apparently relishing this opportunity for fashionable exhibitionism without the risk of unfashionable suntan. Harkman paused for a few minutes, staring down at them. People always seemed to behave the same on a beach, discarding normal behaviour with their clothes.

Beyond the beach, set on its hill, was Maiden Castle: symbol and embodiment of his discontents.

Julia was there, but his jealousy was defensive, and he dared not seek her out.

Standing by the rail overlooking the beach, Harkman felt again the primal instinct that drew him to the Castle. It represented the permanence of time, an inexplicable link with the past.

It came from the past, the real past, the historical past.

Maiden Castle had been there on its hilltop as Dorchester

was being rebuilt after the earthquakes. It had been there as the earth had shaken and subsided, and as the sea crept towards it, submerging the valleys around. It had stood on its hill indifferent to the nations and races of the world, as they argued and warred about territory and money, maize and oil and copper, ideology and torture, political influence and frenetic arms-race. It had been there as the first steam-train followed its bright new iron tracks towards Weymouth in the south, and it had been there as kings struggled with parliaments, and as feudal lords and seigneurs raised private armies to extend their lands. The Romans had sacked it, the ancient Britons had raised it. Time was deposited about Maiden Castle like layers of sedimentary rock, and Harkman could excavate it with his imagination.

It distracted him because it was the focus of his interest in Wessex.

He had not come to find Julia, although he had found her, and he had not come to ride the Blandford wave, although he had done so and would again. The Castle was central to everything: a sense of past, of continuity, of permanence.

If he walked along Victoria Beach from here he would be at the Castle in ten minutes. Harkman tested his courage against his jealousies, and his courage failed. He glanced once more at the glowing green mound, then turned back and walked quickly into Dorchester.

He had been at his desk for no more than ten minutes when the internal telephone rang.

'Mr Harkman? This is Cro, of Information. I understand that the Commissioner has authorized you to examine our archives.'

'I thought Mander was in charge of those.'

'Mr Mander is taking a few days' leave of absence. Before he went I took it upon myself to make sure you received your clearance. Do you wish to use the archives today?'

'Yes, of course. I'll come now.'

He went first to Cro's office, then followed the portly little man to the elevator.

The archives were kept in the basement of the building: a huge storehouse behind a fireproof wall, filled with metal racks that covered all four walls and made artificial aisles across the width of the room. On these shelves were stacked the records: cardboard-boxfuls of papers, books, pamphlets, bound folders, licences, records of births and deaths, notes of court proceedings, file upon file of memoranda from Westminster and the other provincial Commissions, statutes, minutes of meetings, newspapers, government posters, police-records . . . all the dusty memorabilia of service to and administration of the State, and a mouldering testament to the pedantic mind of the bureaucrat, which will never allow anything to be thrown away.

'I'll have to lock you in, Harkman,' Cro said.

'That's all right.' Harkman looked at his watch: it was just after two. 'Come down for me at five, unless I telephone beforehand. And I'll probably want to spend all day tomorrow here.'

Cro pointed to a browned, faded sign above the door. 'You can't smoke in here.'

'I wasn't intending to.'

'You'd better give me your cigarettes, in case.'

Harkman stared at Cro aggressively, fighting to keep his temper. He had had only occasional contact with this man, but he felt he knew and understood him, or his type. Because of Harkman's status as an attached academic, Cro was administratively his junior, but the archives were his domain. To avoid a needless scene, Harkman handed over his cigarettes, aware that he was scowling like a schoolboy caught smoking behind the gym.

He forced a grin. 'I suppose I might have been tempted.'

'I'll keep them for you,' Cro said, and put them on a shelf outside the room. He closed and locked the door, then nodded to Harkman through the heavy glass window, and walked away. Harkman stared thoughtfully through the window at his cigarettes, knowing that if Cro had taken them with him he would have forgotten them. Now he wanted a smoke.

He turned away, intent on getting on with what he had come down here for.

Until now, the only aspect of the archives he had had access to was a part of the index, so he already had a partial understanding of the filing-system, and the numbered codes used to identify different classifications.

He walked up and down the aisles, looking at the boxes and

folders. The newer additions to the collection stood out from the others, for their labels were as yet clean, unyellowed by age. Harkman tried to read the words inscribed on the spines of various folders, lifted the dusty lids of boxes to peer inside. The air in the vault was dry and stale, and even just walking raised clouds of fine dust, making his eyes water and his nose itch.

He worked aimlessly for half an hour, not only unsure of where to look, but uncertain of what it was he was seeking. The rows of dirty folders confused him; the order in which they were stacked appeared to be random, with the court records for one year placed with seeming purpose next to the register of marriages for another, twenty-three years before.

He returned to the index, and chose a few entries at random, trying to work out the system. After some false starts he managed to trace a chosen item: *Housing Committee, Minutes of Meetings, 2117-2119.* He had no interest in the proceedings of a committee sitting some twenty years before, but finding it had helped him understand the system.

Now with more than an inkling of how to go about his search, Harkman settled down at one of the desks with the index in front of him. He had already abstracted a list of certain records he wanted to examine, and he took out his notebook and checked off two or three items of special interest. By a quarter past three he had a list of some forty entries that might contain what he was looking for, and he went in search of them. He couldn't find them all, but he soon had at his desk a land-registry that covered the whole of the twenty-first century, newspaper files, Commission year-books for the last three decades, minutes of Party meetings and congresses, a popular history of the twentieth century, several guidebooks to Maiden Castle, and copies of various memoranda sent between Westminster and the Resources Attaché's office in the last two years.

In this last folder he discovered the first reference to Maiden Castle.

A query had been raised in the Regional Office in London about the power-consumption of the Castle community: the answer, amid much elaborate qualification, said that the community had access to mains electrical supply, but that its consumption was negligible provided certain unidentified equipment was not in use.

Later, Harkman discovered more correspondence in the same folder, this time concerned with a query about the possible scrap- or salvage-value of the research equipment; the Commission's answer – signed by D. Mander – took the form of a letter attached to a printed circular. The circular was a Party directive concerning self-sufficient craft cooperatives, and the desirability of minimal government interference; the typewritten note merely added that the present condition of the Ridpath apparatus was not known, and was assumed to be worthless.

The proper name of the equipment held no significance for Harkman.

In the land-registry of the previous century, Harkman discovered extracts of the deeds by which title to the land on which Maiden Castle stood was transferred formally from the Duchy of Cornwall to the Soviet Land and Agriculture Board. This was in the year 2021. The transfer was one of several hundred, in which all land not nominally State-controlled was handed over to Westminster.

There followed a fruitless search, where he found several documents relating to Maiden Castle, or referring to it, but they were normal bureaucratic fodder: population estimates, land surveys, health reports, an advisory document on education, the findings of a team of sanitary inspectors.

Harkman had not looked at the newspaper file since locating it, thinking of it as a last resort, but on searching through he discovered that in the early years at least of the Commission's administration, there had been diligent attempts to collect items of local interest. There were all sorts of cuttings here: details of a road-building project (since abandoned), the reconstruction of Dorchester after the earthquakes, the first ideas publicly discussed for the development of Dorchester as a tourist centre.

Then, stuffed into a pocket at the back of the file, Harkman found several other clippings from a much earlier period. He pulled them out and unfolded them carefully: they were brown with age, and as dry as the dust that lay on them.

The first one had a lurid headline, set in an old-fashioned type-

face: A JOURNEY TO THE FUTURE! Underneath, written in short
paragraphs and sensational English, was a report on the forma-
tion of what the newspaper called 'an electronic think-tank',
whose members would 'step into the future' and 'contact our
descendants', all with the aim of 'solving the burning problems
of today'.

There were several more of a similar ilk, each one concentrating, presumably for the benefit of a semi-literate audience,
on such ideas as time-travel, exploration of the future, visiting
the ends of time, and so forth. These were in cuttings dated from
the beginning of 1983 until the summer of 1985. Maiden Castle
('shrouded in antiquity') was mentioned several times, and
the name of Dr Carl Ridpath (variously a 'boffin', 'inventor' or
'genius') featured prominently.

Harkman read them in chronological order, learning more
from each one, and recognizing also which elements of the re-
porting could be discounted as sensationalism or speculation.

As he finished the last cutting, Harkman felt that he had found
what he had been seeking. At some time in the late twentieth
century – presumably in 1985 – a scientific research foundation
had developed a means whereby the future could be investigated. It was not a form of travel through time, in the sense the
newspapers used it, but a controlled, conscious extrapolation,
visualized and given shape by Dr Ridpath's projection equipment. The work would be carried out in a special laboratory
constructed beneath Maiden Castle.

Clearly this was the apparatus that was mentioned in the
Commission files!

Harkman was suddenly struck with an intriguing notion, and
he turned back through the cuttings. There was common consent in the reports on one matter: that the chosen period for the
projected 'future' would be exactly one hundred and fifty years.

In other words, they were envisaging the year 2135 . . . just two
years ago!

Harkman wondered wryly what they had made of what they
found.

He stared at the aged newsprint for several minutes, realizing
that these ancient pieces of paper were themselves a link with

that optimistic past, a time when man and his technology had not stagnated, when they could still look forward. Just as Maiden Castle itself had been built for defence against the enemies of the day, and had survived to withstand the decay of time, so these words, hastily written and hastily printed, had outlived their makers.

The men were dust, but the words and ideas lived on.

Harkman shuffled the cuttings into a pile, then slid them back into their pocket in the folder. He felt a slight obstruction, so he pulled them out again and peered inside.

At the very back, concordant by the pressure of the others, was one more cutting. Harkman reached inside, and pulled it out carefully.

He smoothed it with his hand, pressing it out on the desk-top.

It was printed in a different style from the others, with a more sober presentation: from the printing at the top he learned that it was taken from *The Times,* 4th August 1985.

The headline was: MAIDEN CASTLE – AN EXPENSIVE DREAM? Harkman read through the piece quickly.

Today, in an Ancient British hill-fort near Dorchester, a group of intellectuals, economists, sociologists and scientists will pool their conscious minds in an attempt to see into the future of Britain and, indeed, the world. Questions have been asked in Parliament, and much comment has been heard from informed sources, about the expense involved in what to some is no more than an indulgent fantasy of some of the best brains in Britain. Would the money not be better spent, say the critics, on more positive and social research – indeed, the very kinds of research that in many cases the participants have abandoned in order to take part?

In fact, although the Wessex Foundation is partly subsidized by the Government – through the Science Research Council – most of the funds have been raised from private and industrial sources.

There followed a paragraph discussing the financing of the project. Harkman glanced over this, then read on.

Much has been heard about the 'time-travelling' ability the participants will develop when their minds are electronically pooled, but this is strenuously denied.

Speaking at yesterday's press-conference in Dorchester, Dr Nathan Williams of Keele University said, 'We are *imagining* a future world, which is made palpable to us by the Ridpath projector. Our bodies will be inside the projector itself, and will not leave it. Even our minds, which will seem to experience the projected world, will in fact stay within the program dictated by the equipment.'

For the Trustees of the Wessex Foundation, Mr Thomas Benedict, who is himself to take part in the experiment, added, 'In terms of what we hope to achieve, we believe that what we shall learn from the world of 2135 will amply repay every penny of what has been invested here.'

There is a total of thirty-nine participants in the project, and together their qualifications present a formidable array of talent. Many have taken indefinite leave of absence from their university posts to contribute to the Ridpath projection, and several more have left brilliant industrial careers for a chance to deploy their speciality in this experiment.

Dr Carl Ridpath, who developed his mental visualization and projection equipment at the University of London, was unable to attend yesterday's press-conference. Speaking from a West London clinic, where he is recovering from an operation, he said, 'This is the fulfilment of a dream.'

Alongside the article were eight photographs of some of the participants, tiny faces staring out at Harkman across the years. One was of Ridpath, a small, intense expression; another was of Dr Williams, a middle-aged, balding man with a square, intelligent face.

At the very bottom of the double column of photographs were two at which Harkman stared uncomprehendingly.

The first face was his own. Underneath, the caption said: *Mr David Harkman, 41, Reader in Social History, London School of Economics.*

The second photograph was of a dark-haired woman: *Miss*

Julia Stretton, 27, Geologist (Durham University). Miss Stretton is the youngest of the participants.

Harkman's first reaction to this was disbelief, and he closed his eyes and turned away his face, as if this would remove some incredible sight. Then he stared again at the pictures, and glanced through the article, his heart speeding up as his nervous response stimulated the adrenal gland. The photograph was unmistakably that of Julia: the man given his name was undoubtedly himself.

Harkman felt something akin to a jolt of electricity pass through his mind, like a short circuit in the synapses, and his head jerked back involuntarily; reality blurred.

He tried to be calm, tried to understand.

According to the newspaper, a hundred and fifty years ago – a hundred and fifty-two, to be precise – a man called David Harkman had joined this mind-projection experiment. The chosen year was 2135. (*How could they imagine it? On what did they base their information?*)

Julia, or someone with her name and appearance, had also joined the project.

And yet he, the real David Harkman, lived here in the year 2137. Julia lived here.

He had been born in 2094 (*he was 43, like his alter ego would be!*) ... he had been born in 2094, had been educated at Bracknell State School, had studied at the London Collegiate, had graduated in Social History, had married ... this was what he knew!

The year, the world, the people ... they were all around him. He was of this world, this real, uncomfortable and dangerous world.

Was this the sort of world these twentieth-century academics could visualize?

Harkman shook his head, disbelieving. No one could grapple with the innumerable subtleties of an entire social order.

(*1985: before the destruction of the British union, during the last years of the monarchy, before the collectivization of industry and agriculture, before the absorption into the Soviet bloc. No one who was alive then could have foreseen this society!*)

Extrapolation, in the social sense, meant the opposite of history. It implied the ability to draw inferences about the future from observations of the present. Harkman did not doubt the ability of these academics to speculate intelligently, but he knew as a certainty that any speculation about *his* world would be wrong. The history of the last century and a half, with all its complexities, was known to him almost as thoroughly as he knew the story of his own life.

History was the critical order that the present imposed on the past; it could not be created forwards!

This sudden urge to dispute the principles of the theory was his intellect's way of evading the true emotional shock.

Who was this David Harkman?

He stared with renewed amazement at the photograph in the cutting, then reached into the back pocket of his trousers and found his Commission identity-card. He laid it next to the photograph, still disbelieving.

The newspaper picture looked stiff and unnatural, as if it had been taken in a cold studio, and he seemed older than he looked in the identity-photograph. His face was fuller now, his hair was longer and he had greater poise.

Nevertheless, the two photographs were indisputably of the same man.

And he had only to look at the ancient photograph of the woman called Julia Stretton to know that it was her.

Confronted with the impossible, Harkman found that he could not cope. His first impulse was to stand up and walk away from the desk, but he had gone no further than the nearest rack of old folders before he returned. He stumbled as he sat down, nearly fell off his chair.

His hands were shaking, and he could feel his shirt clinging damply to his back.

For a few minutes he sat quite still, holding the edge of the desk in each hand.

At last he looked again at the text of the newspaper cutting, and reread the quoted words of Dr Williams: '... our minds, which will seem to experience the projected world, will in fact stay within the program ...'

For a moment Harkman felt that in these words lay the clue: there had been a mistake, something had gone wrong. All that apparent sensationalism in the other newspapers was, after all, right: *he had travelled in time!*

It seemed to be the only solution to the dilemma, and irrational and incomprehensible as it was it would explain . . .

The notion took hold for a few seconds, then slackened its grip, fell away.

It could *not* be so: he had no memory of the twentieth century, nor of any time before his own life. Forty-three years, perhaps thirty-eight of them remembered with any clarity. No more. An ordinary life.

He looked again at Williams's words: '. . . our minds will seem to experience . . .'

It was possible, just marginally possible, that this was the central statement.

In effect, everything he saw, everything about him, what he ate, what he read, what he remembered . . . was a mental illusion.

Again, he kicked back his chair and walked in torment from the desk and along the nearest aisle.

He paced agitatedly to and fro.

All *this* was reality. He could touch it, smell it. He breathed the musty air of the vault, sweated in the unventilated room, kicked up clouds of ancient dust: this was the world of external reality, and it was necessarily so. As he strode past the seemingly endless rows of files and books, each of which contained its own fragments of remembered past, he concentrated on what he himself conceived as reality.

Was there an inner reality of the mind which was more plausible than that of external sensations? Did the fact that he could touch something mean that it was as a consequence real? Could it not also be that the mind itself was able to *create,* to the last detail, every sensual experience? That he dreamed of this dust, that he hallucinated this heat?

He halted in his fretful pacing, closed his eyes. He willed the vault to vanish . . . let it be gone!

He waited, but the dust he had kicked up was irritating his nose, and he spluttered a great and messy sneeze . . . and the vault was still there.

Wiping his eyes and nose, Harkman walked back to the desk.

There was something else in the cutting, something that had left a barb that snagged at his memory.

He scanned the faded newsprint once again, but couldn't see it. Then he noticed the date. It was printed at the top: 4th August 1985.

There was something incontestable about a date, an impartiality, a known and labelled event shared by all.

The newspaper had described the initiation of the project as taking place 'today' . . . presumably the same date. In which case the projected future would have begun on 4th August 2135.

Where had he been on that day? What had he been doing? He knew the general answer at once: for the last few years he had been in London, working at the Bureau. That would seem to be rejection enough of any but a coincidental link with this twentieth-century experiment, because his roots extended beyond or before the incident date. But he was still not satisfied.

Why was August 2135 a significant month to him?

Then he had it: that was the month he had applied to the Bureau for transfer to Dorchester. He remembered because his birthday was 7th August, and he had filed the application with a feeling of resolution and changed direction, a present to himself. It had felt then like the fulfilment of a long-felt need, but he knew that the decision had been a relatively sudden one. He had become obsessed with the idea three days before, when he had had the realization that until he was able to live and work in Wessex he would never be content.

Three days before! That would be 4th August!

His incomprehensible urge to go to Maiden Castle, feebly rationalized, had started on the very day the project began.

The significance of it was awful, but for the life of him Harkman couldn't see why.

His memories before that date were his hold on reality: so long as they extended before then he knew that his identity was safe.

The memories were there: education, career, marriage, career . . .

Talking to Julia a few days ago he had had the same static memories. The events stood out like check-marks on a list.

They had happened, and they had not happened. In precisely

the same way that Julia had seemed for a time to be an illusion, so Harkman realized that his life until 4th August 2135 had been remembered into existence.

And the newspaper photographs lay on the desk before him, and they told him who he was and where he had come from.

An hour and a half later the door to the vault was opened from the other side, and Cro arrived to let him out.

Harkman barely noticed. He picked up the cutting and slipped it into his pocket, and followed the man to street level. As Cro went on up the stairs, Harkman walked out into the street. The buildings of the town seemed insubstantial, shifting, shadowy.

He walked down to the sea-front. While he had been inside the vault the wind and rain had increased, gusting in from the heaths behind the town. The smoke from the oil-refinery poured over the town, dark and depressing and greasy. There were very few people about and the trees along the front were dulled and dirty.

The tide was going out, and for a moment Harkman had an hallucinatory image of some bottomless drain far out at sea, into which the water was emptying, drawing back from the shore and leaving the bay sodden and bare, the muddy remains of the twentieth century scattered like shipwrecks across the land.

23

After introducing him to everyone present, and outlining the nature of the project, Paul Mason took Mander to see the Ridpath projection equipment. Mander, still bemused by the speed with which not only had he been accepted by the others, but also with which he himself had adapted to the project, followed the young director down a side-tunnel into a long, low-ceilinged hall, lit dimly by two electric bulbs.

'We call this the mortuary, Don,' Mason said, and turned on more lights to illuminate the equipment.

Mander winced mentally at the first-name familiarity; more than a quarter of a century in public service had made him unused to anything more personal than initials.

Spotlights were grouped in clusters at both ends of the long room, and as they came on Mander looked without too great an interest at what appeared to be a row of large filing-cabinets set against one wall. Mason, and some of the others, were interested in the mechanical process by which the futurological projection would be achieved, but for Mander it was the psychological implications that were fascinating. His years in the Regional Service had left his early training behind, and all that he retained was an instinctive understanding of human mental processes which, in his moments of greatest self-awareness, he knew he used best in interdepartmental politicking – and a rudimentary and probably out-dated vocabulary of psychologists' jargon.

He had joined the Regional Service in the naïve belief that trained psychologists had a useful rôle to play in the sometimes delicate administration of State affairs: that, at least, had been the policy of the Regional Office in Westminster when he had taken the appointment, but successive changes of Party leadership – both in England and in Russia – and subtle reshadings of ideological colouring had progressively eroded any useful function he might once have had. Now, twenty-seven years later, routine promotions had provided him with a stable income and a position of authority, and the rather ambitious twenty-seven year old industrial psychologist had developed into a reliable fifty-four year old administrator.

Paul Mason went to the nearest of the drawers and pulled it open, pressing one hand against the body of the machine for leverage. After initial resistance, the mechanism slid open smoothly enough, as if the roller-bearings of the drawer had stayed free over the years of disuse.

'It's inoperative at the moment,' Mason said. 'You can try it if you like.'

'You mean I should climb on?'

'Well, we normally refer to it as climbing in.' Mason smiled at his own pedantry, and Mander felt again the instinctive liking he had had for the young man from the moment they met. The popularity Mason enjoyed was total; it was as if everyone involved in the project had become captivated by the young man's good looks and personality. 'Nothing can happen to you until the power is switched on,' Mason went on, and to demonstrate he laid his hand across the bright metal points of the neural contacts.

Mander said: 'If I were to climb in, what would happen to me?'

'Nothing at the moment. You don't suffer from claustrophobia do you, Don?'

'Not at all.'

Mander shook his head at once, anxious to make it clear that not even a minor neurosis existed to prevent him from joining the team. In the short time he had been at the Castle he had developed a strong wish to be accepted.

Until that man – what was his name, Nathan Williams? – had called on him at his office, Mander had had no notion that there was anything at all going on at the Castle. Now some inner voice urged him to join the others, become as one with them.

'You see,' Paul Mason was saying, 'the inside of each projection unit is cramped, and although the person inside will be unconscious, some people might find the idea disturbing.'

'Let me try it,' Mander said, sensing a trace of doubt in Mason's voice. He was anxious to prove his worth in the eyes of the project director.

There was also the matter of his age; during the introductions someone had pointedly asked him about this, and although the reactions had been civil he had been left with the impression that some might think him too old.

Willingness to show interest, keenness to participate, these were the qualities he was hoping to communicate.

Mason helped him to lie down on the drawer, and showed him how to rest his shoulders in the supports. Mander felt the neural contacts pressing against him, blunted by the fabric of his clothes.

'It will be uncomfortable,' Mason said, 'but don't struggle if you get an attack of claustrophobia. I'll pull you out again after a few seconds. Now, are you ready?'

'Yes.'

'There's no air circulating inside. That's because the fans are off. And it will be dark.'

Mason put his weight against the drawer, and Mander felt himself sliding. He passed into the darkness of the interior, and moments later the drawer halted against spring-loaded clamps.

He raised his head instinctively, to try to look around, but at once his forehead struck something smooth and cold and hard directly above him. He felt with his hands, moving them out from his body, but they hit the metal sides of the drawer and he realized that with only a few millimetres leeway he was all but confined. It was cold and airless inside the machine. He had not lied about the claustrophobia, but when he had been inside for several seconds it occurred to him that he had only Mason's word to trust, and that if he chose to leave him here he would be trapped.

To his relief, before he was put to further test, he felt the drawer move, and grey light shone in around the end of the drawer by his feet. He looked to each side of him and saw a wire-mesh grid, some metal tubes extending the length of the tiny cubicle, grey paintwork slightly tarnished.

Looking up he saw, fleetingly, a reflection of his own face ... but then the drawer was pulled right out and he was staring up at Paul Mason. He felt foolish lying there, like a body on a slab awaiting dissection, and he remembered the wry nickname given to this place.

'Well? Do you feel up to it?'

Mason helped him down from the drawer, and as his feet touched the ground a slight dizziness came over him. He concealed it by turning round, banging a hand expressively against the cool metal, 'It's an odd experience.'

'You're with us then?'

'Of course.'

His dizziness had been caused by something quite other than the containment in the dark. There had been that glimpsed reflection of his own face ... an instant of self-recognition, a face in a circular mirror.

Mason slid the drawer back into place, and the line of grey-painted cabinets became uniform again. There was a cool surgical efficiency to this machine, lying unused beneath the Castle for a century and a half; a legacy from a richer age.

They walked slowly down the row of cabinets, Mason occasionally reaching out to brush his fingers lightly against the metal handles of the drawers.

'How many are there in all?' Mander said.

'Thirty-nine. This gives us an effective limit to the number of people involved.'

'Do you have a full complement yet?'

'Thirty-six so far. Thirty-eight, including you and me.'

Mander was on the point of remarking on the obvious, that there was still one more person to find, when he detected the subtle emphasis on the thirty-six confirmed participants. He was still not quite accepted.

He brooded on this as they reached the end of the long line of cabinets, and turned back.

'Paul . . . are you not concerned that I work for the Commission? Someone in the conference room said – '

'It makes no difference. I'm for you.'

'Your decision alone?'

'No, there was a vote. If you wish to take part in this, you may. Do you have any reservations?'

'Not at all.'

'Then what were you thinking?' Mason said.

Mander looked guardedly at the other man, but his gaze was met with a frankness that disarmed him.

'The dissident nature of this project,' he said. 'I know Party policy about research projects as well as anyone. I have only to go back to Dorchester and telegraph to Westminster a list of the names of all the people I've met today, and within a couple of hours you'll all be under arrest.'

'But you wouldn't do that, would you, Don?'

Said by anyone else there would have been an undertone of threat in the words, but because it was Mason saying them it became a straightforward question. It was one to which Mander had a straightforward answer.

'No, I wouldn't. But I wondered if you were aware of the possibility.'

'It was discussed.'

'And . . . ?'

'I've told you. You have been accepted, without reservation.'

They left the mortuary, and Paul Mason switched off all the lights but for the two embedded in the concrete ceiling. They walked back towards the conference room.

Mander was thinking: I am accepted, as I have accepted them.

Now that he had made a break with his life at the Commission it felt an absolutely right thing to have done. He recognized the people here. Even the strangers, the people he was told had come from other parts of the country, behaved in a friendly, familiar way towards him, as if he was already a colleague. Then there were the others: the people he had often seen around Dorchester, whose names he did not know but whose faces were known to him. The young woman on the stall, for instance; he had spoken to her for the first time and learned her name: Julia Stretton. Inexplicably, she seemed to be one of those most in favour of his inclusion in the project, and while some of the others had been questioning him about his career at the Commission, she had sometimes offered a spontaneous defence on his behalf.

These early reservations aside, Mander had been astonished by the evident rapport within the group. He could feel it growing in himself, paralleled by an excitement at the possibilities of the project. During his long career with the Party, Mander had sometimes been complacent about its achievements, but when he was younger he had often been critical of the means by which it achieved its ends. Those discontents had never really been removed, but as he grew older he realized that the worst result of the Soviet regime was the fact that English culture and society had stagnated. The country was ready for a social revolution of the same scale as the political revolution that had taken place at the end of the twentieth century. The problems of that troubled period were as far in the past as the years themselves, but no society was ideal. A glimpse into the future might suggest a course to be taken.

'We're still one member short, Don. Do you have any idea of someone we might approach?'

'Couldn't you use your usual procedure?'

'Oh yes. That's why I'm asking you. Selection is based on the recommendation of other participants.'

Mander shook his head. 'I don't think I'd know anyone suitable.'

They had reached the end of the side-tunnel, and were standing at the corner. A damp draught sprang from somewhere, curling around Mander's legs. A few metres away the door to the conference room was open, and light and voices spilled out.

'You understand that I'd like the project to start as soon as possible. Later today, I think.'

'So soon?' Mander said. 'But proposing someone for work as important as this . . . Would it be only at my suggestion?'

'The group will decide. That's how it is always done. Offer a few names. We'll know as soon as we hear the right one.'

'May I ask how?'

'In the same way that we recognized your name as soon as it was put forward.'

'I really don't know many people in Dorchester,' Mander said.

His solitary private life, which for years he had seen as a psychological bulwark against the strains of his daily work, suddenly seemed a social disadvantage. As he and Paul Mason walked into the conference room, Mander was thinking over his few acquaintances and trying to visualize them here. As soon as each name came to mind, he automatically discarded it.

An open forum session was in progress, a relaxed meeting of all the chosen participants, in which their ideas about the future world were expressed and discussed and eventually pooled. Mander and Paul Mason found two spare chairs, and joined in . . . and at once Mander detected a shift in the emphasis of the discussion. Instead of speaking across the room, people turned towards Paul, and it was he who led and shaped. Seen here, in the company of the others, Paul Mason was the obvious leader. The respect they had for him was transparent: he had only to start speaking to bring silence to the others, and if he made a suggestion it found ready approval. In spite of this, Paul did not abuse his position, seeming open to ideas, receptive to the suggestions of others. In all, he conducted the discussion with good sense and humour, and Mander found himself admiring his intellect and warming to his personality.

Only one person showed the least resistance to the group's natural leader, and that was the young woman from the stall, Julia. She happened to be sitting opposite Mander, and on the occasions when she spoke he was aware that she was looking in his own direction. Because she was moving against the psychological current of the meeting he began to wonder why. At first he suspected that some conflict existed between her and Paul, but there was nothing of this sort apparent in what she was saying. Later, he observed a momentary look on Paul's face when speaking to her, and he guessed that something more than a working relationship was going on. That might account for it.

Once, when Mander himself put forward an idea for discussion, it was Julia who responded first, seeming eager to agree with him. He found this pleasant, though oddly puzzling. A few minutes afterwards he made a second suggestion to test her response, and again she spoke first.

There came a break for coffee, and during this Mander noticed that Paul took Julia aside and spoke to her at some length. She smiled and nodded and seemed to be agreeing with him, but Mander noticed that the knuckles of her hand showed white with stress.

Mander used the break to talk informally to as many other people as possible.

One man he was most interested to meet was a former research chemist from York Collegiate, who was presently masquerading as a fisherman in the nearby village of Broadmayne. The man's name had come to Mander's notice at the Commission, because his frequent absences from his cottage had aroused the suspicions of a neighbour that he was selling fish for private gain. In fact, some quirk of absent-mindedness had made Mander overlook the complaint, and the papers lay unread in a wire basket on his desk.

When Paul Mason returned to his chair it was clear that the break had finished, and everyone else sat down again.

'Before we can proceed further,' he said, 'we must select the last member of our team. Does anyone have any suggestions?'

Mander felt the weight of responsibility on him, but he decided to listen to the others. There was a general discussion of the type of personality deemed suitable for the work, but no names were proposed.

Paul looked in his direction.

'How about you, Don? Any ideas?'

'I told you, Paul. I don't seem to know many people around here.'

No one said anything, but Paul continued to stare at him.

Then Julia said: 'Somebody at the Commission, perhaps . . . ?'

Mander shook his head at once. There was no one there.

Again Julia spoke. She said: 'Don, I'm sure you can think of someone.'

Paul glanced at her sharply as she said this, and Mander noticed that her hands were clenched tightly across her lap. Once again he was sure that she was suppressing some deeper tension.

'Well, I don't know,' he said. He thought of Commissioner Borovitin, of Cro, of one of the clerks in the front office he sometimes lunched with. 'There's only . . .'

'Who, Don?'

'An historian from London, doing some research here. David Harkman.'

Someone said: 'He's the one!'

It was as if a draught of cool fresh air had swept into the stuffy room. Julia laughed, as if with relief, and Mander felt for the first time a true sense of empathy with her, with everyone on the project. David Harkman was right, he was the missing participant. With him, the project would be complete.

People were talking across the room, and several got up from their chairs.

Only Paul Mason was unmoving, looking silently across the room, first at him, then at Julia. Mander stared back at Mason, and noticed a wildness in his eyes, a fanaticism, that had not been there before.

24

The memory of Paul's angry face haunted Julia as she hurried down the last of the Castle's ramparts, bending her head against the rain. Paul, smiling reasonably; Paul, suggesting that Don Mander should go to find Harkman; Paul, standing by the door of the conference room as if to hold it open for her, while actually trying to block her way without the others seeing.

She had defied him, though, and she had done it with silence.

'Why not let Don go, Julia?' No answer, Paul. 'How will you recognize him, Julia?' No answer, Paul. She alone in that room had detected the undercurrents of his apparently pleasant manner: for the first time in the three years he had lived with her at the Castle, Paul suspected her of something.

No answer to that, Paul, because this time, the first time, there was cause.

The others were hypnotized by Paul, just as she had been hypnotized by him when he arrived at the Castle ... but all that had changed for her since David.

She ran through the long grass, wetting her feet and legs, and came to the concrete sea wall that enclosed the shore at this point. Julia could feel Paul's influence fading, to be replaced by a joyful anticipation of David.

After the confined and damp surroundings of the tunnels, the open air smelled fresh and clear, but it was only relative. In spite of the wind and rain, there was the usual dirty haze in the air, muting the landscape with a mottled grey film and saddening the grass and trees.

She had borrowed a raincoat from Marilyn, and as she walked along the puddled, rust-streaked concrete wall, Julia thrust her hands deep inside the pockets, trying to keep warm and dry.

The tide was going out. As the sea receded it left its usual scum at high-water mark: a black smear of oil spillage, driftwood, plastic containers, the bodies of seabirds and fish. There was always a smell of acidic chemicals during an ebb-tide, as if the sea, on drawing back, laid bare the new noxious compounds and poisons it had itself created by reacting with the mud and grit of the filthy beach.

Ahead, through the veils of dismal rain, Julia could see the source of much of the bay's pollution: the unloved town of Dorchester: oil-town, spoil-town, used and usurer.

At Victoria Beach the pipelines came ashore, four dead metal worms crawling out of the sea, and where they crossed the sea-wall there was a military guard-post. Julia passed through unchallenged, and she glanced down at the black welded pipes, which, where they rose from the sea, created an artificial breakwater, making the waves sluice greasily along the channels between them. There were only two sentries in sight: one standing on the parapet of the sea wall, his rifle slung over his shoulder, the other waiting by the doorway of the guard-post. Both soldiers were staring out into the bay, watching the constant traffic of lighters and diving-ships and helicopters, swarming like jungle vermin through the flooded forest of drilling rigs and platforms.

Inland from the sea wall, the four parallel pipelines turned together towards the refinery that dominated the landscape behind Dorchester: a bizarre agglomeration of rust-red and silver, towers and gantries and cables, lights and flames and fumes, white-painted storage tanks standing in lines across the countryside, modern tumuli rich in fossil deposits.

Julia, thinking of David, remembered the lovemaking on the heath.

She was following the long curve of Victoria Beach, seeing the grey ribbon of the seawall turning towards Dorchester on its bayside hill. The wind came across the heath, drenching her with drizzle. She was out of breath from hurrying, drawn towards the town because of David, repelled by it because of what it was. Leaving the Castle was like escaping from some dungeon; not the twilight incarceration of the tunnels, but the uncanny psychological embrace Paul put around her. When she was with him he managed somehow to exclude David from her life, as if he knew ... but not until a few minutes ago, when Mander had uttered his name, had Paul ever had the least intimation of David's existence.

Now, almost as if it were against Paul's will, but with the empathic support of the others, David could join the project.

She started to run, her feet splashing in the puddles that cratered the causeway at the top of the wall.

Then: 'Julia!'

The wind took the words, but she recognized David's voice at once. He was close but she couldn't see him, and something made her look out to sea, towards the skeletal rigs black against the drizzly sea, orange fireflies of burning waste gases jetting from their heights.

'Julia, down here!'

She turned at once, laughing, and saw David running towards her on the land side of the sea wall. She called his name, feeling again a sensation she had had at the Castle when she heard Don Mander speak his name: it did not contain the man, nor any words the love.

He reached the bottom of the wall below her, looking from side to side for a way up to her. On the seaward side the wall had been smoothly angled, with a concave lip to turn back storm waves, but on the other side the builders had left it rough and perpendicular. In certain places concrete steps, like those built against harbour walls, had been placed against the face, but none was anywhere near.

'Along there!' she called, pointing back towards the Castle, knowing that where the oil pipelines went through the wall there were several places where access to the top could be gained.

He ran at once, and she ran too, keeping abreast of him and looking down.

He reached the bottom of the first flight of steps, and took them two at a time. Panting and laughing she went into his arms, and they kissed as if it had been six years, and not six days, since they had seen each other. She felt his lips, cold and wet from the rain, against her face and neck, and his hair, when she put her hand against it, was dewed and crisp.

'What are you doing out here?' he said, drawing back from her. 'I thought you'd be at the Castle.'

'I'm looking for you,' she said, and tightened her hold on him, pulling him down so that their faces nestled side by side. She kissed his ear, felt the wetness of his hair against her forehead. 'Come to the Castle, David. It's all changed now. They want you there.'

He said nothing.

'David? I told you: it's what you were asking for.'

He moved back from her and stood by the edge of the sea-wall, looking across the miserable, rain-swept country towards the refinery.

'I don't want that,' he said. 'Not any more. And I don't want you there.'

She stared at him uncomprehendingly, then took his hand.

'It's *right*, David. It's right that you should be there. Paul, Don Mander . . . all the others. They need you. I've come to find you.'

'Just because the others want me?' he said, glancing at her.

'No. I came . . . because I can't stop thinking about you, and you wanted to live with me at the Castle.'

'Or the alternative. Live with me away from the Castle. In Dorchester, anywhere. Not there.'

'David, I have to go back.'

She said it quietly, scared of the same impasse they had reached the last time they were together. She could face up to Paul if David was with her . . . he mustn't let the fear of that prevent him from going.

Another squall of rain swept across the wall, and they both turned their backs to it. David was wearing his office clothes, and they were soaked through. He looked so cold and depressed: she went to his side, put an arm around him.

'David . . . let's go back to the Castle. Just to get out of the rain. We can talk there.'

'No, we'll talk here. I don't want to go to the Castle.'

'You were going there just now.'

'To find you and take you away.' He pointed down at the base of the wall on the land side. 'Let's get out of the wind, Julia. For a few minutes.'

The rain had laid a sheen of wet over his face, and she could see the darkening of his collar against his neck. 'All right.'

She followed him down the concrete steps, and as soon as they were below the level of the wall the sound of the sea lessened. At the bottom they sheltered under the steps.

David said: 'Tell me what's been happening at the Castle.'

'You mean the work we're doing?'

'Yes.'

She felt she was trapped. And yet . . . she didn't mind that with David.

'There's a man called Paul Mason. He's in charge of the project, and he's – '

'I know. You don't have to tell me. He's the one you live with.'

She took both his hands in hers. 'David, I promise you, I haven't slept with Paul since I met you.'

'But you still live with him.'

'I have to . . . I can't change it just like that. As soon as the work is over, I'll move out. It has to wait until then.'

'You'd better tell me about the work, in that case.'

'We've got a total of thirty-eight people there. In the next few days we're going to use some equipment that's at the Castle to create an imaginary future. I don't know how the machine works; Paul handles all that. I can't really explain, but all the people there have a sort of, well, a special understanding. I'm not putting it very well. Everyone's in accord . . . it's like empathy.'

Harkman had been watching her as she spoke. 'Julia, these people. What are their names?'

'You wouldn't know them.'

'I might. You mentioned Don Mander just now. Is he one of them?'

'Yes. He's the only one you'll know.'

'Is Nathan Williams there?'

Julia, taken off-guard, said: 'How do you know Nathan?'

'I came across the name. Tell me some of the others.'

She gave him a few names, sometimes having difficulty remembering surnames. He recognized only one: Mary Rickard's.

'Mary Rickard. The biochemist, from Bristol?'

'That's right. But how – ?'

'What about Thomas Benedict? Or Carl Ridpath?'

Neither name meant anything to her, although the first had a hauntingly familiar ring to it. Harkman seemed puzzled, but pressed her no further. He said: 'We can't go to the Castle, Julia.'

'Why not?'

'Because I'm scared of what might happen there.' There was a strange look in his eyes, and he was standing over her in the confined space, blocking her. She felt a tremor of alarm. 'Listen, Julia . . . do you know where we are from? Do you know how we got here?'

'Of course I do!'

'I don't mean your background . . . something else. Wessex, Dorchester, the Castle! I thought I knew where I was, where I was from. But not now.' He was speaking quickly, and his meaning was lost on her. 'Do you remember? When we last met . . .what did we do?'

'We went on the heath and talked.'

'Yes, and we made love. There was a storm coming, but while we were there it was warm and dry. Do you remember that?'

'Yes, David.'

'And so do I. I remember loving you out there, on the heath.' He pointed suddenly. 'Just there, where the refinery is!'

She saw the silver-painted towers, and the fumes and the tanks.

'We were nowhere near the refinery!'

'Do you remember seeing it?'

For the last six days Julia's memory of the lovemaking on the heath had been all that she had to help her resist Paul.

'It was there, David . . . but somewhere behind us.'

'Are you sure?'

'I think so. . . .'

The refinery was there, it had always been there.

'And I think so too. I'm not sure, though. I know that the refinery has been here for years, that when Dorchester was rebuilt it was as an oil port, and that the economy of Wessex depends on the wells here. But do you remember the tourists?'

'What? Here in Dorchester?' She laughed.

David said: 'I was amused too, when I remembered them.'

'There have been one or two,' she said. 'They visit all parts of Britain.'

'Britain?' David said. 'Or England?'

She shook her head. 'Don't! Please don't!'

'Then listen, Julia, try to understand. You say you are working on some kind of experiment to project a future world, so you must see the consequences of that. If it is to work, if it is to have the least degree of consistency, then it must be a whole world, a *real-seeming* world, one with people you don't know and events you don't understand. And if you are to move in that world, *you too* must be a part of it, with a whole new identity and probably no memory of your existence here.'

'How do you know all this?' she said.

'It's true then?'

'Paul says that will happen to us. But it will be only temporary, for as long as the projection lasts.'

'However long that is to be,' David said. 'Julia, this afternoon I came across some newspaper files. In those I read that the equipment at the Castle, the very same equipment, was used once before. During the twentieth century. A group of scientists, thirty-nine people, with names like Nathan Williams and Mary Rickard and David Harkman and Julia Stretton, started a projection of *their* future. The world they projected was this world ... today, here!'

Julia felt as if she was about to laugh again, but the intensity of his expression was enough to subdue her.

'Do you see, Julia? You and I were in that projection ... you and I are figments of our own imagination!'

And then he moved unexpectedly, reaching into a back pocket. He pulled out a limp piece of yellowed paper.

'This is what I found. It's genuine, I'm sure it's genuine.'

She took the paper from him, and saw that there were eight photographs printed at one side. She looked at the bottom, saw herself and David. Saw the others ...

She read the text. One of the names stood out for her.

'Tom,' she said. 'It mentions Tom Benedict ...'

'Do you know him?'

'No, Tom's dead ... I think ... He ...'

Suddenly she couldn't remember, and simultaneously she could. There was no photograph of him, but the name was somehow enough. A trustee ... a Wessex Foundation ... it was all buried, laid within her unconscious mind.

'I can't understand,' she said. 'I know most of these people. They're at the Castle now, waiting for me.'

'All of them?' David said.

'Not Dr Ridpath. I don't know him. But the others ... look, here's Nathan, and Mary. But it doesn't mention Paul. That's odd, because he's the director ...'

Thoughts started and died in the same instant; reactions were immediately supplanted by contradictory instincts. This was her, but it could not be her. It spoke of Tom, but she knew no one of that name. Paul was not mentioned, but how could any report omit him? These people were alive *now*, not a hundred and fifty years ago . . .

David said: 'Does anyone at the Castle know of this?'

'No one's mentioned it.'

'Then like you and me they have no memory of it.'

She turned on that. 'But I've known some of them for years! They were all born here. I was, you were!'

As she said this an automatic memory came of her mother and father: like a photograph, wordless, motionless. They were there, somewhere in the limbo of her past.

The limbo of her past: it was a phrase she sometimes used lightly, to dismiss her upbringing, to dissociate herself from her background. But did it contain a deeper truth?

'Don't you see what this means for you and me, Julia? We don't belong here, although we think we do. But it's all we know! There's no way back.'

Julia, still struggling for a hold on her own reality, shook her head.

'All I know is that I'm bound to the others. Just as you are.'

'Not me.'

'If you were at the Castle you'd feel it.'

'That's why I want you away from there. Julia, I'm in love with *you* . . . you're here and so am I, and I want nothing changed. Don't you see that? It's enough for me. Reality is what I have and hold, and that's you. We can make a life here.'

She moved towards him, and he put his arms around her.

'I don't know, David,' she said, and they kissed. She wanted to relax, to surrender, but there was too much tension, and after a few moments they drew back from each other.

'I'm all mixed up,' he said. 'What are we going to do?'

'If you believe this piece of paper,' Julia said, 'why can't we go back to the Castle?'

'Because I'm frightened of it. Ever since I've been in Dorchester, I've been drawn to the Castle . . . it's been haunting me. I didn't know why, and then I read that. I wanted things to be understood more clearly, and although I think the paper is genuine it confuses me. I understand it, but I can't face up to what it implies.'

'So you want to run?'

'With you, yes.'

'Why, David?'

'Because I see no alternative.'

She was still holding the newspaper cutting, and it was trembling in her fingers. Rain was dripping from the steps above, and two large drops were spreading through the flimsy paper, like oil in cotton.

'Don't you think we should show this to the others?' she said.

He shook his head, and took the paper away from her. He crumpled it with his fingers, and tossed it on the rain-soaked ground.

'That's my answer,' he said. 'There's no alternative.'

Julia stared at the little piece of screwed-up paper on the ground. It was already soaking up the rain. She bent down and picked it up again, stuffing it into the pocket of her coat. David made no attempt to stop her. She stepped away from him, and walked out from under the shelter of the concrete stairs and into the drifting rain.

When she left the Castle she thought she had resolved the dilemma. She wanted to be with David more than anything else in her life, and whereas for a time she had seen Paul as someone who would have prevented that, she now knew that if David was with her Paul could be resisted.

It had all seemed so simple, yet David, with his scrap of newsprint, wanted only to run away. That would be denying everything she felt within her, and would resolve nothing.

She looked back at him, standing with his shoulders hunched and his hands in his pockets, sheltering under the concrete steps, watching and waiting. She turned away.

The newsprint cutting was in her pocket, and she took it out and straightened it. A tear had appeared across it, and it was wet and dirty.

Shielding it from the rain with her body, she read it through. Then she read it again, and then a third time. She tried to ignore the fact that a photograph of herself was staring out at her.

It evoked no memories. Try as she might, for her the cutting was no more than an artefact of the past. But the names couldn't be avoided . . . and there was one in particular.

Thomas Benedict. It was a name from a forgotten past, long

forsaken. It reminded her of a hot summer, of laughter, of kindness. It was a memory of the undermind, unattainable by the conscious.

She discarded reason – which disallowed knowledge of Tom Benedict – and responded to the irrational. Soon, there were more memories.

There was a tranquil past; another summer she had known. A time of warm blue weather, of crowds of tourists milling through Dorchester, of a loving idyll with David. There was an inlet by the Castle, where David swept to and fro on a skimmer, and where she lay naked in the sun. There was a stall by the harbour, and the heat would rise from the pavement and expensive yachts would moor at the jetty, and foreigners in strange and colourful clothes would haggle with her over prices.

Thomas, Tom, was there in none of these memories, but he was everywhere.

Then, as if her conscious mind was reasserting itself, she looked again at the words on the newspaper cutting, and she saw the date at the top.

In 1985 a man called Nathan Williams had said: '. . . our minds will seem to experience the projected world . . .'

Wasn't this precisely what she and the others were planning to do at the Castle?

They were seeking to examine a future . . . a better world. Their model for it, a fact asserted again and again by all the participants, was the Britain of the late twentieth century.

They looked to a time, one hundred and fifty years in the future, when Britain had *again* become a constitutional monarchy, when Britain *again* was a unified state, when the world was *again* a keenly competitive place, when the balance of power was *again* between Soviet Russia and the U.S.A., when there were *again* the seemingly insurmountable problems that gave life a challenge and purpose, when technology and science *again* had a vital rôle to play in the world's development . . .

Was this to be a future modelled on a period of the past, and so very similar to it?

Or was it to be the past itself, the *actual* past on which they were basing their scenario?

David had said: '. . . it must be a whole world, a real-seeming world . . .'

He had been talking about Paul Mason's project at the Castle, but it applied to their world of Wessex too. This life was real . . . and a hundred and fifty years ago a twentieth-century experiment had set out to create a real-seeming world.

David believed that her life, like his own, was a product of this semblance of reality. And so were the lives of the other participants; they were all of the twentieth century.

If so . . .

Then she saw it: Paul's project at the Castle would not take them to an imagined future. It was a homing urge. To enter his projection would take them to the past, to the year from which they started!

She walked back to David, knowing that whatever he now said or did, she would go back to the Castle.

She handed back the rain-sodden slip of paper. 'David, we – '

'I know what you've decided,' he said. 'I think I have too. I don't want to stay here, there's nowhere to go.'

As David returned the piece of paper to his pocket, she said: 'Do you think you can face up to the implications of that?'

'I still don't know,' he said.

25

As they reached the top of the second earth rampart, and Julia pointed out the entrance to the underground workings, David Harkman looked across at the plateau that was the top of the hill-fort. He had expected to see some kind of habitation here – houses that the participants used, perhaps – but the grass grew long and was untrampled. There were no houses, no tracks, no people. The clouds, scudding in from the west, low and leaden, seemed no higher than an arm's length above them.

He looked towards the east, across the bay with its clustered drilling-rigs and wells. It looked dark and cold, fouled by man and his endeavours.

'I wanted to swim there once,' he said, and Julia looked at him in surprise. 'There used to be a sport here, sometime in the past, I think. People would ride on motorized boards, and try to stay on top of the Blandford wave. When I came down here I was interested in trying it.'

'I've never heard of it,' Julia said. 'And the wave is just a large rip-tide. You couldn't ride on it.'

'I'd like to have seen it, though.'

'Come on, let's get inside,' she said.

He followed her down the slope, trying to rid himself of a dreamlike memory: the swell of the wave beneath the board, the high-pitched whine of the engine, the white thunder of the collapsing breaker . . . but it had an elusive quality to it; at once remembered, but not in his experience.

The long grass brushed wetly around his trouser legs as he followed Julia, and he shivered. He had been out in the rain for more than an hour, and he was wet through. This open windswept place seemed to offer no promise of warmth or dryness.

There was no door to the concrete construction. It stood open, and the wind funnelled in. Pools of dirty water spread over the floor, and much mud and rubble lay about. Julia led the way down a flight of steps.

Walking through the rain, she had tried to explain why she was so adamant about returning to the Castle. She talked of a way back to the twentieth century . . . but neither of them had any emotional link with that past. They were both of Wessex.

Harkman had his own reason, though, and it had been the one that persuaded him there was no hope in trying to escape. Maiden Castle still exerted its power over him. As long as he lived he would feel its compulsion.

Now he was in the very place that summoned him. Here was the focus of the invisible, radiating source that beckoned him. And, like a reaction to the body of a much-coveted woman suddenly bared before him, he felt a simultaneous sense of fulfilment of long-held desire, and a vague disappointment now that the mystery was removed. The tunnel at the bottom of the stairs was cool, and ill-lit. There were doors on each side, all of them closed and apparently locked. There was litter on the floor: discarded pieces of paper, a few bottles, fragments of broken mirrors, a pair of shoes. The walls were clad in concrete, but there was a pervasive smell of soil or clay. ·

'You've been down here for the last six days?' he said.

'It's better in the conference room,' Julia said.

'The whole place is damp.'

'We don't come here for our health.' They had reached a door by the end of the corridor, and Julia held him back. 'David ... you're going to meet the others. Are you going to show them the newspaper cutting?'

'What do you think? Should we?'

'I'm not sure. I'm convinced that this is the way back to the twentieth century, and if I'm right and it's where we came from, then we'll understand when we arrive. Do you think anyone will be expecting us there?'

'I can't answer that.'

He made a move on, but Julia caught his arm again.

'You're going to meet Paul in a moment,' she said. 'You're not going to make a scene, are you?'

'Is there any reason why I should?'

'No,' she said, and kissed him on the cheek. 'You know what I said, and you know what I want.' Still holding his arm, but gently now, she opened the door behind him. 'This is the conference room.'

Harkman walked in, looking around, expecting to find it full of people ... but it was empty. The lights were on, and it was warm and slightly stuffy. Many books and printed papers were scattered over the tables, and used cups and saucers had been left on the floor next to the chairs. Someone had left a jacket hanging from a hook on the door.

Harkman said, wryly: 'Do you suppose they heard we were coming?'

Julia looked around the room again, as if searching would find.

'I only left two hours ago,' she said. 'They must still be here.'

'In one of the other rooms?'

'They're never used. They must have all gone to the projection hall.'

He followed her down a side-tunnel towards a doorway,

through which bright light was pouring, and as they went into the hall beyond Harkman felt the heat from the lamps glaring down on him. Holding out his hand to shield his eyes, Harkman looked around the room, but it was several seconds before he noticed that someone was waiting: at the far end of the hall, standing beneath one of the clusters of lights, was a man.

He said nothing to them, but watched as they walked in.

On Harkman's left, running for the length of the hall, was a bank of large drawers, painted grey. In the centre of the room, and, for some reason, at the place where the beams of several lights converged, was a large pile of discarded clothing. Harkman thought, whimsically, that it looked like the scene of an orgy that had been interrupted by a police raid.

'Is that you, Paul?' Julia said, narrowing her eyes against the glare of the lights.

The figure made no movement or sound for nearly half a minute – during which time Harkman stepped forward, to be restrained by Julia's hand on his arm – but then at last he came slowly forward.

'They've all gone,' he said. 'The project has started.'

'Already?' Julia said, in evident surprise. 'But you were going to wait –'

'I had all the people I needed. No point delaying.'

Julia glanced up at Harkman, and he saw a strange fear in her expression.

She said: 'Paul, I've found David Harkman. You remember, Don Mander proposed him?'

'David Harkman, is it?'

'David, this is Paul Mason, the director of our project.'

'Mason?' Harkman extended a hand, but Mason ignored him and looked at Julia.

'So this is the David Harkman that's so valuable to my project? Well, it's no good, we've started and it's too late for anyone else.' He turned away, and went to stand beside the cabinets. He reached back with both hands, and pressed his palms against the smooth metal.

'I don't know you, Harkman. Where are you from? What do you want here?'

Harkman, irritated by the man's manner – which lay somewhere between psychic disorder and plain rudeness – felt the
temptation to give a sharp answer, but he saw Julia flash a warn-
ing look at him, and he remembered her request not to make a
scene.

He said: 'I've been working at the Regional Commission,
Mason. I was sent there from the Bureau of English –'

'I don't trust the Commission, Harkman. Nor anyone in it.
What do you want here?'

'Paul, he was approved by the others.'

'The others have gone. You and I are the only two left. I want
to know what this Commission man wants here.'

'We want *him*, Paul!'

'So you say. I select the participants for the project, not you.'
Julia looked at Harkman again, this time with an expression of
puzzled despair, then went forward to Mason. He turned away
from her at once and walked down the line of metal cabinets,
running a hand obsessively along the metal surfaces.

With all that had happened during the day. Harkman had had
no preconception of what he might find at the Castle ... but this,
with Mason apparently distracted beyond sense, was something
he had no way of knowing how to deal with.

'Julia, is he sick?' he said quietly.

'I've never seen him like this before,' she said. 'When I left he
was angry ... but I hadn't expected this. And where is everyone
else?'

Harkman said: 'What shall we do?'

Julia was silent, staring down the long room at Paul's strangely
neurotic figure. He was standing once again under the cluster of
lights, his hands pressed against the nearest cabinet.

Looking at him, Harkman could see why Julia had once been
attracted to him. He was probably about the same age as she was,
and was possessed of undoubted good looks, in a dark-haired,
clean-cut way, but there was an ugliness to his mouth and a narrowness to his eyes that made Harkman dislike him. The fact that
his dislike was evidently reciprocated came as no surprise: this,
after all, was the other man in Julia's life, and such confrontations
were supposed to be charged with suppressed feelings.

'Do you know how this machinery works?' Harkman said to Julia.

'Yes . . . Paul was explaining yesterday.'

'He seems incapable of explaining anything at the moment. What happens?'

'Each participant has a drawer to himself. Mine is that one.' She pointed towards the drawer about eighth or ninth from the nearer end, and Harkman realized that this was one of the three that were still not fully closed.

'How do you know that one is yours?' Harkman said. 'They all look the same.'

'Because . . . I'm not sure.' Julia looked at the other two, shook her head. 'I *know* it's mine, because it feels like mine. I can't say why.'

'But why is one different from another?'

'It's to do with neural and cerebral patterns. Dr Eliot – '

She broke off suddenly, and looked at Harkman in alarm.

'What is it?' he said.

'Dr Eliot should be here! And Marilyn. And the rest of the staff. Paul was emphatic about this . . . the project mustn't be started without medical supervision.'

'Then where are they?'

Julia called up the room: 'Paul, where's Dr Eliot?'

Paul said something inaudible, but did not turn to face them.

Harkman said: 'Go on, Julia. What happens to the participants?'

'We have to lie down in the drawer, and when it's closed lights will come on inside. That will trigger some kind of cerebral response which will link our minds to the projector. There are electrodes inside.'

They went to the drawer Julia had said was her own, and pulled it open. At the sound of the metal runners, Paul turned round to face them.

'What are you doing?' he called. 'My experiment is in progress. I don't want it interfered with.'

Harkman said: 'Take no notice of him, Julia. Go on.'

She pointed out the padded rests for head and shoulders, and between them an array of short, pointed electrodes.

'We have to lie so those press against the skin,' she said. 'I've already tried it. They prick the skin, but otherwise don't hurt.'

Harkman glanced at the pile of clothes in the centre of the floor. 'And we undress for this?'

'Of course.'

Harkman stared at the drawer with uncertain feelings; the bright lights and Mason's mad words; Julia's earnestness. But he was being infected by it; he was at the centre of his obsession. There was a drawer in this cabinet for him, and he knew which one it was. Like Julia, he didn't know how he recognized it . . . but he knew which of the two remaining drawers was his.

Paul Mason was still standing under the battery of lights, watching them.

'I've killed the others!' he shouted. 'I'll kill you too. Keep away, Julia . . . you know what will happen to you!'

'Does he mean that?' Harkman said.

Julia, who was clearly disorientated by Paul's irrational behaviour, said: 'I don't know. Help me with this.'

She laid her hands on the drawer next to hers, and together they pulled it open. Lying inside was the unconscious body of a naked young man, and so still was he that for a moment Harkman thought he was indeed dead. Julia bent over his face and put her cheek beneath the young man's nostrils. She placed her hand on his heart.

'He's still breathing,' she said.

'Then what did Mason mean about killing everyone?'

'David, I don't know. We have to ignore him. I don't understand what's gone wrong with him . . . he was perfectly all right this afternoon.'

But Mason wasn't to be ignored, for he started coming slowly towards them, pressing his back against the bank of drawers. He was mouthing words, but incoherently.

'Why is he unconscious?' Harkman said, looking at the young man on the drawer.

'Because he's projecting, I think. I'm not even certain of that.'

Harkman realized with sudden surprise that he recognized the young man. He was the peddler with the mirrors, the one he had sometimes seen about the streets of Dorchester.

'Who is this?' he said.

'His name's Steve. I don't know much about him.'

They pushed the drawer closed again.

'What shall we do, Julia? Are we going to go through with it?'

She looked back at Paul, who was still working his way towards them, muttering to himself.

'I'm frightened, David. Nothing makes sense any more ... we've only that old newspaper cutting to believe.'

'Do you believe it?'

'I have to. And so do you. Everything else is insane.'

'Julia, I'll kill you if you get into the machine.' Mason was beside them now, staring at them with wild eyes. 'I planned all this ... it has to be you and me alone together. That's what we agreed!'

Harkman said: 'Get undressed, Julia. I'll keep Mason away from you.'

He stepped to the side, standing between her and Mason. Instantly, Mason leaped at him. He threw an arm around Harkman's neck from behind, and tugged his head back. With his other hand he clawed at his eyes. Julia screamed.

Harkman, taken by surprise, felt himself dragged back. The hand closed over his face, groping fiercely across his nose and eyes; a finger went into his nostril and started pulling. In an instinctive fear, Harkman snatched his head to one side and slammed an elbow backwards into Mason's stomach. At once the grip around his neck loosened. Harkman turned, and with an awkward untrained blow, hit Mason sideways across the temple. The other man staggered back, and fell weakly against the bank of drawers.

'David, are you all right?'

'I'm O.K.,' he said, but his heart was racing and he was out of breath. 'Please, Julia ... get into the machine. It's all we can do now.'

'I can't go by myself. I'm terrified of what will happen.'

'I'll be with you, I promise. I'll follow you.'

Behind them, Mason suddenly let out a howl of rage, and tried to get to his feet again. Harkman turned to face him, clenching his fists. He was no fighter, and Mason's insane behaviour was scaring him. As Mason levered himself up, Harkman kicked out at the man's legs, making him fall again.

'Do it, Julia! I'll keep Mason off you.'

She hesitated a moment longer, then undid the buttons of the raincoat. Her arm got caught in the sleeve as she pulled it off, and Harkman helped her. She was watching Paul, and her fingers fumbled with her dress.

'*Julia!*' Mason cried. 'Don't go!'

'Paul, it's what we planned.'

'You'll die, Julia! You'll be killed!'

'Don't talk to him,' Harkman said. 'It makes him worse. Stay calm, and let me handle him.'

They managed to get the dress off her at last. She swept back her hair, which was still damp and tangled from the rain, and reached up to kiss Harkman briefly.

'Come straight away,' she said. 'Do you know which is your drawer?'

'That one, I think.' He was pointing towards the one he had recognized as his. It was just beyond where Paul Mason still huddled on the floor.

Julia said: 'David, this is right! We both feel it.'

'What do I do, though?'

'You can pull yourself in,' she said. 'There's a handle inside. And a large mirror above you . . . look into it.'

Mason was trying to get up, but he seemed dazed and his movements were uncoordinated. Harkman glanced down at him, wondering whether to knock him over again.

'Get into the drawer, Julia. I'll help you.'

He made sure the drawer was pulled right out, then Julia sat on the metal surface and lay back. She shifted her head and shoulders a few times, apparently trying to settle herself comfortably, and pushed her hair out of the way so that it did not interfere with any of the electrodes.

'I'm ready, David.'

He bent over her and kissed her lightly on the lips.

'I love you, Julia. Are you frightened?'

She smiled up at him. 'Not now. This is what we have to do.'

'I'm not frightened either. Are you ready?'

On the floor a short distance away, Paul Mason groaned.

'Yes, I'm ready.'

David pressed against the drawer, and felt it slide smoothly into the body of the machine. He looked down at her, hoping to catch her expression, but she had turned her eyes away from him, was looking to the side.

The drawer closed. In the last instant Harkman saw a bright light turn on inside the cabinet, and as the drawer settled into place he saw the brilliance outlined squarely.

Mason was on his feet, and he had moved away from the cabinets.

'Where's Julia, Harkman?'

He tried to ignore the man, stepping round him, but Mason side-stepped to block his way.

'You're not interfering any more, Harkman. Who the hell are you, anyway? Where's Julia? What have you done with her?'

'Get out of the way, Mason.'

'You're not getting into the machine. I'll kill you.'

'You can't stop me.'

They stood facing each other, and Harkman's heart started to race again. Mason was crouching, as if ready to leap on him. Then Mason looked away, and stared towards Julia's drawer. The brilliant internal light was fading, and as both men watched it dimmed and went out.

Mason turned towards the cabinets, and Harkman took a step forward.

26

There was a bell ringing in darkness, then a jerking, sliding motion, and light shone in her eyes. People were moving about, and it was hot.

'It's Miss Stretton!' somebody said, and another voice shouted above the clatter of metal and hubbub of voices: 'Nurse! Bring a sedative!'

Julia opened her eyes, and her first impression was the customary one: that the drawer of the Ridpath projector had opened the instant it was closed, and that she was still in Wessex . . . but there were too many people about, and there was no Paul, no David.

A man in a white coat was standing over her, his head turned away and his arm reaching out impatiently towards someone hurrying across to him. He held Julia's wrist in his other hand, his fingers on her pulse. The nurse put a hypodermic needle into the doctor's outstretched hand, and bent over to swab the inside of her elbow.

Julia wriggled, trying to move herself away. Pain shot down her back.

'No!' she said, and her voice felt as if it was breaking through lips swollen with sores; her nasal passage was dry, her throat was hurting. 'No . . . please, no sedative.'

'Hold her still, nurse.'

'No!' Julia said again, and with all the strength she could find she managed to wrench her arm away, and fold it defensively across her stomach. 'I'm all right . . . please don't sedate me.'

The doctor, whom Julia recognized as Trowbridge, took hold of her wrist again as if he were about to pull her arm forcibly away, but then he looked closely into her eyes.

'Do you know your name?' he said.

'Of course . . . it's Julia Stretton.'

'Do you remember where you've been?'

'Inside the Wessex projection.'

'All right, lie still.' He released her wrist, and passed the hypodermic back to the nurse. 'Find Dr Eliot,' he said to the nurse, 'and tell him Miss Stretton has apparent recall.'

The nurse hurried away.

'Can you move your head, Julia? Try it very slowly.'

She made to raise her head from its support, but as soon as she did a sharp pain snatched at her neck.

'The electrodes are still in contact,' Dr Trowbridge said. 'I'll ease you away.'

He leaned over her and took both her shoulders in his hands. Moving her a fraction of an inch at a time he raised one of her shoulder-blades, and so lifted her away from the electrodes on that side. By the time he had done this Dr Eliot had arrived, and together the two men lifted her painfully away from the needles.

Soon, she was sitting up in the drawer, her head down between her knees, while one of the doctors dabbed the inflamed area of her neck and spine with a soothing ointment. Somebody put a blanket over her, and she hugged it around her.

As awareness grew in her, and she realized what had been happening, Julia felt a conflict of intense emotions: anger and confusion, mixed with the pain. Her fury was directed at Paul; how he had interfered with the projection, how he had distorted the world of Wessex, how he had so effectively intruded and destroyed. Confusion, because the projection hall was crowded with people, most of them medical staff. Peering up between her knees she saw somebody being wheeled way on a trolley, with two orderlies holding oxygen equipment alongside. Another person was being carried away on a stretcher, and while Julia's neck was still being treated she heard Dr Eliot's name called, and he walked quickly away.

But above all this, through her suppressed rage, Julia held a memory of David. In spite of everything, Paul and his insane distortions, and all the changes in Wessex he had wrought, David was the same.

'David? Is David out?' she said.

'David Harkman? He's not here at the moment.' Dr Trowbridge pushed her head down between her knees again. 'Keep still.'

'I've got to talk to someone,' she said. 'Please . . .'

'You can speak to Dr Eliot. In a moment.'

'But at least tell me what's happening here.'

'There's a full-scale emergency. Something must have happened to the projection, because everyone's returning at once.'

Dr Trowbridge's name was called, and he left Julia with the lint lying loosely on her neck.

Under his strict injunction not to move, Julia was unable to watch what was happening, but she listened to him speaking to two of the nurses a short distance away. She heard her name mentioned several times, and 'no apparent traumata', and 'we haven't tested her motor functions, but they seem normal', and 'as soon as Dr Eliot is free he'll have to speak to her.'

A nurse finished cleaning and dressing her neck, and while this was going on Julia tried again to look to either side of her. She was still sitting up on the surface of the drawer, and her view was obstructed by the many people moving around her, but it seemed to her that most of the drawers were open. She was trying to discover whether David's had been opened yet, but it was too difficult to see.

The nurse fixed the lint in place with some sticking-plaster across her shoulder-blades. 'That's finished, Miss Stretton. Remove the dressing tomorrow.'

'May I get down now?'

The nurse looked across to where Dr Trowbridge was leaning over someone lying on a trolley. 'Has the doctor released you yet?'

'No . . . but I feel all right.'

'Let me see you move your arms.'

Julia flexed her muscles, and turned her wrists, and apart from the customary stiffness after retrieval there seemed no difficulty.

'I'll find you an orderly,' the nurse said.

At that moment, Julia saw a small group of people come into the room.

'There's Marilyn,' she said. 'She'll help me.'

Marilyn spotted her before the nurse could beckon, and called out her name and walked quickly across the room to her.

'John Eliot said you were all right!' she said, and kissed Julia on the cheek. 'What happened to the projection, Julia? Do you know?'

'Yes, I saw it all.'

'You *can* remember it then?'

'Of course I can.'

'Julia, something terrible has gone wrong with the others. They're suffering from amnesia.'

'But . . . how?' Julia said.

'We don't know. There's been such a rush. Everyone was returning at once. And one after another, none of them has had any memory of who they are, where they've been, what's happening to them now. Most of them are being taken to Dorchester General Hospital, but a few have gone to Bincombe House. And amnesia is the least of the problems. Dr Eliot says he suspects brain-damage in some cases, and Don Mander has had a stroke.'

Julia stared up at her in horror. 'What on earth has happened?'

'No one knows. You're probably the only one who can tell us.'

She looked at Marilyn, thinking of David inside the projector.

'Is David out yet, David Harkman?'

'I don't think so ... wait a minute, I'll check.'

Marilyn went over to Dr Trowbridge and spoke briefly to him.

'No, he's still in the projection,' she said when she returned.

'Marilyn, help me down. I've got to speak to John Eliot.'

She put an arm round the other woman's neck, and lowered her feet to the floor. She stood up, supporting her weight on Marilyn, but after a few seconds of uncertainty found that she could manage on her own. She leant against the metal wall of the nearest cabinet, clutching the blanket around her.

'Who else is still in the projection, Marilyn?'

'Just one other ... Paul Mason.'

Julia remembered the brightly lit hall, a future analogue of this one. She remembered Paul's mania and his threats ... and she thought of David alone with Paul, in Wessex.

She shook her head weakly, not knowing whether she wanted David to stay there with him ... or return to this. He had now been inside the projection for more than two years; what the physiological effects would be on him when he returned were too horrid to contemplate, and never mind the amnesia Marilyn had spoken of. Brain-damage, strokes ... did these await him on his return?

She felt an almost uncontrollable urge to climb back on her drawer, to pull herself inside the cabinet ... to return to the future.

'Are you all right, Julia?'

She opened her eyes, saw Marilyn standing beside her.

'Yes ... I'm just a little cold.'

'Let's see if we can find your clothes.'

'A surgical gown will do. I must talk to Eliot.'

They walked together through the hall, then had to stand to one side as another trolley was wheeled out. As it passed, Julia tried to see who was on it, but an oxygen-mask was being held over the person's face. Knowing it was one of the participants, a sharer of her private world, Julia felt a sense of close identification. She wanted to know who it was, but she couldn't even see whether it was a man or a woman. She turned away, looked at the wall until the trolley had passed out of sight.

As they reached the main corridor, Eliot appeared from one of the rooms.

'Julia!' he said. 'Have you been examined?'

'Yes, I'm all right.'

'Thank God for that! You do have total recall?'

'To the last detail,' she said, thinking of the grim ironies of those details.

'Come to my office as soon as you've dressed. We must find out what went wrong.'

'Paul Mason went wrong,' she said, but it was to herself. She and Marilyn went to the cubicle she used for changing in. The clothes she had been wearing were still there, but a feeling of transience that she wished to preserve turned her away from them. A considerable part of herself was still in Wessex, still with David. Until he was back safely she wouldn't feel safe or permanent in the present.

There was a surgical gown folded up in the cupboard, and she put this on.

They went to Eliot's office immediately, because Julia was anxious for news of what had been happening ... but all Eliot told her was what she had already heard. The participants had been returning for the last two hours; all, except her, had suffered acute mental or nervous disturbance. She was the last to return so far.

'Of course, this must mean the end of the projection,' Eliot said. 'I cannot imagine any circumstances under which it could be revived now.'

'But what about David?' Julia said at once.

'The projector will have to be kept in operation, of course. At least until he and Mason are retrieved.'

'Is there any attempt being made to get them out?'

Eliot shook his head. 'I can't allow anyone inside now.'

He told her that three of the trustees would be arriving in Dorchester the next day, to take over the supervision of the projector.

Julia, listening to this, was experiencing the uncanny overlap of realities that always followed a retrieval. Nothing had changed: there were still trustees, and there was still a Foundation. Outside the Castle there was the twentieth century and the world she knew, and it awaited her inevitable return.

But this world was no longer hers. She had ceased to be an organic part of the real world from the day she had first entered the projection. She belonged to the future; life could never again be stable except in the Wessex of her mind.

She could never accept that the future had ceased to be, for it was real to her. Wessex was a world of timeless safety, of certain stability, of unconscious harmony.

These were the qualities of the real Wessex, not the nightmare perversion that Paul's malign consciousness had created.

'Julia,' Eliot said, 'what happened to the program? Why did everyone return?'

'Because of Mason,' she said, thinking of Paul, thinking of David. 'Because it was what he wanted, what he intended.'

Remembering the evening on the heath with David, which was the exact moment when she had rejoined the projection, she began to speak of the changes Mason had made to Wessex, either consciously or unconsciously. Reliving those few days in the future she experienced again, this time with the perspective of whole awareness, the sense of growing confusion that the protean world had evoked in her. The destruction of Dorchester as a tourist resort; the appearance of the refinery and the oil-wells; the pollution and filth; the countless tiny changes in scenery and populace; the disappearance of the village at the Castle, and of most of the auxiliary egos.

All these . . . and the major change. The madness in Mason.

'While I was back before – a week ago – Paul Mason told me that the trustees had authorized him to change the projection. He didn't say how, not directly. But now I've seen it. He set up a *second* projection, using the Ridpath equipment that exists in Wessex. I can't imagine what he hoped – '

'You didn't report this to me or the others,' Eliot said. 'You had every opportunity.'

Julia fingered her throat, felt the swelling that was still there from Paul's attempt to rape her.

'I couldn't ... not then.' She remembered the guilt and confusion Paul had caused in her: the internal conflicts, the long struggle towards self-control and a sense of her own identity. 'He was, well ... blackmailing me. We used to live together, years ago. It lasted two years, and in the end I ran away from him. He's never forgiven me.'

'Julia, it was your duty to tell me this. You know the rule about –'

'It wouldn't have made any difference, John. He had the trustees behind him. Anyway, he turned the rule against me when he found out about it. He made me believe that if I revealed this to you, then it would be me and not him who would be excluded, because of his status with the trustees. I couldn't risk that ... Wessex is too real to me.'

Then she started to cry, reliving the agonies of the dilemma that Paul's reappearance in her life had produced. All that she had feared had come to pass: Paul had once again destroyed everything she possessed.

Eliot waited in embarrassed silence while she cried, and Marilyn comforted her and found her a tissue.

'You see, this is what Paul has done. It was because of me!' Julia held the tissue in her fingers, compressing it and feeling it shape itself wetly into a ball. 'He had an unconscious will to change what *I* had in Wessex. He offered some sort of plan to the trustees, but that wasn't his real intention, because he didn't recognize it himself! He's unstable and neurotically inadequate. I've always known it!'

Calming herself, she told Eliot about the project that Paul had constructed in Wessex. The other participants had been drawn in, unable to change his will. Most of them had had no idea that someone new had joined the projection; the sudden presence of a strong personality, obsessed with itself, had overpowered any resistance they might otherwise have put up. So, drawn into his mania, they'd worked with him to create a new projection ... one that was based on their buried memories of the real world.

'Paul was directing this! Not only consciously, because he cast himself as project director, but at the same time he was unconsciously diverting everyone else towards an obsession with the present. We all went along with him, because his influence was so powerful.'

She paused then, remembering the charismatic personality that Paul's projection of himself had possessed. He had seemed so likeable, so genuine, so strong.

The memory was deeply offensive to her, as if someone had importuned her sexually. In those few days of Wessex – in Paul's version of Wessex – she had seen Paul's unconscious image of himself, and it was one that in her real life she had hated him for.

'Julia, you can't believe that one man could bring all this about.'

'I saw it, felt it.'

Eliot had never fully understood the real subtleties of a projection. No one who had not been to Wessex could. As she tried to describe what she had experienced, she could hear her own words as if objectively, and she knew they sounded paranoiac. Eliot was being gentle, and trying to understand, but he would never know until he had felt it for himself how one personality could so insidiously influence another.

'You seem to have resisted him yourself,' he said. 'Why is it that you alone have retained your memory?'

Julia knew: it was too strong to ignore. 'Because of David Harkman.'

'You know Harkman is still in the projection?'

'Yes, of course.'

'And did he become involved in this second projection?'

'No . . .' Julia tried to find the way to explain, a way that would be true to herself.

Then she chose a half-truth to express a whole truth: 'John, my alter ego has fallen in love with David Harkman.'

Half the truth, because her alter ego did love him . . . but so did she.

She went on: 'In the projection Paul was trying to possess me, but because of David he couldn't reach me. He overloaded the minds of the others, but he couldn't touch me and he couldn't touch David. He was unconsciously trying to close the projection by returning the others, but he always intended that I should stay in Wessex, alone with him. He said something like, "I planned this for the two of us". But he didn't really understand about David.'

'Why not, Julia?'

'Because I never told him . . . I never told anyone. Paul didn't realize what David had become for me.'

Just then, the telephone on Eliot's desk rang, and he picked up the receiver. 'Yes? Ah, Mr Bonner.'

Julia remembered the name: the trustees' legal adviser.

Marilyn, who had been sitting quietly to one side through all this, said: 'Do you need another tissue, Julia?'

'No thanks.' But she realized that tears were still trickling down her cheeks, and she took the second tissue from her.

Marilyn said: 'Do you know why all the others have lost their memories?'

'I suppose it was too much for them to cope with.'

Even to herself it didn't sound convincing; the human brain wasn't like an electrical appliance that could blow a fuse.

She tried to listen to Eliot, but he had turned away from them and was talking quietly into the telephone, answering questions, listening to Bonner.

The loss of memory was like the loss they all experienced inside the projection: a total severance from their real lives, and an assumption of a new identity. After two years of experience she had come to terms with it, but on her first retrieval Julia had been frightened by the awareness: the memory of the amnesia, so to speak.

Paul's alter ego had warned them of it. One day, as they planned their project, Paul had said: 'On emergence in the future' – he had meant the present – 'you will lose your present identities and take on new ones.'

He had understood that much of the working of the projector, at least. And it was as he had said: the participants had returned without their memories.

But why? They had all returned from the projection before . . .

and they had had total recall then. Julia tried to think why this time it should be different.

The young men with their mirrors, the hypnotic triggers.

That was it. Other retrievals were achieved through hypnotic suggestions placed in the present, in the real world. This retrieval had been achieved in an altogether different way. The projector had been fully functional, used as it was in the present. Even the two retrievers had programmed themselves to take part; Julia remembered seeing Steve inside his drawer, projecting with the others.

No mirrors had been used, except those inside the cabinets.

In the world of Wessex, projected from the present the participants had created a second projection. They *imagined* themselves into the past. They had become projections of themselves!

Julia recoiled away from the idea.

This was the *real* world, was it not? This was not a projection?

She looked at Marilyn sitting a few feet away from her . . . and at Eliot, talking on the telephone. They were of the real world, of the twentieth century . . . they were not figments of the imagination.

But they had been in Wessex for a time, *inside the projection!* Paul, or one of the others, had imagined them into existence as auxiliary egos! Julia remembered Eliot at the conferences, remembered borrowing a raincoat from Marilyn.

Marilyn said: 'Are you feeling all right, Julia?'

She reached out and touched Marilyn's arm. It was solid, real. She jumped, and snatched away her hand.

'What is it, Julia?'

She stood up, and pushed back her chair. Suddenly she wanted to see the outside world, to see the Frome Valley and the inland town of Dorchester, and the white trails of overhead jets, and the railway-line that passed the Castle, and the roads and the traffic . . .

Was the world as it was? Was it still there?

She ran out of Eliot's office and into the cool, earth-smelling tunnel. At the far end were the iron gates of the elevator: the way to the outside. She ran towards them, fulfilling a terror of the unconscious.

The days inside the projector had weakened her, and she staggered as she ran, and when she reached the elevator gates she leaned against them, gasping for breath.

Her resolution failed as her body had weakened, and she went no further.

The world would be as it was. It would still be there.

It would be real, or *real-seeming*. It made no difference. It would be as it was, or as she expected it to be . . . and it therefore was of no importance.

She leaned against the gates, trying to recover her breath.

Marilyn had left Eliot's office, and was walking down the tunnel towards her. 'Julia, what are you doing?'

'It's all right. I'm O.K. now. I just wanted some fresh air but I changed my mind.'

'Let's go back and wait in the office.'

Still out of breath from her dash down the corridor, Julia looked again at Marilyn. She realized that even if she were to spend the rest of her life in the company of the other young woman, and saw and spoke to her every minute of every day, she would never again be convinced of her true existence.

If she turned her back, would Marilyn vanish? Would she re-appear as soon as she looked again?

'Is David Harkman out of the projector yet?' she said, trying to make her voice sound normal, unexcited.

'Let's talk to John Eliot again. He'll know.'

'All right, Marilyn.'

They walked back together towards the office, but as Marilyn opened the door, Julia ran again. She ran down the tunnel, further into the heart of the Castle. She heard Marilyn shout her name, then call urgently to Dr Eliot.

Julia turned the corner, past the conference room, and ran into the projection hall.

Calm and order had been restored, and Julia was brought up short by the quietness and emptiness. The emergency seemed to be over.

Two more trolleys were standing by, and two teams of order-lies were waiting beside them. Oxygen bottles and blankets were ready near by, and drugs had been set out on a tray. Dr Trow-bridge was standing near the orderlies.

As she walked in, he turned towards her.

'Have you seen Dr Eliot?' he said.

'Yes,' Julia said. 'I'm passed as fit.'

She was fit because she wanted to be. Imagine herself ill, and she would become ill.

'You should be resting,' said Dr Trowbridge.

'I've got to wait here . . . for John Eliot.'

Trowbridge turned away, and Julia walked slowly – and with contrived idleness of purpose – down the length of the row of cabinets. Now that most of the drawers were opened, it looked as if some mammoth burglary had taken place, with the contents of the drawers rifled indiscriminately. Two drawers were still closed, their precious living contents hidden away from the world.

She tried to imagine what the minds of the two men would be making. It was a projected world of two personalities, and one that would reflect an intense conflict that would be expressed in every way, from the unconscious id, to the conscious mind, to the physical body. She remembered Paul's violence as he attacked David, she remembered his madness.

Julia went to the nearer of the two drawers, the one that David was inside. She saw his name, printed in small black capitals on a white card affixed to the front.

Dr Trowbridge had his back turned towards her, and he was talking to two of the orderlies. Julia put her hands on the handle of David's drawer, but immediately she snatched them away.

She wanted to see him again . . . but dreaded doing so.

The emotion that had welled up when she was talking to Eliot flowed again, and she let out an involuntary sob, which she choked back by swallowing. She pretended a cough . . . but Trowbridge, still speaking, took no notice.

She took hold of the handle again, but this time pulled it as strongly as she could manage. The drawer resisted for a moment, then it slid smoothly out.

The body of David Harkman lay before her, and on the instant she saw his face Julia cried aloud.

He was still and stiff, as if dead, but his eyes flickered behind closed lids and his chest was moving steadily up and down. His body had been allowed to deteriorate even further than when she had last seen him here: his naked skin was pale, and his flesh was soft and seemed as if it were waterlogged. His hair was long and matted, and his fingernails curled back towards his palms.

She sank down and laid an arm across his chest, loving him, loving him.

Something unspoken told her that he would never return; that his permanent place was the Wessex of the mind: that he had become as one with the world he had helped create.

She was crying because he was there and she was here, and because she wanted only to be with him.

He had been watching her from under the shelter of the sea-wall, waiting while she read the crumbling piece of newsprint. Of course she remembered it now: the newspaper had carried the story the day the projection began, more than two years ago. 'It's genuine, I'm sure it's genuine,' he had said. She wanted to tell him now that he was right ... but what did it matter? She no longer knew what was real, no longer cared. David was her only reality, but David was in Wessex.

Julia cried, and wiped her eyes with the soggy tissue she still clutched. She kissed David's unresponsive face, then stood up. She walked to the front of the drawer, put her weight to it, and in a moment it slid slowly and smoothly home. He was safe again.

She walked numbly towards her own drawer, and found it.

The surgical gown was held with three simple laces at the front, and she slipped it off. Then one of the orderlies noticed, and pointed it out to Dr Trowbridge.

'Miss Stretton ... what are you doing?'

She made no answer, but reached behind her and found a corner of the sticking-plaster across her shoulders. She pulled, wincing at the pain. It wouldn't tear back, so she tugged harder, and at last it came away. As she dropped it to the ground Julia saw that there were spots of blood, mingling with the yellow stain of antiseptic.

Her drawer was beside her, and so she sat down and drew up her legs.

'Julia!' It was Eliot, who had appeared at the entrance to the hall. Marilyn stood beside him. 'Julia, get down from there. Trow-bridge, get her away from that!'

'I'm going back, John!' she shouted.

'I told you, no one is to use the projector again. I've had instructions to close it down, to turn it off.'

Trowbridge had crossed the room and was standing a few feet away from her, apparently uncertain of what to do.

'You can't turn it off with people inside,' Julia said. 'You know that would kill them.'

'I've had instructions from the trustees.'

Eliot had been walking slowly towards her as he spoke, and Julia knew that where Trowbridge hesitated Eliot would act. She knew what she wanted. She knew more certainly than anything she had ever known in her life.

Wanting it, she stared her defiance at Trowbridge ... who turned away.

Wanting it, she stared at Eliot ... and he came to a halt.

From the doorway, Marilyn called: 'Do it, Julia! Take care!'

Julia closed her eyes. She lay back on the drawer, settling herself on the supports, and she gasped with pain as the electrodes went into the old sores. She reached behind her, found the handle inside the cabinet. As she pulled, the extra strain caused the electrodes to snag and tear at her flesh ... but the drawer was moving, taking her into the dry, warm darkness.

The drawer closed and bright internal lights came on, and Julia stared upwards into a circular mirror.

27

Julia ran down the main tunnel beneath Maiden Castle, the coarse fabric of her dress chafing against her legs. Her memories were intact.

For the first time since the projection had begun, Julia had full knowledge of herself and her place. She could remember Paul's mania in the projection hall, and the shouting and fighting: she could remember her return to the world of the 1980s; she could remember running down this tunnel away from Marilyn, with the woman shouting her name.

But this was Wessex, and there was no Marilyn, no Dr Eliot.

She reached the end of the tunnel, and no one called after her. She was alone.

The glaring lights of the projection hall shone down the side tunnel, and she slowed, not knowing what to expect. Were David and Paul still in conflict? Was Paul still cowering in his corner, babbling of death and power?

All was silent as she walked into the long hall. It seemed like only a few moments before that she had walked in the same way into the same room, desperate for a sight of David. And so it was again: shielding her eyes against the brilliant spotlights, Julia looked for David.

The hall was empty. Along the side, the drawers of the cabinets were closed, a uniform wall of finality. When she left Wessex, two drawers had been opened: one for David, one for Paul. Now all the drawers were closed, their secrets contained.

In the centre of the floor, picked out by the lights, was the pile of discarded clothing.

'David?' she said, her voice unsure and sounding tremulous. This was the first noise she had consciously made since walking into the hall, and at once she was alarmed. She had a sudden irrational fear that it would bring Paul out from some hiding place.

The room was silent, with only the background hum of the projection equipment.

Because she had expected to find the two men here, Julia was disconcerted by their absence. What had happened to them? Because they hadn't appeared in the present, she had assumed they were still in Wessex. Where were they?

But their drawers were closed: could they have returned to the present without her knowing it? But no, her memory was quite clear: neither had appeared. She remembered the two closed drawers, the two trolleys and the orderlies waiting. And she had seen David's body only seconds before she climbed into her own drawer.

Nagging at her, though, was the knowledge that the transfer from present to future, and vice versa, was instantaneous. It *could* have happened ... Paul and David could have returned at the same moment as she herself rejoined the projection.

How else to explain it?

She walked across to the drawer that she knew was David's, conscious of the way in which she was continuing to retrace the steps of her alter ego in the present. *That* Julia had walked to this drawer looking for a David she had lost, and that Julia had not found him. With the same instinctive dread, she pulled her hands away from the drawer before she could act.

She stepped back, turned away. Alone in a world that was entirely hers, Julia felt the terror of the unknown.

The pile of discarded clothes was next to her, and she looked down at it. Lying on the top was a jacket she recognized at once as David's. Beneath it, neatly folded, were the rest of his clothes.

She touched the jacket, and it was damp from the rain; she lifted it up and pressed it against the side of her face, holding it as if it were the last trace of him.

In total misery she dropped the jacket on the pile, and cried out his name.

Then, very muffled, she heard: 'Julia . . . ?'

It was David's voice . . . and without a thought she ran across the hall and took hold again of the drawer handle. She pulled with all her strength, and at once his naked body slid into view.

That he was conscious and alert was instantly obvious because he moved his head before the drawer was fully extended, and bumped his forehead against the metal edge.

He winced with agony, and his head fell back.

She looked at his healthy body, his ruddy complexion . . . and the expression on his face, pain and pleasure, comically mixed.

She laughed aloud, almost hysterically, relieved beyond words that he was safe.

'Oh, David . . .'

'Don't laugh! Help me out of here! I thought I was stuck forever!'

She knelt down and put an arm across his chest, pressing the side of her face against his. She was still laughing, but crying too . . . and David put his arms around her, pulling her down against him.

Then he winced in pain again. 'These needles . . . pricking me.'

She moved back and helped lift him away from the shoulder

supports. He sat forward, in the way she had been made to sit by Dr Trowbridge, and rubbed the back of his neck with his hand. She looked to see, but the needles had barely penetrated the skin, and there was a faint pink rash along the upper part of his spine.

She hugged him for several minutes, thinking only of him, and being with him.

But then she said: 'David, what happened? Why didn't you go back to the present?'

'I did as you said . . . but nothing changed. I stared into a reflection of my own face, wondering what the hell was supposed to happen, and how I was going to get out, until I heard you outside.'

'But you should have returned instantly. Has the projector been turned off?'

'Not as far as I know. I certainly didn't touch it, even if I knew how.'

'Then Paul must have tampered with it.'

David shook his head. He swung his legs to the floor, and walked over to retrieve his clothes. He said: 'Mason's in the machine.'

'Was there a fight?'

'Not after you left. He was still ranting away, but he ignored me completely and was talking about projecting himself into the future, trying to follow you. He went to the cabinets on his own, I waited until he'd filed himself away . . . and then I tried to come after you. But as you see, it didn't work.'

'Why not, David?'

'Perhaps I'm immune.'

He said it jokingly, but it struck a resonant chord in Julia's memory; her new memory, the one that stretched back to the twentieth century.

The last time she had been out of the projector, during the meeting when Paul was there: Andy and Steve had come back from Wessex and reported that David had been shown the mirrors but that he'd resisted it somehow.

(And a deeper memory, several layers down, folded back under itself: a morning at the stall in Dorchester; David exhilarated from having ridden the Blandford wave, and trying to talk about it as the tourists gathered around the stall; Steve appearing with a mirror, and trying to show or sell it to David; herself taking the mirror from him, and smashing it on the ground; David unconcerned, wanting to see her later in the day; Steve going away from the stall.)

David had been in Wessex continuously for more than two years; had the deep-hypnotic triggers been lost? Was he as resistant to the mirror inside the projector as he was to the ones carried by the retrievers?

David said: 'You must be immune too. You're still here.'

'I'm here because I chose to come back. Everything you talked about was true. Look . . .' She took his trousers from him just as he was about to put them on, and felt in the back pocket. The newspaper cutting was still there. 'This, David . . . it's true. When you put me inside the projector I went back to the twentieth century. As soon as I was there I *remembered* all that's true about us. Neither of us is real, but it doesn't matter! We are real to each other. I saw what was happening in the present, and I couldn't stand it. I had to come back.'

She was wondering how to begin telling him what she could remember. The trustees; her past life with Paul Mason; the damaged minds of the other participants.

And David's real body: pallid, bloated, uncared for. If he ever went back, tried to assume his real identity, could he survive?

'David, this is the only reality left! What Paul Mason did . . . I can hardly explain. He set up the second projection here, and I thought it was a way home. But what he is projecting is an *imaginary* twentieth century . . . one where that newspaper was printed!'

David laughed nervously, and took the newsprint from her. 'First I'm told by this that I don't exist, and now you tell me this doesn't exist!'

'That's right.' She remembered the emergency as the participants returned. 'Most of the other people have gone mad . . . in that projected world.'

'But not you.'

'No . . . I had something to believe in, something I knew to be real.'

'What was that?'

She shook her head, and smiled at him. 'If you don't know, David, I'm not going to tell you.'

He had all his clothes on now, and was straightening the collar of his shirt: a concentration on a familiar, mundane task to avoid thinking about the unthinkable.

'David, don't you understand? The newspaper was right about us at one time, but it's wrong now. When we met, our identities were projections from the past. But Paul Mason changed that. His project, this one, is *imagining* the past. Not the one we're from, but one very like it! And Paul's projection is a complete success; I know, because I've been there! It's a two-way projection ... people in Wessex, who were projected from the past, are projecting the past from which they started. It's been too much for them. They've lost their minds.' She ran a hand through her hair, and found that it was still damp from the rain of an hour before. 'I think I'm beginning to lose my own!'

She went to the cabinets, and took hold of the handle of the first drawer she came to.

'If Wessex is still a projection, David, this drawer should be empty. The alter ego that was projected would either vanish, or resume its normal life in Wessex, when the mind of the participant withdraws. But do you know what's inside this? Is someone here ... or is the drawer empty?'

As she had been talking, David had left his shirt-collar alone, and was watching her thoughtfully. The piece of newsprint had slipped from his fingers, and lay on the pile of clothes.

'Julia, I don't think you should open that drawer,' he said.

'I've got to!'

She pulled, felt the familiar resistance ... and a moment later the drawer slid out.

Lying inside was the body of Nathan Williams. He was still, but alive. His chest rose and fell steadily, and behind closed eyelids his eyes were moving.

Julia said: 'He's projecting, David. His mind is functioning.'

She opened a second drawer, a third. Both contained living bodies of people she knew.

Thinking of their destiny, thinking of what had happened to

those minds, Julia closed the drawers again. She had seen their projection.

'Have you looked in your own drawer, Julia?'

'No!'

'You should. Is your drawer empty?'

'It must be . . . I'm here!'

'Are you a figment of your own imagination, as I am of mine?'

'David, I don't want to know!'

He had turned her own argument against her in a way she could not face. She stepped back, and further back, until she reached the further wall. Between her and David lay the pile of clothes . . . and she saw, lying beside a damp raincoat, there was a plain, brown dress, identical to the one she was wearing. She looked down at herself. The bottom of the dress, that had not been covered by the coat, was dark and wet from the rain. She remembered the chafing against her legs as she ran down the tunnel.

The dress lying on the pile was also damp.

She alone had visited the projected past, and had not been harmed. She alone had returned to reality. Her memories were whole. She was in Wessex. The future, the present, the now.

David pulled open the drawer she had used, and stared inside. For several seconds he didn't move, but then he said: 'I think you had better look, Julia.'

'No, David. No!'

She could see, from where she was standing, that there were two white and naked legs stretched out along the drawer. The rest of the body was hidden by David standing over it.

'You're the same as the others, Julia. You lie here and project, and you stand there and are projected.'

'Close the drawer, David. *Please!*'

He turned to look at her. He was grinning.

'You're very beautiful naked,' he said. 'Come and see what I mean.'

She couldn't move, couldn't turn her head away. 'David, please close that drawer!'

The momentary roguishness on his face had faded, and with a sober expression he put his weight to the drawer and slid it back into place.

'I don't understand, Julia. Are you real? Am I?'

'I can't think about it any more,' she said. She felt as if she were about to faint, or to suffer the same loss as the others. 'We are as real as we think we are. I only know that I love you. Is that reality?'

'It is for me.'

He went across to her and put his arm around her shoulders. 'I'm sorry, Julia,' he said. 'I shouldn't have done that . . . with the drawer.'

'I think you had to. We had to know. It doesn't seem to make any difference.'

'What shall we do?' David said. 'Can we leave here?'

'Do you want to?'

'I said, *can* we.'

'We can do whatever we wish,' Julia said. 'We are utterly free, for the moment.'

'What do you mean by that?'

'When I was in . . . in the present, I heard that the Ridpath projector was going to be turned off.'

'It means nothing to me. What effect would that have?'

'Nobody's really sure,' Julia said. 'Ridpath himself believed that it would kill anyone inside. It's never been tried.'

Then a stray thought – comforting? confusing? – hovered for a moment like a flying insect. As she left the present, Eliot had said the trustees had instructed him to close the projection. But that was in the world she believed was being projected from here! Would that have any effect here? Where was the present from which Wessex was being projected? Were they the same . . . or was the system now closed? Did one world project the other, each dependent upon the other for its own continued reality?

David said: 'Julia, I think we should leave. I've got everything I ever wanted. We're together . . . that's enough for me.'

Julia, distracted by the uncertainty of her thoughts, felt David's hand on hers. She shook her head, as if to throw off the intruding notion, then saw from David's expression that he had taken this as a negative response to what he had just said.

She tightened her fingers around his hand, and said: 'I'm sorry. It's what I want too.'

'Come on, let's go back to Dorchester.'

She felt a sudden fear about what might lie outside the Castle, and who might be there, but knowing David was consciously neglecting to think about this, she made the effort too.

'Do you think it's still raining?' she said. 'Should I take the coat?'

'Is it yours?'

'No. I borrowed it . . . from Marilyn.'

The auxiliary ego Marilyn, the one who had been in the Castle for a time. Marilyn had vanished, but her coat was still here. As she looked at it, Julia remembered that the real Marilyn, the other Marilyn, had a coat just like this.

'You won't need it,' David said. 'Leave it here.'

They walked together towards the doorway, talking about the coat and the possibility of rain. It was like David straightening his collar: a hold on a plainer reality, a need for the prosaic.

As they stepped into the tunnel, Julia pulled herself away from under David's arm, and turned to face back into the projection hall. Something had been worrying her, nagging at her.

'What is it?' David said.

'Paul Mason!' she said. 'What happened to him?'

'I told you: he joined the projection with the others.'

'But no . . . he didn't. I was there. He didn't return. I'm sure of that . . . they were waiting for him.'

'Is he immune too?'

'No. At least, I don't think so.' She grasped David's hand, gripping it tightly in sudden fear. 'Are you *sure* he's inside the projector?'

'Of course . . . I saw him close himself in.'

'When was that?'

'A few minutes after you. Two, three minutes . . . I'm not sure.'

'But . . .' Julia looked at David in despair. 'But Paul *didn't* return,' she began again. 'I'm certain of that. The doctors were waiting. There was just you to return, and Paul.'

'Then he's trapped inside, like I was.'

David pushed past her, ran back into the hall.

Something inhuman in her made her say: 'Don't let him out, David!'

'If he's trapped, I've got to. This is his drawer, isn't it?'

'I think so, yes. . . .' She hardly dared look.

David pulled the drawer, and she saw pale legs stretched inertly out, the feet slightly splayed. As the chest, and then the face, came into sight, Julia started to tremble and she leaned against the tunnel wall. The inhuman instinct was still there: a desire for dreadful revenge on Paul for all those years of humiliation, to slam the drawer closed with him inside, to trap him forever inside the cabinet, alive or dead.

David was bending over the body.

'Is he alive?' Julia said, her fist clenched over her mouth.

'He's breathing . . . his eyes are closed.'

'Is he projecting?'

'I don't know . . . you'd better look.'

She had been unable to look at her own body inside the drawer, and she was unable to look at Paul. It was he who had dominated all her adult life, first by his presence and then by his absence. He had dominated the projection, he had destroyed.

Now there was a primal dread in her: that she would *never* be free of him.

'Close the drawer, David.'

'Not until you tell me what's happening to him.'

'Are his eyes moving? Flickering . . . under the eyelids?'

'A little, yes.'

'Then he's projecting.'

David continued to stare at the unconscious body of the man, and seemed uncertain of what to do. Julia waited in the tunnel, but David kept the drawer open.

'Close it, David. Please.'

'But if you say he didn't return to . . . to the past, where *is* he projecting to?'

'For God's sake!' She turned from the tunnel wall, ran into the room. She pushed David aside, and put her hands on the front of the drawer. Then she saw Paul's face.

She paused, realizing that he was indeed projecting. She had been impelled by fear: the idea that he might be lying there pretending, waiting to take some new form of retaliation against her. But her paranoia was unfounded: Paul was as deep inside the projection as all the others. He could not escape; there was no way back.

She stared down steadily at him, gaining strength. She knew

she would never see him again, never ever. Looking at him thus, directly and unflinchingly, she pushed against the drawer, and it closed.

David was watching her face, perhaps beginning to realize the order of her fear of Paul. She looked back at him, and forced a smile.

'I'm sorry, David . . . I had to do that. I thought he might sit up again and start threatening us. Like he did before.'

David took her hand. 'I don't ever want to know what Mason did to you.'

'It doesn't matter any more,' she said, and she knew that this time she could say it and know it was true.

'Let's get outside,' David said. 'I've had enough of this place.'

They walked out of the projection hall, leaving the lights burning.

Halfway down the main tunnel, Julia said: 'He didn't return to the present. He really didn't.'

'Then where is he?'

'In the future? All by himself?'

Paul alone believed in a second projection; Paul alone failed to realize, on an unconscious level, that the future he was planning was actually the past; Paul alone believed in the future as a reality.

As they reached the bottom of the lift shaft and began to climb the stairs, Julia wondered what any world of Paul's making would be like; one which he alone imagined, and in which he alone exercised unconscious will. Would he take an image of her along with him, an auxiliary ego of his own? Or would he make the world itself auxiliary to his own ego? Would anyone exist in that world who would resist him, who wasn't subservient to his will, who wasn't the butt of his malice and destructive criticism?

Julia felt she had lived once before in that kind of world, and knew it well. But that was in the past.

28

The rain had stopped, but the wind was chill. When they reached the top of the earth rampart, Julia and David paused to look down across the bay towards Dorchester. It was a heavy, clouded night, and the town itself was mostly in darkness. Only the harbour was brightly lit; white arc-lamps flooded the port with brilliance, because it was never still. Throughout the nights the endless business of the oil-rigs was conducted, with supply-ships and lighters moving to and fro across the bay.

Behind the town, spreading untidily across the heaths, the refinery was at work, throwing up a pall of smoke that glowed orange from the floodlamps beneath it. Connecting the refinery to the sea, the pipelines crawled in parallel lines, their path flood-lit for security. Out in the bay, the dozens of drilling-rigs could be seen, standing squarely in the sea as far as the horizon; lights flared whitely and randomly on the superstructure of the platforms, lights for working by, lights for navigation. Seen from the Castle, the rigs looked like a stationary armada, lying-to offshore, waiting for the tide before sailing in to invade.

Beyond all this, beyond the bay and the town, the Wessex hills lay black against the night horizon.

'Let's wait,' David said, and he sat down on the wet grass. Julia sat beside him, oblivious of the cold and wet. She snuggled under his arm, drew warmth from his body.

Time passed, and they did not move. The ground seemed less cold after a while, as if it were they who were warming it. Julia, reaching round with her hand, found that the grass had dried.

'I'm not cold now,' she said.

'Neither am I. I think the wind has dropped.'

It had slackened to a gentle breeze, one that barely touched them, one that was warm from the day.

'Where shall we live, Julia?'

'I suppose it will have to be Dorchester,' she said. 'It's the only place I know.'

'We're completely alone now?'

'Yes, I think so.'

Some time later, David pointed out that the orange flame above the refinery, the torch of burning waste-gas, was dying down. Soon it went out, and around it a cluster of floodlamps were also extinguished. For a long while there seemed to be no reaction within the refinery, and normal work went on.

'Look at the pipeline, David!'

The floodlamps above the four great pipelines were going out, one after another, those nearest to the refinery dying first. To David and Julia it appeared that the pipelines were slowly shrinking away from the refinery, drawing back into the sea whence they had come.

As the last of the pipeline flood-lamps was extinguished they saw that in the bay the rigs were turning off their lights, systematically and without haste. Soon only one rig was visible: the large supply-platform in the centre of the bay.

Piece by piece the refinery was vanishing into the dark of the night; lights and flares went out, and with them disappeared the tanks and pipes and gantries. In the town, the arc-lamps of the harbour dimmed quickly. The supply-platform was soon the only light showing; it too vanished in time.

Overhead, the clouds were clearing, and the stars came out. Dorchester, dark and silent, remained on its hill. Its streets and buildings were unlit, the harbour was still.

For a long time nothing more happened, and Julia, still held in David's arms, began to doze. It was warm and comfortable on the rampart of the Castle, as if its glowing life was radiating from within. There was a smell of flowers in the air, a heady, summery smell, anticipating day.

Suddenly, far away, there was a loud explosion, and the sound of it echoed to and fro across the bay, from Purbeck Island to the Wessex Hills, seeming to zig-zag across the funnel-shaped bay.

Julia, stirred by the noise said: 'What was that?'

'The cannon at Blandford. The tidal bore is coming through.'

It was too far away, and the night was too dark, for them to see the wave, but they both had the same feeling about it: that the incoming tide was refreshing and renewing the waters of the bay, flooding in from the north with the weight of the ocean behind it, cold and clean and alive.

Coloured lights flicked on in Dorchester, the lights that were strung in the trees along the front. They reflected in the sea, which was calm and still, as yet undisturbed by the flooding tide.

Street-lamps came on in Dorchester; windows and doorways

became squares of golden light. The harbour moved again: yachts and cruisers, bobbing at their moorings. Across the silence of the bay Julia and David heard music and voices. A group of people were laughing, and as the lights above Sekker's Bar came on, they could just see that the tables on the patio had been cleared away, and that a large crowd was dancing and jostling in the warm night air.

They both slept after this, secure on the Castle rampart, holding each other.

They woke about an hour after dawn, when the sun was still low over the English hills: a brilliance of yellow in a clean, azure sky.

Holding hands, Julia and David went down into Dorchester, and walking along Victoria Beach, where the white sand was showing again as the new tide receded, they heard the muezzin calling from the mosque.

Later, as they walked along Marine Boulevard, looking at the cafés and stalls shuttered for the night, they saw the fishing boats coming across the empty bay towards the harbour, heavy with their catch.

29

There was a sharp wind from the south-east and the waters of Blandford Passage had a deep swell, with white foam rippling back from the southerly mouth of the channel. Protected from the elements by his wet-suit, David Harkman could not feel the wind, although as he left the harbour at Child Okeford and steered his skimmer into the centre of the Passage he was almost upset from his board several times by the swell.

Wave-riding conditions were perfect. It was now too late in the season for all but diehard riders, although the recent spell of fine autumnal weather had brought tourists back to Dorchester in sufficient numbers to persuade the cafés and bars to reopen, and for the last three days Harkman had had to share the wave with no more than about a dozen other riders. The consequent absence of jostling for position on the wave-crest, together with the southeasterly wind and the spring tides, meant that he had had four excellent rides in the last week alone.

He still sought the perfect wave, though . . . one that would set the seal on the season. Now that he was able to wave-ride more frequently, he had become known to many of the regulars in Child Okeford, and heard much of their lore. There was always the quest for perfection: a combination of height, speed, daring, timing.

For David Harkman it would be enough to execute a ride for the whole length of the Passage, and not be caught by the curling wave as it broke into the bay. He had still to achieve this; either he fell behind at the last moment, or he was trapped by the thundering pipeline as it rolled on top of him. The fact that he was regularly riding waves of a height and speed that would daunt anyone less experienced was of no consequence to him. Whether the wave was thirty metres high or, as had been the case for the last week, nearer twice that, he needed for his own satisfaction a wave-ride which he completed.

The height of the wave was, nonetheless, a major consideration. The stewards had been talking recently of prohibiting further rides until the waves became weaker; several riders had been injured in the last few days. In the clubhouse at Child Okeford, older hands were saying that the only waves bigger than these were the winter storm-waves, and no one had been known to ride one of those and survive.

With the regular practice Harkman's proficiency had naturally increased, but as he was waiting for the firing of the cannon he moved to and fro across the Passage, trying to gauge the strength of the swell, getting used to the pressure of the wind.

The wind was an enemy while he climbed the wave; an ally once he reached the crest.

At last the cannon fired, and Harkman and the other riders looked northwards to the Somerset Sea, estimating the distance of the wave. It had been in sight for some minutes; the spring-tides gained body further out in the Sea, and when Harkman looked he saw the advancing swell like a huge cylindrical drum, rolling towards him half-submerged.

He closed his face-mask, turned on the oxygen.

There was time for one more straight run against the swell, and a flip-reversal from the top of one wave to another ... and then he felt the rising push of the tidal bore. As usual, Harkman had placed himself on the Wessex side of the Passage, and further down towards the mouth than most of the other riders, and by the time he was accelerating before the wave most of the others were at least halfway up.

On a wave as large as this, the engine had to be at full throttle for the whole ride. Harkman drove down and to the side, flipped back and accelerated again, tacking and sheering away from the crest ... but each time he turned, each time he looked for the crest, it was nearer. The wave was piling height on volume, and the immense speed at which it was hulking towards the gap meant that each turn of his skimmer took him ten or twenty metres higher up the wave: height that had to be lost again if he was not to reach the crest too soon.

Several riders had fallen already, pitched from their skimmers by the ragged swell. Once a rider fell he had almost no chance of regaining the wave, for even if he could mount his skimmer again quickly enough, his engine would certainly lack the power to take him up the reverse side to the crest.

They were now less than a hundred metres from the mouth of the Passage, and Harkman was in the water most broken by the wind. Every swell, every line of foam, was an obstacle to surmount. Each time he flipped the skimmer, and it leapt across the trough from one swell to the next, he could feel the wind beneath the board, lifting and blowing him.

He was judging it exactly right; with less than fifty metres to go to the mouth of the Passage he was almost at the crest of the wave, and he throttled back the engine and let the wave lift him towards its sharpening peak.

As he reached the crest the wave was starting to curl, and he accelerated again, keeping abreast of it. He was heading directly into the wind, feeling the nose of the skimmer being lifted as the wave itself was being held back from breaking.

They passed the mouth of the Passage, and the wave, curling, frothing, continued to rise.

Harkman pushed forward, out to the very edge.

He threw his weight forward, slicing the skimmer down and sideways, diving it through the thinning foam; a moment of grey-green confusion, the suck of water about his head . . . and then he was falling through the air.

Beneath him, the rising inner wall of the wave was almost vertical, and Harkman shifted his weight, bringing the nose of the craft down against the wind, trying to match the gradient.

Above him, the wave was breaking at last: slowly, it seemed, and with great and terrible majesty.

A freak gust of wind came from the side, raising the skimmer's nose, overbalancing him. Harkman, inside the wave's pipeline, windmilled his arms, felt his foothold on the board loosen . . .

But then silence fell.

The howling vortices of the wind, the persistent whine of the engine, the thunderous roar of the wave . . . they all died away.

Harkman, falling back from the board, was in the air.

He was frozen in flight, naked and alone in a sky. His arms and legs were free, he could turn his head.

Slowly, slowly, he swum around, twisting his abdomen, trying to face down.

Beneath him, the wave, the cliffs and the sea had vanished. He was floating above countryside: a gentle, green, undulating landscape, with meadows and cottages and hedgerows. There was a road down there, and he could see a line of traffic moving along it, the sunshine glinting up from the metal bodywork. Behind him, where Blandford Passage had been, a little town lay in the valley between two hills yellow in the autumnal haze. He could smell woodsmoke, and petrol-fumes, and mown grass.

He felt he was about to fall, and he thrashed his arms and legs as if this would save him . . . but he only turned laterally until he was facing towards the south. Hovering in this alien air, he looked across the Frome Valley towards the Purbeck Hills, and beyond these to the glistening sea, silver and sunlit.

He closed his eyes, forcing the sight away from him . . . but when he opened them again nothing had changed.

Looking towards the ground, Harkman felt for the first time the vertiginous effect of his height, and as if this had released something which until then had suspended him, he began to fall.

The air roared in his ears, and he felt the pressure of wind on his arms, legs and stomach. The ground seemed to rise up to strike him, and in real fright he clawed at the air with his hands, as if grasping for a rope or a net.

At once his motion ceased, and he was suspended again in the air, although noticeably lower than before. Now he could hear the traffic on the road; a motorbike was overtaking an articulated lorry, and the sound of its exhaust hammered at him.

Harkman wished himself higher ... and at once he felt the pressure of the wind on his back, and he soared upwards. When he had attained his former height, he made himself turn around again ... and he stared across at the quiet countryside, with its wooded hills and its verdant fields and pastures.

What he saw had no meaning for him: it was the product of some unconscious wish that he could not control.

It was something that had excluded him, something that he had in turn rejected.

Because it was from the unconscious past, unremembered, it was at once wholly intimate and voluntarily relinquished. It was the landscape of his dreams, a world that was not real, could not ever become real.

As once before, when he had unconsciously rejected this phantasm from his life, Harkman exercised a conscious option, and expelled the dream.

He looked down at his body: the shiny wet-suit appeared, and was clinging to him, the drops of salt-spray scintillating in the bright sunlight. There was a tightness across his chest, and a weight on his back. Something black and soft and padded wrapped itself around his head, and his vision dimmed as the visor of the helmet fell across his eyes.

Oxygen from the cylinder on his back began to hiss, and he breathed deeply.

He turned himself in the air until he was upright, and he felt for and found the roughened upper surface of the tide-skimmer. The throttle control wrapped itself around his right foot.

He made a few corrections of attitude: leaning forward and tipping the nose of the craft downwards.

The wind started to blow, and the streamlined shape of the

skimmer responded, planing in the currents. Harkman kept control, shifting his weight and balance to maintain the craft on an even keel.

A penumbral darkness fell as the Blandford wave curled again over his head; below, the almost vertical rising wall of the wave was a multifaceted frozen mirror of sunlight.

The wave began to move above him, starting and stopping, like the frames of a film inching through a projector. Harkman, truly afraid of the wave's elemental violence, halted the motion, still seeking to balance the skimmer in the cross-current of wind.

He began to fall, and he lost control of the wave. The nose of the skimmer was pushed up by the wind, and with a desperate outbalancing of arms he managed to bring it down again. The skimmer slapped heavily against the water, and at once he gunned the engine, staggering for balance. He glanced up, saw the black pipeline curling down above him . . . and in terror of the wave he raced the skimmer down the slope, down and down and down.

Seconds later, the wave crashed behind him, and foam and spray deluged him, reaching out to clutch him. He was still upright, still racing the wave, still outdistancing it by a few crucial metres that saved him from being overwhelmed by the crushing, swirling spume. He was in the open waters of Dorchester Bay now, the skimmer leaping in spray from the crest of one swell to the next . . . but still the wave tumbled and crashed and flooded behind him, dwarfing him even in its collapse.

As the wave spread and flattened it lost its forward speed, and soon Harkman had left it behind him. He turned the skimmer towards the west, and headed for Dorchester. In time he was passing the beaches, where a few tourists still sprawled beneath their multi-coloured umbrellas, and Harkman waved meaninglessly to the people, trying to convey the excitement that was in him.

He raced the tide all the way, and when he skimmed smoothly into the shallow waters of the harbour the visitors' yachts were still grounded on the mud.

When evening came that day, he and Julia walked down to Sekker's Bar for a meal of local sea-food, and on the way they paused to look at the goods on sale at the Maiden Castle stall.

Mark and Hannah were standing behind the counter as usual, but today there was a new assistant serving with them. She looked at David and Julia with curiosity but failed to interest them in buying anything.

As they left the stall, a young peddler dressed in the clothes of Maiden Castle stepped out of the crowd and approached them.

'Would you look at a mirror, sir?' he said, and held out a small circular glass before Harkman's face.

'No, thank you,' David Harkman said, and Julia, holding his arm, laughed and pressed herself closer to him. As they went up the steps to the patio of Sekker's Bar, they heard a young woman's voice shouting angrily, and a few moments later there was a tinkling of broken glass on the paving-stones.

CPSIA information can be obtained
at www.ICGtesting.com
Printed in the USA
LVHW032106290122
709587LV00001B/71